A Possible Life

Also by
Simone Chaput

La vigne amère
Un piano dans le noir
Le coulonneux
Incidents de parcours
Santiago

A Possible Life

a novel by

SIMONE CHAPUT

TURNSTONE PRESS

Turnstone Press
Artspace Building
018-100 Arthur Street
Winnipeg, MB
R3B 1H3 Canada
www.TurnstonePress.com

Turnstone Press gratefully acknowledges the assistance of the Canada Council for the Arts, the Manitoba Arts Council, the Government of Canada through the Book Publishing Industry Development Program, and the Government of Manitoba through the Department of Culture, Heritage and Tourism, Arts Branch, for our publishing activities.

Canada Council for the Arts
Conseil des Arts du Canada

Canada

Cover design: Jamis Paulson
Interior design: Sharon Caseburg
Printed and bound in Canada by Friesens for Turnstone Press.

Library and Archives Canada Cataloguing in Publication

Chaput, Simone
A possible life : a novel / by Simone Chaput.

ISBN 978-0-88801-332-3

I. Title.

PS8555.H39827P68 2007 C813'.54 C2007-906902-9

pour France et Doug

grazie mille

What will survive of us is love.
—Philip Larkin

In love, we are beasts of infinity.
—Rhona McAdam

A Possible Life

Vancouver
Tuesday 12 February 2002

I can't sleep. Gale force winds are blowing off the Strait, rattling these hotel windows and my Scotch-drenched old bones.

Had hoped for a respite, a slow, idle slide into spring, but it appears that is not to be. While she spoke, while her eyes lit up with unmistakable urgency, I felt it, too, that jarring of the heart, that sudden slowing in the wide, wide wheeling of the blood.

The book is taking shape, even now, while outside my window, the waters of Juan de Fuca roil in winter storm.

Magda, Magdalena is her name, like the beautiful adulteress of the Talmud, *she of the mouth of watered wine, of hands, hollow, pale and blue.* And she did speak to me of harlotry, while I looked on in astonishment, but a harlotry not her own. Her husband—that is, her ex-friend, ex-dream, ex-lover, ex-spouse—appears to be an old lecher of the old school. A sculptor and a respected member of the Faculty of Fine Arts, he seems to be pathologically incapable of resisting the charms of the sweet young things that swing their hips and flick their long pale hair in his studio halls. Sex, Magda said to me tonight in words sharp as bloodied cut glass, is his heroin. He gets stoned on the bodies of young women. He's a cunt addict, a pussy junkie, just one more cheap whore.

Bitterness deep enough to have anchored me, I would have thought, pulling me firmly to ground. And yet, I kept floating off in spirals of dull amazement. It was, it is, inconceivable to me that any man could be drawn away from the beauty that is Magda by the promise of a casual thigh. She is, simply put, the kind of woman at whose altar candles are burned. She is nothing less than sacrament, and one should approach her, and take her, only in a state of grace.

(Christie, my beloved, this is a beauty you, too, would understand.)

And that's when the world jolted to a stop.

I was gazing—dumb and helpless and distracted—at her closed face when she suddenly looked up at me again and smiled. By the new light shining in her eyes, I saw it was over. The goat was gone, he'd been dismissed, never to be mentioned again.

On her lips, instead, was the name Masaccio.

It fell upon my ears—and my heart—like a summons. I cocked my head like a faithful spaniel and waited for more. And she did not disappoint me. Magda is steeped in the art of the early fifteenth century, like ladyfingers in sherry. She is sweet on it and drunk on it, and blushingly round with it. And her *engouement* with the enigmatic Tommaso of Florence is nothing short of infectious. There is something so engaging about the man—about his absent-mindedness, his messiness, his marvellous gift for artifice. But to me, an aging writer in a transient world, what is most fascinating about him is the brevity of his time among us, and the fixedness of his ambition.

My hand aches tonight to begin a story about the light of Tuscany.

Fletch has been pleased with the turnout at every stop along the tour. He says it's quite impressive, really, for a book of short stories. In the same breath, however, he makes sure to remind me that it's still novels that sell best. I wonder what he'll say when I tell him the main character in my next book will be a fresco painter of the Italian Renaissance. Will probably sniff once and reach for the Bunnahabhain before telling me he's noticed of late the readership prefers, hmmm, shall we say, more recent stuff.

It struck me again, this evening, how reading one's work in public is an act both sacred and profane. It is at once a prayer, a profession of faith and humility, and a common striptease. When I stand before a crowd and speak aloud the images I conceived, alone and away, I am like the young stripper, *la petite effeuilleuse,* dancing towards nakedness with hope in her heart and a ripping fear in her guts. As, one by one, the veils drop away from her body and each new expanse of flesh is exposed, it suddenly becomes clear to her that the revelation to which she is moving is intended, not so much for the crowd that watches and whistles out there, but for herself. She will learn, by way of the leers and the laughter, the nudges and the sighs, the more and the less of her appeal. Thus, she will discover that the shrug she found so provocative in the indulgent reflection of her bedroom mirror strikes the crowd as parody. Or that the baring of her belly takes a little too long and comes a little too late.

But if she is lucky, she may also discover that a trick she has with feathers inspires new and deeper lust. That certain, small, cunning gestures of the finger, the lip and the thigh arouse to unsuspected heights.

In the same way, tonight, as I stripped before the anonymous crowd, parading my freshly forged words, it was to me that revelation came.

I am a striptease artist of the soul, watching your face as I bare it all, waiting for the quickening pulse, the betrayal of the fluttering lash.

It is three a.m. and my glass is empty. I wait for nothing now, but sleep.

Vancouver, still howling
Wednesday 13 February

Woke up thinking about Nick. About his fragile, blue-veined wrists and the unforgiving face of the Goat's Eye. Before he packed up his board and left, Alex bet me the kid would come back from spring break with one or the other bone in a cast. Hope he's wrong. Hope there's a Providence for skinny, uncoordinated boys who attempt to fly on snow.

Have to catch a turbo-prop to Victoria at ten a.m. One reading and signing tonight, then it's back home at last. Ten o'clock. Still too many hours away. Useless time, good for nothing but remembering and cringing.

(Your first question to me, Christie, when we'd slip into bed after I'd been away on tour. We'd be lying there, do you remember lying there, Christie, with our bodies still pulsing and our flesh damp and our hearts sore with too much love, and you'd curl your fingers into the greying hairs on my chest and tug, ever so slightly, and ask for them all. All the cringers I had collected along the way and was madly scrambling now, with mud-stained hands and broken fingernails, to bury deep in the oblivion of memory. And I would turn to you and hide my face against your breast, and moan as I remembered. But you would listen as I dredged up every embarrassing thing I'd said, each faux pas and every indiscretion and, before long, I would feel your body quaking with gentle laughter.... I would give up all the earth, and heaven too, to hear that laughter now.)

I had an uneasy moment last night, when she reminded me that, three years ago, I'd signed her copy of *The Dovecote* with a quotation from Nietzsche. I groaned, then started to apologize for my very transparent attempt at claiming for the novel a depth of meaning it did not possess, but she shook her head. Listen, she said, to what you wrote. And she recited from memory:

> To green-eyed Magda.
> *We have art so that we shall not die of reality.*

And then, above my name:

From one survivor to another.

What I want to know, she said, is how you knew.

I couldn't answer her. I didn't know then in which country of grief she had made her home. But what fills me now with amazement is that, three years ago, when my heart lay mangled in my chest (like your poor body, Christie, among the wildflowers of the highway ditch), I could have imagined that I'd not died.

Her symposium ends on Friday. We've agreed to meet for drinks back home. We shall talk of art. Of survival. Of the art of survival. We shall talk of Masaccio.

~

I suppose I should add that when Magda and I parted last night, I didn't kiss her or even shake her hand. No, to my everlasting confusion, I gave her a pat on the shoulder, the way old men do to women they wish they had world enough, and time, to love.

Victoria

Thursday 14 February

Am reading *Austerlitz* by *le très regretté* W.G. Sebald. (Have I told you, Christie, that he, too, was taken from this place in the crush of flesh and metal?) This one sentence leapt off the page at me this morning, and set the tone for the rest of the day: "... the darkness does not lift but becomes yet heavier as I think how little we can hold in mind, how everything is constantly lapsing into oblivion with every extinguished life, how the world is, as it were, draining itself, in that the history of countless places and objects which themselves have no power of memory is never heard, never described or passed on." (It is because of these lines, because of the anguish they woke in my heart, that today you were everywhere I looked. It was a warm island day—the daffodils and irises are already out, here, Christie, and the old folks gladly linger in the sunshine. I was making my way to the bookstore when I passed a couple seated at an outdoor terrace, and though everything was wrong—from the salty smell of the wind to the sound of traffic all around us—something about the way they looked into each other's eyes reminded me of us. We were—you and I—immediately transported to another island, in another springtime. The leaves of the poplar trees whispering all around you were the tender shade of green you love best. Behind you, and beyond the thin strip of forest, the channel waters ran fast between the island and the mainland, they squinted and shimmered in the sunlight, they slapped against the shingled limestone of the shore. The air was sharp with the raucous trilling of red-winged blackbirds. A broad-tailed hawk rose on an updraft, a blue heron lifted with a squawk out of the brittle phragmites at the water's edge. As you spoke, you paused to turn an ear, or catch a glance, your pretty head angling away from me, taking it all in, not missing a thing.

The gear was still all piled high at the dock. We had unloaded the Beaver, unlashed the canoe from the floats and pushed it off to one side. Before heading back to pack up the car, take the cable ferry off the island and drive home to the city, we were sitting there at The Landing, waiting to be served, savouring the feel of paddle-broken hands and river-run bodies.

It had been a good trip. The Pigeon had proved quick but generous, the nights, savage with northern lights, the days, long and languorous things that had caught in our fingers as they drifted by. And as I'd watched your back tense with the movement of the paddle, seen you lift your face to the blue-drenched sky, I'd felt with a keen biting edge the joy of knowing that you were, and always would be, the strength and the rhythm of each one of my days.)

It seems impossible to me now that I could have presumed so much. And I recognize now, with an unspeakable ache in my heart, that my arrogant faith in the future, in the goodness of the world, in the rightness of our place in it, and, yes, in the indivisibility of us, blinded me to the fleeting perfection of the moment. Because I thought we were Forever, I as good as missed the Now.

(You came to me a second time, Christie, when I was in the bookstore. It was the pen again. I'd taken it out, read the inscription and felt, once more, somewhere near my heart, a thick, warm rush of tears. So even as I made small talk, smiled and signed, I was aware of nothing but loss. But then, suddenly, I saw you standing in the crowd among the stacks of books, looking lithe in your little black dress, your blonde head tilted in quiet conversation, your wineglass loose in the cup of your hands. As the line shifted forward, in the pause between two signings, I imagined I could look up from the book I held open before me and catch your eye. To tell you, in one quick, secret glance, how much I wanted you, how much I needed you, and to share with you a small, heretical smile at all this phony famous writer stuff.

When it was over, I did look up, but you were gone.

Some days, Christie, I can't bring back the memory of the light in your eyes, or the texture of your skin, or how it felt to fold your body into mine in the warm bed of our love. And tonight, I could not even hold on to the vision of your face in a blank and faceless crowd.)

Memory is a paltry thing, and even words, old Yeats, are not a certain good.

It will be a relief to be home again. With the boys, with piles of term papers to mark, with Masaccio, with new, small and lesser loves, to fill the empty, howling spaces in my heart.

Winnipeg
Friday 15 February
Nearly wept when I caught sight of the boys waiting for me at the bottom of the airport escalators. (They are no longer boys, Christie, your children are now men. Can you see them, Babe, can you see how your beautiful sons have grown?) Sent up a prayer of thanksgiving when I saw that Nick's limbs were still whole, and nearly wept again. What, oh what, in God's name, is turning me into this maudlin mess? Alex noticed my shiny eyes—gave me a quizzical look before folding me into one of those awkward public hugs.

Was glad to see it is still decidedly winter here. Haven't yet had my fill of those moody, grey, battened-down February days, just right for faded cords and ragged sweaters, for poking around in musty old books, Scotch well in hand. In a very short time, long stretches of sunshine will settle into the back garden, and I will feel the pull of restless root and saucy green tulip blade and, with some regret, trade my pen and ink for the cool, cool crumble of earth in my hands.

Alex whipped us up a great late-night omelette, with toast and marmalade and old cheddar and coffee, and we sat around till two, comparing notes. Nick met tons of people, of course, but there seems to be one girl in particular who caught his attention. She's into theater, too, and had some suggestions for him about summer stock. He says auditions have already begun—are already over in some places—so he has to, quote, get his cute little ass in gear, unquote. Alex spent the week studying for mid-terms, taking time out, I am absolutely certain, to entertain the nubile young Stephanie in the comfort of my home, with the inhibition-suppressing effects of my Scotch. (Am I being naïve, Christie? Are there really no twenty-year-old virgins left? Is our son past the point of furtive caresses and well into the Kama Sutra? Can a student in engineering leave his laptop long enough to engage in a little lap-dancing? Whatever that is....)

While neat-freak Nick was piling up the dishes in the sink, Alex hung around long enough to ask me if I'd met someone—you know, he said, a fervid fan, or a pretty lady reporter, or maybe some sexy poetess with wild hair and a long, thin, black dress. I turned to him, a smile on my face, ready to say, no, no, no one at all, when all at once I remembered Magda. And then, I felt it, a hot surge of blood suffusing my face. I looked down, a little busy with my hands just then, but I could feel Alex's eyes on me, taking in every single shade of red. When I cooled off a bit, I looked up and caught his grin as he sauntered out of the kitchen. I felt a little laughter loosening up inside of me, but, when I turned to look at Nick, the sound died in my throat. He was bent over the sink with an unsmiling face, and a deep, deep furrow chiselled into the middle of his perfect young brow. My heart clenched in my chest, and I wanted to tell him, no, Nicholas, no, don't even think it. I promise you, she will never be replaced.

And now that I need so badly to sleep, I am kept awake, haunted by the memories. (Of the look on his face when we found you at last. Of his bony boy's knees pressed into the muddy grass of the ditch. Of his fingers that stroked, without touching, your cheeks, your eyes, your lips, your perfect, unbroken hands.)

While we are—Epicurus said—death is not, and when death is here, we are not. Tell me, old man, if you will, how it is that I lie with it, and eat and drink with it, sleep with it and dream of it, ache with it and smile with it, listen and hope and wait with it, and still I am.

Saturday 16 February

Spent the day trying to mark papers. Kept wandering off to the bookshelves, looking for references to the quattrocento. Discovered, to my dismay, I have a very unsatisfactory collection of art books. But in all the articles on the Italian Renaissance I managed to dig up, Masaccio is mentioned in glowing, eulogistic terms. It is a measure of my ignorance that I felt only a twinge of embarrassment, the other night, at having to admit to Magda I'd never heard of him. According to some writers and historians, he is nothing less than the initiator and creator of modern painting. It has been said of him that, in his painting, he conquered the world of light. High praise, indeed.

What interests me is, why him? Why was it on him that the gift was bestowed? What heightened perception allowed him to grasp what had escaped painters before him, what experience, what depth of emotion? It is the question we ask of all genius.

Einstein said that the mysterious is the source of all true art and science. Proust believed it all depended on a quality of nerves: *Tout ce que nous connaissons de grand nous vient des nerveux.* And Plato understood that human love is the gateway to all knowledge.

And what was the source of the great Masaccio's inspiration?

In these days before I begin any serious research into fifteenth-century art, or life in Tuscany during the Renaissance, before facts about the real fresco painter Tommaso di Ser Giovanni de Mone Cassai can taint my imagination, it is pleasant to speculate on the man himself. I imagine him largish, with a scraggly beard and long, unkempt hair, dressed in almost monastic robes, barefoot or in rough sandals, his hands wide and blunt, his fingernails ragged and rimed with paint. There is probably nothing remarkable about his face, except perhaps for his eyes. And I wonder if they are vampire eyes. If, in their darkness, they conceal a hunger that feeds on everything they contemplate. I wonder if his friends feel sapped, bled dry, by the intensity of his gaze. I wonder if they can guess, those painters and architects with whom he breaks bread and drinks Trebbiano, from the brooding, dark violence of his eyes, that he is not long for this world.

I will look for a premonition of death in the work of his hands. Perhaps I will find in his frescoes the air of melancholy one senses in the paintings of Watteau, or in the last poems of Keats, he *whose name was writ on water.* Perhaps I will find nothing of the kind.

1401–1428. I look at his dates and marvel that he has reached across six centuries and touched his brief life to mine. Leaving me to struggle with the callous indifference of time, with the paradox of infinity in a quick, hard breath of air.

Sunday 17 February

She called me this morning and invited me to brunch. Told me, without apologizing, that she's like that. Very last minute, very impatient with the squander of aimless hours. Though my craven willingness to rush off at her bidding did awaken my suspicions, I was not prepared for the way my heart leapt inside my chest when I first caught sight of her. She is that beautiful.

Her writing was going badly. She is preparing a lecture for a convention she will be attending in May and, this morning, before calling me, she erased everything she'd written yesterday. She talked, but I hardly listened, distracted as I was by the fall of her lashes on her cheek. She ate, but I played with my food, intent on watching the quick lick of her tongue on her lips. Who was it—Byron, I think—who could not bear to watch a woman eat? I think had he sat a moment at that table in the sunshine across from Magda at her tea and honey, he might have experienced one more of those explosive turns of feeling he loved so well.

Like all true *passionnés*, she is not surprised at my interest in Masaccio. I question her like a schoolboy, pressing for biographical details, mining her knowledge of all things fresco, unabashedly asking for translations of the Italian terms that pepper her conversation. Her eyes flash when she speaks of him, especially when she evokes for me the first time she lifted her gaze to the walls of the Cappella Brancacci. In the Chiesa del Carmine, Firenze, Toscana. I tell her that, one day, I will have to see them for myself.

Her eyes shine as she nods her gorgeous auburn head in emphatic agreement.

As we were finishing our coffee, she told me that, this afternoon, she is going to a production of *River* with a friend. Ah, I said. Joni Mitchell. My wife loves her music. (I really said that, Christie. Just like that. In the present tense.) Magda cocked her lovely head, looked me in the eye and said, with a hint of alarm in her voice, "I guess I'd misunderstood. You *are* married." And then I had to explain. (About the month of May, and the new road bike I'd bought you, and the guy in the semi who hadn't yet adjusted his vision, or his margins, or his sympathies for springtime solitary cyclists. I didn't cry, Christie. But she still stretched out a hand to give mine a squeeze.)

Then she said something heartless. She said, "I envy you your grief."

I felt as though she'd hit me hard across the face. (Didn't she understand what it meant to me, this losing you? I decided then, Christie, I had no time to waste on her and made a move to leave.)

But when I looked into her eyes and saw the coldness there, I suddenly understood. I saw that, for her, death would have been easier to accept than betrayal. Where I could grieve, she could only hate.

Monday 18 February

Between classes, I scoured the university library for books on the quattrocento. There is a good selection—everything from general texts on the civilization of the Renaissance in Italy, to very specific works on all the paintings of Masaccio—all of them old and dog-eared, zealously underlined, highlighted and annotated. In nearly every one of them, Giorgio Vasari, the sixteenth-century Italian writer, painter and architect, is quoted thus: "Masaccio was born in Castel San Giovanni di Valdarno. He was most careless in external matters. He had his mind fixed on art and could by no means be induced to care for worldly things, such as his own personal interests, and still less for the affairs of others. He gave no thought to his clothing and did not collect debts owed him until he was actually in want. Because of this, he was called not Tommaso—which was his name—but Masaccio—Slovenly

Tom—. He was so called without malice, simply because of his negligence, for he was always so friendly and so ready to oblige and be of service to others that a better or kinder man could not be imagined."

It seems to me that, in this thumbnail sketch, I have the whole man. The novel will write itself, I think, as the mystery, the passion and the tragedy of Masaccio's life seem to grow, as in so many cases, out of the matrix of character. (Have I jinxed myself, Christie? When, several years hence, I am still battling with the stubborn recalcitrance of a life lived in a time so unlike my own, will I rue the day I wrote these words? And yet, I don't know how to explain it—in some strange way, it seems to me this is a book I already know by heart. As I think about Masaccio, I find myself yielding again and again to a feeling that has taken root somewhere deep inside me—a feeling that his story is, in some ways, very like ours, Christie, yours and mine.)

Our hero-infatuated culture has made much of the absent-minded genius. We smile indulgently upon the lapses of men and women of accomplishment, to give us—the dull, the ordinary, the uninspired—a patronizing edge. But in our condescension, there is also an element, I believe, of deep and abiding gratefulness. While we go about our small lives, it is reassuring to know that some of us, despite the constant betrayals of our very mortal natures, are somewhere on another level, trafficking with greatness.

This book will be an attempt to flesh out three days in the life of the very gifted, very absent-minded Tommaso of Florence.

And it will begin with a departure.

Tuesday 19 February

Ran into Magda at the art gallery, completely *par hasard*. She'd been doing a little research in the archives. I stopped in over lunch to catch Robin's show. I was startled to discover it was a series of self-portraits. When he was in one of my classes, a good ten years ago now, I had been struck, of course, by his very remarkable face. I understood today exactly how remarkable it is. As we wandered through the rooms—and how enlightening it is to visit a gallery with an art historian at one's side—Magda mentioned to me in passing that Masaccio, too, had left a self-portrait in one fresco of the Brancacci chapel. It is a large painting, she said, depicting St. Peter's resurrection of the son of the king of Antioch, who had been dead fourteen years. After the miracle, St. Peter is seated by the king on a throne and crowds have come to honour him. It is among the people of that crowd, Magda said, that Masaccio painted himself standing with friends: Masolino da Panicale, his mentor and confrère; Leon Battista Alberti, an Italian architect and writer; and the great Filippo Brunelleschi, architect of the dome of the Cathedral of Florence. I just stood there, staring at her, my mouth no doubt agape. She took one look at my face and smiled. I have some reproductions, she said. I'll show them to you some time.

Back in the classroom, I found it hard to concentrate. Something Magda had said kept rising to the surface of my thoughts, then vanishing before I could take hold of it. The distractions of the day buried it deep, but it came floating back up to me this evening. According to Magda, the fresco of the resurrection of the son of King Theophilus was never finished by Masaccio—some of the characters depicted in it were painted fifty years later by Filippino Lippi. And I knew then in what state of mind my Masaccio would be the morning of his departure for Rome. Like so many artists, he would have been plagued by the fear of failure and incompletion, haunted by the spectre of wasted time. Like da Vinci, he might have had as his mantra, "Tell me, tell me, if anything got finished...."

I have lots of notes already on the man and on the age, and I feel the story building, as always, in phantom shapes on some half-cleared back lot of my mind. And yet I hesitate to begin. It seems to me there is a vein here I still have not mined, a motherlode that waits patiently in a still and pregnant earth. It has to do, I believe, with the problem of time.

(We marvel, sometimes, at the secret workings of the body's memory, of fingers that remember the intricate manoeuvres of a fugue long after the mind has mislaid the notes, of bones and blood that shift and tilt and level in the unblind search for balance. But since you were taken from me, Christie, I have grown in intimate knowledge of the body's disgraceful forgetfulness. That, my love, and nothing else, is what we mean when we speak of the limitations of the flesh. Not sin, not disease, not even death. But the inability to re-member. Your bodily presence has been excised from my life as ruthlessly as the tumour the scalpel cuts away, as permanently as my boyhood face. Though it seems impossible to believe, our thousand embraces left no trace upon my flesh. My body is powerless in the face of my desire to summon you as you lived and breathed in the shelter of my arms.)

And at the core of this humiliating fact lies the mystery of time. And of the unbearable truth of our subservience to it. It seems to me that, with a bit of effort, God could easily have conceived of a universe in which time flowed a little more tractably, a little less rigidly. He could have made it a soft, permeable medium, like a water one swims in, or a light through which one moves, with present collapsing into past, *now* slipping backward into *then*. But because the gift of every moment is lost, is being lost, even as it is lived, our lives are only memories, dreams that are over before they've begun. And is this, then, what heaven will be—a long, nostalgic look back at a life fulfilled, in short, an eternity of dull remembering, or will it be, instead, each best second of our lives relived intensely for an eternity of time?

I am reminded of Joyce's priest and his definition of eternity: if the sand from all the world's beaches was gathered in a pile and once every million years a raven came and took away a single grain of sand, by the time he'd done away with every grain, just one second of eternity would have passed. (Time enough, do you think, for us to love, and to know we are loving? In the here and now, and not, no more, not ever, through the filmy gauze of faint remembrance? My memory, Christie, that unfleshly thing, is a fake and a fraud. It evokes only to betray. It says, Look, look, then blinds me with false light. It says, See how immutable the perfection, then fills my mouth with the taste of ashes. And with each passing day, I watch with anguished heart as the images grow fainter. Soon, lover, your face and every one of its beloved lineaments will have all the resonance of a description read, many years ago, in some old, yellowed copy of Henry James.)

Consume my heart away; sick with desire
And fastened to a dying animal
It knows not what it is; and gather me
Into the artifice of eternity.

Precisely, Magda would say, the very thing: the consolation of art. The painting that fixes for eternity a changing fall of light. The phrase of music that captures and contains the soul's small exaltation. The poem that sounds forever the sighs of our mortal heart. Colours, notes, words that transcend the strictures of time and aspire to infinity.

Did it once occur to Masaccio, as he stood, perhaps, in the golden Tuscan twilight, that the spot of radiance he caught on a chapel wall would long outlive the memory he had of a thousand nights of love?

~

A novel about immortality, then, and therefore about love. And let it begin and end with light.

CHIAROSCURO
A NOVEL

by
Daniel Clevenger

Look at the light and consider its beauty.
Blink your eye and look at it again:
what you see was not there at first, and
what was there is no more.
Who is it who makes it anew
if the maker dies continually?

—Leonardo da Vinci

PART ONE

I

LIGHT POURED DOWN FROM THE TUSCAN SKY AND PAINTED Tommaso's tousled head in sharp relief against the garden wall. Seeing the crown of his wild hair there in shadow on the brick, he raised a hand to comb it with his fingers. But the crescent of green paint beneath his thumbnail caught his eye and as he put it to his mouth, he remembered, and felt sadness wash over him, thick as morning light—he was off to Rome, to Masolino, to the rotten blue air of the south. To make matters worse, he'd slept badly. In the room next to his, Giovanni and his new wife hadn't left off cavorting till nearly dawn and, as he'd tossed from side to side, watching with anxious eyes as night paled on the linen pane of the window, he'd grown by turns feverish, then icy cold, at the thought he might never return to finish the work he'd started in the chapel of the Carmine.

He'd hoped to get away before the others woke. He hated leaving, hated saying goodbye. As it turned out, it was a very good thing Giovanni had eased himself away from his woman's arms to see his brother off. Tommaso was leaving as he was, without scrip or shoes, set to walk barefoot the hundred and seventy miles to Rome. Giovanni sent him back into the house to get his wooden clogs and the packet of provisions Isotta had prepared for him while he fetched the horse. Then, looking evenly into his brother's sleep-smudged eyes, the good Giovanni had said, "O you Masaccio, you! A little water on that ugly face of yours wouldn't have hurt."

Then he'd wrapped him in his big arms and sent him on his way.

Leaning into his brother's chest, Tommaso had felt the wineskin squeeze against his side, had known by the yielding in the pouch he held beneath his arm that Isotta, bless her soul, had filled it with the fleshy cimarrón olives he loved best. Over Giovanni's shoulder, he could just see Isotta in the doorway of the house, her nightdress slipping and slipping off her shoulder and he reminded himself to take a closer look at her when he returned. There were planes in her broad Luccan face that caught the light just so. And her breasts, he thought, might be the small round ones he liked best to paint.

With a tweak of the mare's tail, Giovanni had set his brother off towards the edge of town and Siena. By the time he'd sat down to a breakfast of bread and apricots soft as Isotta's flesh, he'd already imagined him trotting calmly among the cypress trees of the countryside, away from the sun-washed air of Florence into the haze of the south. He would have been surprised to learn that Masaccio had given in to an irresistible urge, had turned his back on the silvery olives at the city gates and led the mare past the goldsmiths' shops and the *botteghe*, past the rose and golden campanile, across the Ponte Vecchio, right to the door of Santa Maria del Carmine. He'd decided he could not leave Florence without looking one last time at his own face on the chapel wall.

His assistant was already at work. The last patches of *intonaco* painted by Masaccio were dry this morning and Andrea's task today was to apply the blue *a secco* to garment and background. Scaffolding covered the better part of the wall, and seeing it there, in all its ugly clumsiness, filled Masaccio with helpless anger. Besides blocking the fresco from view, it reminded him of how much work had yet to be done. Del Giusto could be depended upon to complete the details of costume and anatomy in the frescoes of the left wall of the chapel, but who would paint the bottom sections of the right wall, those huge expanses below Masolino's masterworks, if for some reason he, Masaccio, never returned from Rome? Once again, he felt his belly fill with cat's claws, the anxious raking at his guts that all the night long had wracked his sleep. And then, he made up his mind. Tearing off hood and cloak, he picked up an assistant's apron, slipped it over his head, and began to move sacks of plaster to the right side of the chapel, where the wall was not encumbered by scaffolding, where Masolino's Adam and Eve hung waiting in the garden high above his head.

When Andrea heard the trough being dragged across the chapel floor, he moved to the platform's edge and looked down, his scowling face a dark smudge in the shadows of the church. At first he thought it was another one of the assistants, come in to clean up the tools on this the last day of work, but then a ray of light fell on the fingers gripping the handles of the water buckets, and he recognized Masaccio. Seating himself on the board then, he folded his arms, a paintbrush daubed with blue held aloft in one hand, smiled down at the master and said, "O Tommaso! What, may I ask, are you about down below?"

"What does it look like I'm doing? I'm fetching water for the *arriccio*. Today I begin a new story, and I will see it finished before I go."

"A new story, Masaccio! But this one is not yet finished! Look here. *La resurrezione* is far from being finished! You shall go, make no mistake, and the walls of the Brancacci Chapel will bear here and there the traces of Masaccio's brush, but nowhere will Masaccio be complete. You would leave your work for some artisan to finish? You would leave your light to be dulled by some dilettante's shade?"

Dropping the clattering pails to the floor, Masaccio crossed the chapel once more, and stood beneath Andrea del Giusto's dangling feet. Perhaps the man was right.... It would be foolish to begin yet another fresco some other hand would have to finish. Looking up then, he caught between the fir boards of the scaffolding a glimpse of the painting of the resurrection of the son of the king of Antioch and of St. Peter enthroned. Masaccio grimaced as he looked up into the face of Theophilus—it was no imaginary head he had painted there but the effigy of the notorious Giangaleazzo Visconti, one of the most feared tyrants in Florence who, *Deo gratias*, had been taken off by plague twenty-six years before. Then, shifting his feet, Massacio looked up and away to the side, and smiled as his eyes lit upon the faces he had come to see one last time before leaving for Rome. He had painted St. Peter deep in ecstatic prayer, seated on a high throne in a niche carved out of the bare wall and, close at hand, from left to right, the portraits of his friends Masolino, Alberti and Pippo. He himself stood among them, stretching out his doubting hand to touch the saint. And so, he thought, as he strained to see their faces in the imperfect light, it *had* been a fine idea to include them in the fresco, to immortalize their friendship on the walls of the *Cappella Brancacci*. He shifted his feet again, let his contented gaze drift across the painting once more time and suddenly was seized with horror. There upon the chapel wall, for all the world to see, was a huge error that had somehow escaped his scrutiny. His eyes growing wide, Masaccio saw that for himself and for his three brothers in art, he had painted *only one shadow*. He started at the mistake, felt his blood run cold and, in a quick breath, understood that all was as it should be: one brotherhood, he thought, one light, one single shadow.

He untied the paint-spattered apron, then wrapped himself in his clumsy cloak once again, and left the chapel without a backward glance. As the doors heaved closed behind him, he heard Andrea del Giusto's whistle rise up into the high, clear stillness between the chapel walls.

‡

He supposed it would always be this way. He, at twenty-seven years of age, no better than a *discepolo*, at the master's beck and call. It had been difficult enough, the first time, to leave his grandfather's house in Castel San Giovanni to go live with the other shopboys in Masolino's atelier. It had seemed to him at first quite impossible he should live without the smell of pine boards and olive planks, or the reassuring noise of hammer and plane, or the golden fall of wood dust from his grandfather's hands. Paint and plaster had struck him as such foreign things. He had hated grinding the gessos, had quietly despaired of all the time wasted stamping and gilding. But what had held him there, in Tommaso di Cristoforo Fini's workshop, was the early morning hour spent drawing. In the stroke of charcoal upon wood, he'd found amongst the shadows a light he'd never thought to look for.

Then, when Masolino had closed the shop in Valdelsa to open a *bottega* in Florence, Masaccio had followed. Both teacher and pupil had been comforted to find that in the city on the Arno, spring rains coloured the slopes with the same flowers as in the Valdarno. That while the river froze over and snow drifted down from the Apennines, the crisp, blue vault of winter shed the same clear light as back home. And now, as he rode down the city streets, past the old market and the silk-twisting mills, through the pungent smells of wet wool and dye and autumn's ripe fruit, Masaccio wondered if he could love anything enough in Rome to compensate for losing Florence, his beautiful scarlet mistress. And in a small voice, he damned Masolino for calling him away.

The Church of San Clemente awaited him in Rome. And the bad air that gave Masolino headaches. And ruined temples and mosaics, and everywhere the smell of burning marble. He'd heard of the wolves and foxes that took shelter in the woods within the city walls, of the malaria-infested poor who fed on the hares they caught down in the streets. As the mare's nostrils flared in the bright air of the Chianti hills, and Masaccio tipped the Trebbiano to his lips in ever-lengthening draughts, he felt his spirits grow heavy with yet another thought. Masolino would not be alone in Rome. He would most certainly have Miuccia with him there. Lying in wait for Masaccio, with warm breast and unforgiving heart.

II

IT WAS NIGHTFALL OF THE SECOND DAY BEFORE HE REACHED SIENA. He could smell the spas in the dark, the alum- and iron-rich waters of Bagno al Morbo and of Vignone, and he began to think of Blessed Catherine and her hot purgatorial baths. This, in turn, reminded him of the glimpse of lake he'd painted in *Il Tributo* on the Carmine chapel walls and soon, he could think of nothing else but water. Deep, hot water for the aching, horse-bruised muscles of his back and bottom. At the inn, when the hostelier told him a bath could be had for a few *soldi*, Masaccio bolted his supper of cheese and vermiglio and quickly made his way to a back room where the innkeeper's wife and daughter hurried to fill an oaken tub. As he drew off his dusty clothes, the salty smell of sweat lifted off his skin in waves. He looked down in disgust at his pale legs and his dirty feet, began to feel ashamed of his ugly naked body here in the presence of strangers, then immediately forgot everything—the women, his nakedness, the waiting bath. Distracted by the shadows cast upon his belly by the candle's flickering light, he watched the play of chiaroscuro as his rib cage rose and fell. Off in the corner, his head bowed upon his chest, he stood entranced while the women laughed and gestured behind his back.

The texture of his skin, there, where it dissolved in darkness, seemed to him exactly like some other skin he'd touched before. Casting about amongst worlds of images, he eventually found the figure of Adam, shamed and stricken at the gates of Paradise. It was on Adam's face and neck, Masaccio now recalled, that he had painted shadows as deep as those carved in his own flesh by the dance of candlelight. And then he found himself wondering once again whether he had seen and then painted, or else painted and then seen. Perhaps Paolo—or was it Pippo?—was right after all when he said the painter does not seek, he finds.

The water was steaming hot, the wood of the tub felt smooth against his skin, the women bending over him were plump and comely. A grateful Masaccio let his greasy head sink into the bath, let the bony road and the horse's stony rump ease out of his body. Below the surface, he could hear the servants' voices humming like cicadas in summer sunshine, while heartbeat filled his head with summer thunder.

Drowning must be a lovely way to die, he thought. He had heard people pulled at the penultimate moment from the roiling waters of the Arno speak of colour bursting before their eyes and intense white light and peacefulness warm as wax suffusing their souls. Gone, he supposed, all thought of what they'd left behind them on this nearer shore: bare walls, unfinished stories, dry paint and broken plaster. As he rose up gasping for air, it occurred to him that life was perhaps not so much about learning how to live, but about learning how to die. Something maybe Rome would be able to teach him.

The innkeeper's wife had set a slab of black soap on the edge of the tub, dark as the rosaries of black amber he had seen wound 'round Felice Brancacci's wife's hands. As he tried to coax up a lather, Masaccio remembered those hands and the black snake writhing through its fingers and suddenly felt a shudder of cold. Letting his shoulders slide into the warmth of the bath, he remembered there had been serpents in the frescoes in the great hall of the silk merchant's mansion, and fanged vipers painted on the lid and the sides of the house's many *cassone*, and he was surprised now to realize that was the reason he'd felt such distaste for the place. Hurrying to erase the image from his mind, he plunged his face into his soapy hands, rubbed hard at the road dust caught in the creases of his mouth and eyes, and immediately went blind. After a few frantic minutes spent screaming and thrashing about, he risked parting first one lid then the other, and what he saw then, in the bleary light of his bloodshot eyes, made his breath catch in his throat.

He sat in the scummy depths of his bath, blinking and blinking his streaming red eyes, trying to focus on the vision before him. In the wide doorway leading to the kitchen, beneath the blackened beam of the roof, the innkeeper's daughter sat on a stool in the golden glow of firelight. She held some great, gallinaceous bird under one arm, its tail feathers a spray of speckled sword blades, its head a sorry, red and wattled thing. She'd turned it upside down and, with a quick hand, was plucking its breast, dropping clumps of feathers and down onto a piece of cloth stretched at her feet. Beside her rose a heap of game—rabbits and thrushes and ducks—all lit up, as were one side of her face, her bare arm and the falling folds of her dress, by the yellow light of the kitchen fire.

Masaccio heaved himself up out of the water, made his way to the pile of clothing he'd left on the chest in the corner of the room, and dug about amongst pouches and pockets till he found a small piece of charcoal and a roll of parchment squares. Then, settling into the tub once again, he began to draw the girl's bleached arm and hair and face, the transformations wrought upon her unsuspecting shape by the magic and mood of firelight. And as he drew, the porous stone held high in his hand, he spoke to the girl as she broke wings and twisted necks, he asked her after which saint she had been named.

"Cecilia. But I neither sing nor play the lute. As you can see, I haul water and gut hares and drakes. And ruin my fingers scouring."

"Ah, Cecilia. Do not be bitter. Now, you work in your father's house. Soon, you will be mistress of your own."

She lifted her chin to consider a moment, and the flames lit up her throat, soft and downy as a swan's neck. Masaccio grazed the paper with the fine edge of the charcoal and made the dip at the base of her throat beat with a warm pulse.

"No, *signore*. I will leave my father's house to go work in my husband's. He is a taverner, and wants me for his serving wench."

"This pleases you?"

"No, *signore*. Though the wedding is but twelve days from now, I have not yet discovered the means by which to avoid it. I have given much thought to slipping away in the night, but having nowhere to run to, and no money with which to keep body and soul together, I think it best to resign myself to being a tavern-keeper's wife."

This Cecilia had very high cheekbones that caught on their crests the full glare of the fire and plunged the hollows of her face in darkness. Shadows moved across her face and described it. As Masaccio studied and delineated their direction and the character of their edges, the planes upon which they lay found definition under his hand. He made her pouty bottom lip shine and softened the hard line of her chin. Then he moved to the gathers in her bloodied apron and skirt, spread wide between her parted legs. It stuck him then how young she was.

"How old are you, Cecilia?"

"Fifteen, *signore*."

Puzzled by the flatness of the bird he'd drawn in her arms, he left off speaking for a moment, tried to swell the thin lines he'd sketched to suggest the thing, tried to make them round and fat and full of shape-giving shade. But the pheasant resisted and so absorbed Masaccio's attention that he continued to speak to the girl without hearing what he said. While she cut off paws and plucked out feathers, Masaccio spoke of Rome and of the frescoes he had been called upon to paint there. He told her he and Masolino needed models for their work and, if she wanted, she could meet him by the stables at first light, before her father woke, and he would take her with him to Rome. His voice rose soft as smoke in the dark room, the girl's hands lay still in the folds of her apron, a small white feather floated noiselessly onto the surface of the water. Letting the drawing and the piece of coal fall to the floor, Masaccio watched the feather drown as he rose out of the cold bath.

It had suddenly occurred to him, as he'd lain back in the water, that here in Siena, he was surrounded by masterpieces of fresco—

the works of Berna in St. Agostino, those of Simone Martini in the palace of the Signoria, of Ambruogio Lorenzetti in the cloister of the Friars Minor. Amazed he had not thought of this before, he dressed quickly, thinking now only of bed and of the early morning hours he would spend in quiet communion with frescoed saints and the traces of the gifted hands that had brought them to life.

As he left the back room of the inn, he barely glanced at Cecilia or at the mound of dimpled pink flesh at her feet. A newly arrived pilgrim was hurrying towards the tub, dropping cloak and robe as he went, and calling in a loud voice for fresh water and soap. As he made his way to his room, Masaccio heard the innkeeper's wife swear as she struggled to hang another great pot at the fire.

He slept badly. His clean skin gave good purchase to the bed lice and his wet hair kept his head cold the whole night through. Despairing, at last, of waiting out the sleepless hours, he rose shortly before dawn. The last shreds of darkness found him on his knees on the pavement of the Duomo, where he attempted to decipher by the paling light of a crescent moon the figures Duccio had set out there in marble. As the sun lifted, watery and weak, out of the dark mass of the mountains, he began to make out the shapes the master had captured in stone. He watched in awe as the ascending light made the pavement dance. And he remembered, with a stab of sad pride, that the face of the Christ child he had painted in the Church of Sant'Ambrogio had been, like Duccio's marble, brought into relief by the light. The one he'd thought to paint there—a brilliant stroke of sunlight cast upon the wall. Full of nostalgia, then, for the work he'd left behind, grieving at once the done and the undone, he led the mare with a quiet clucking sound to the southern gates of Siena.

It was only when he was far away, on the road to Bolsena, that he remembered and felt a pang of guilt. All those other masters he had meant to visit and pay homage to, all the frescoed glories of Siena. And then, too, there was the small matter of the unsettled account at the inn. He grimaced at the memory, but, recalling the excellent drawing he'd left on the wash-room floor, wondered if it might be considered payment enough. Then reaching for the wineskin and finding it empty, he turned all his thoughts to great, full casks of mellow Trebbiano.

Sunday 3 March

Went to Brendan's fiftieth birthday bash last night—took a bottle and a card and considered myself well armed, ready for anything. It had been a while since I'd seen anyone from Christie's side of the family—the boys go for a drink with their cousins from time to time, and Sheila still calls once in a while or sends over a casserole or a pie—but I thought, by now, it would be easy. Well, I was wrong. As soon as Brendan opened the door, I glanced up at his face and found myself looking into Christie's eyes. My expression must have changed because Brendan didn't say a word. He just clasped me to his chest till I thought I would choke. And he said, I know, man, I know. She never even made it to bloody fifty. So we set our minds to getting stinking drunk.

I don't remember much of the early part of the evening. Brendan kept pressing drinks into my hand and introducing me to the same people over and over again, and the boys kept leaving their game of snooker to come see how I was doing. They'd make sure my glass was full, put their big leering mugs into mine, then disappear again. I also sort of recall hitting on a young brunette who hovered around me with platters full of food, insisting that I eat. She was probably Liam's girlfriend, all of eighteen, for God's sake, and I hope I wasn't a complete ass. If she was as patient with me as I seem to remember, it's probably because Sheila explained to her about the poor, old widower uncle, the lonely writer, who drinks in order to forget.

Also have a vague memory of repeatedly putting my fingers to Brendan's face. He'd be deep into a discussion with two or three people, I'd be standing on the edge of the circle, not contributing, not really listening, either, and suddenly I would find myself stretching out a hand and touching Brendan's face. The first time, he was a little startled, sort of drew away but, when he saw it was me and as he got progressively drunker, he stopped minding, even leaned in for me to get a better feel. (Your brother's skin, Christie, is so much like yours, I wonder now why I haven't spent more time with him since you've been gone. Just to pretend, for a moment, that you're around the corner in the kitchen, giving Sheila a hand, just to fill my eyes with a living, breathing reminder of you.)

All evening long, I drifted in and out of conversations, leaving sometimes in the very middle of a sentence, bored, bored, bored out of my skull. I walked around the house, even poked into the kids' rooms, shut myself up in Brendan and Sheila's bedroom for what seemed like a very long time. All the guests' coats were piled up on their wide double bed and I had to fight the urge to crawl under them, make myself a nest there and fall asleep. I remember looking at my face in their big dresser mirror, checking out my grey hair, my pouchy skin, the wilderness of wrinkles that has cropped up at the corners of my eyes.

A woman came into the room and shut the door quietly behind her. I watched as she lifted her skirt and adjusted a stocking to conceal a run. I'd noticed her before, her excessive makeup, her very short, very narrow skirt, and I'd cast my gaze around the living room, trying to decide which of the paunchy, red-faced men might be her husband. I was trying to think up an excuse for my being there, alone, amongst the winter coats and their pockets full of wallets, car keys and coins, when she suddenly walked straight up to me, grabbed me by the back of the neck and pulled my face into hers. She kissed me full on the mouth, softly but insistently, somehow chastely, too. And as unbelievable as it sounds, I felt that old familiar stirring in the loins and suddenly I could see the two of us, buried in the furs and the melton cloths on the bed, going at it like a couple of monkeys. But before I could set my drink down on the dresser and slip my hands up her dress, she pulled away from me, looked me hard in the eyes and said, "You poor, poor baby." Then she quickly walked out of the room.

I've had the time, in these three long years, to discover it really is true: experience of death destroys sexual desire. I have lived like a monk since Christie has gone and can honestly say I have not missed, how does Cheever put it? carnal congress, and the game of seduction, and above all, the obligatory casual banter that gives a veneer of civility to the hard, hot fact of animal connection. (I cannot get past that one, Christie, no matter how hard I try. Small talk seems to be growing smaller and more insipid all the time. Remember how we used to dream, you and I, of building a simple house on a remote northern lake, far from the crowds and the rush and the noise of the city? I am more than ever drawn to the vision of the secluded life. When I try to imagine what my days will be like when the boys have settled into careers and marriages, I picture a brown and bearded man, sitting alone on a sand esker, reading a book beneath the midnight sun. That'll be me, Christie, without you. A barmy old hermit, hunkered down somewhere between the treeline and the tundra, talking aloud to someone only he can see. And every day I will awaken to the regret of not having told you often enough, when you were here, when I still had the chance, how much I loved the sound of your voice.)

After everyone had gone home, Brendan and I sat down with what was left of the Scotch and spent the rest of the night passing the bottle back and forth between us. He's taking it hard, this business of turning fifty, and I didn't have the heart to remind him some people aren't so lucky. And besides, I sympathize. I even quoted Yeats to him: *What shall I do with this absurdity—O heart, O troubled heart—this caricature? Decrepit age that has been tied to me As to a dog's tail?* It's the decline of the body that we are forced to stand back and witness, the waning of potency, it's the feeling of being out of phase, of missing the point, of suffering the effects of a narrowing peripheral view. It's also, of course, the sense of having lived so long and accomplished so little. The abyss yawns, and we do not feel prepared, just yet, to slip off the face of the earth and disappear forever.

I poured another drink and told him that at thirty, Matthew Arnold had written that his heart was three parts iced over. "Ha," Brendan said. "I wish it was only my heart." But that was the Scotch talking. (He really does know, Christie, nothing matters so much as the heart.)

Before going off to bed, Sheila sat with us for a minute and, with the earnestness of the mildly drunk, enjoined me once again to think about ME, to carry on with MY life. She told me I was still young and still so beautiful (Her very words, Christie, not a word of a lie. That's how drunk she was.) and I should think about marrying again. I told her, like I tell everyone who worries about my romantic life, that my days are very full, with the boys, with teaching, with writing. (I told her, too, as kindly as I could, that no one could ever replace you.) Then she said, with tears welling up in her eyes, "Sometimes at night, when I'm curled up beside Brendan, I think about you all alone in your cold, empty bed and feel my heart ache." (I wanted to tell her, Christie, that in the interests of avoiding heartache, it would be best not to think about me at all, then, in that or in any other place. What I told her, instead, again, was not to worry. "Remember," I said, "that when I seem to be most alone, and withdrawn, I am in fact engaged with my whole heart in the exalting effort of retrieving every last particle of Christie." "But that's what I mean," she said. "You never can, you never will." And then her voice softened and she said, "It's time, Daniel, for you to forget about Christie, to make room in your life for someone else." I gazed at her with what I hoped was an indulgent look on my face—that's when I noticed her teeth were blackened from too much wine, there was a smudge of cake icing on her écru sweater, and her cheeks were full of rucks and seams like after a long and sleepless night. It was clearly way past her bedtime. So I smiled at her, Christie, gave her a chuck under the chin, and started talking about Masaccio.)

It was a mistake, of course. I could see their eyes glazing over, but that perverse desire to persist in the face of undisguised resistance had taken hold of me and wouldn't let go. "Can you explain," I asked in a belligerent voice, looking from one closed face to the other, "how it is that an artist who is recognized, in learned circles, as the innovator of modern painting remains to this day a virtual unknown? How it is," I demanded, my voice rising, "that the names Michelangelo, Raphael and da Vinci are familiar to all of us, even to Joe Six-Pack down there on the street, when the name Masaccio is not? Consider this," I said. "Masaccio was the first to follow the laws of perspective in painting, the first to create relief by the use of light, the first, in fact, to place an inscription at the bottom of a fresco. His name, however, and you'll agree with me here, is hardly a household word."

They were in no position to agree or disagree. Sheila was fighting a losing battle with eyelids suddenly grown stupid and heavy and, behind a closed and quaking fist, Brendan's face was slowly dissolving in yawns. They were both grey around the mouth, they had a waxy sheen to their skin, and their bodies looked as rumpled as their clothes. But that didn't deter me—I was in hot pursuit of an idea that had glimmered for a second in my field of vision like a stray reflection on darkened glass, and I was not prepared, despite the lateness of the hour or the blurring of my thoughts, to let it slip away.

"My question, Brendan"—by this time, in order to fix his attention, I had him by the arm, my long fingers grasping the flesh of his right arm in the death clutch of the very drunk—"is this: why him? Why was it given to him to make these incredible advances in the evolution of painting? What did he have that others did not? What insight had he been given that all his predecessors, his venerable brothers in art, had not?"

Rousing himself, Brendan shoved his pudgy fingers through his thinning fair hair, wiped his slack mouth with the back of one hand and said, "Isn't there a school of thought that espouses the theory of critical mass? About ideas, I mean."

A noble effort, so early in the morning, with blood so dangerously thin, and bones like clear jelly. I was proud of him. I urged him on.

"Well, notions build, don't they? Through the ages? A tiny insignificant concept could raise its pinhead one day and slowly start rolling, gathering weight and substance as it moves through time, absorbing influences, attracting ideas like a black suit picks up lint, growing bigger and bigger till critical mass is reached and the thing has to be noticed before it explodes and dies. And it's a matter of chance, really, who does the noticing. A random thing. Your guy, here, this Masaccio, was simply in the right place at the right time. The thing—the light thing, the perspective thing—was probably so huge by the time it reached him he'd have had to have been deaf, dumb and blind to miss it."

It sounded good, but I wasn't convinced. "No," I said. "Listen, Brendan." My face was in his, and our breaths there, commingling, must have been incendiary. "There had to have been something in the man himself that allowed him to seize upon what were, after all, mere abstractions, and give them fully realized life."

"Okay," he said, grimacing as he pushed away from me and my big warped face. "How about this: it was a genetic thing. Like in Shakespeare or Beethoven. These smart genes being passed down from one generation to another and becoming more and more concentrated, more and more potent till, in the fullness of time, they reach the pitch, the intensity of brilliance we lesser mortals call genius. And that was your guy, Daniel. Just the last in a long line of Johnny Brightlights. Once again, a question of numbers: *un coup de hasard.*"

I was gathering my thoughts with the intention of demurring—as gently as I could. The guy was fifty after all, quite thoroughly drunk, and an orthodontist to boot. I was very touched by the willingness he had shown to work with me on this, a subject that falls, I feel sure, quite beyond the compass of his usual interests. But Sheila had made coffee; it was time for me to be heading home. I filed away my glimmer of insight (it has since been irrevocably lost), gave Brendan an amicable pat on the shoulder, told him he was probably right, and reached for the steaming cup with grateful and trembling hands.

Came home, slept a bit, woke with a raging headache and spent a miserable afternoon listening to my brain slide around in my skull like so much silver slush. A complete write-off, of course. Except for this. It occurred to me this evening, as I sat down to a dinner of tuna surprise—it was Nick's turn to cook—that Masaccio might in fact have lived like me. With one foot in time, the other in eternity. He probably did not carry on an epistolary love affair with a departed one, as I do, because words were not his medium. He probably corresponded with her, with him, through images. Through light. As I take myself off to my empty bed tonight, I go comforted by the thought that the lonely *dipintore* might not, in fact, have been alone, that his notorious absent-mindedness might simply have been the outer manifestation of a deep and satisfying involvement with a luminous vision of infinity.

Wednesday 6 March

Went to O'Driscoll's class today to talk about writing. The usual comments about my inconclusive endings and my obsession with hands, and one startling, almost poignant query from a diffident young man with long, curly blond hair. He raised his hand at the end of a discussion about Sarah's decision to renounce art—Chapter II in *Gabriel*; I had to ask for the reference, it's been so long since I've reread *The Dovecote*—and asked me if I really believed, as my novel seems to suggest, that a talent will cause your death if you try to hide it. I don't remember what drivel I offered up in guise of an answer, I was that taken by the look in his eyes. But when I paused, another student turned around in his seat, glared at the kid and said, in a tone that struck me as being a bit offensive, "Why in the world would you want to hide it? There's nothing at all romantic about the reluctant artist."

The boy glanced up at me with apology written all over his face and said, "Well, some people might consider talent an occasion for sin. They might want to refuse the temptation of worldly fame or, like the hymn has it, man's empty praise."

(I took that one like a punch to the heart. We've talked about this so often, Christie. And I'm still not sure of the impulse—full of grace or devil-inspired—that drives me to write. But in the face of this boy's implicit accusation, I became defensive and immediately dismissed him—another Catholic, I thought, or a Mennonite, with that tiresome, overdeveloped sense of guilt.)

Then another student, a girl this time, raised her hand and answered the boy's question by directly addressing me. "You, Dr. Clevenger, obviously do believe that suppressing a talent will eventually kill you. After Sarah's initial exhilaration at being freed from the constant need to paint—you refer to it, I think, of having rid herself of the cynical monkey on her back, with its ambitious claws sunk into her flesh—she becomes indifferent, neglectful, almost losing her life as casually as one loses one's keys. To rephrase the question, then. Is it really a matter of life and death?"

I looked beseechingly at O'Driscoll, sitting high up in the lecture hall, hiding a smile behind his elegant, manicured hand. And refusing to help. Something wicked tore through me then, very like anger or, maybe, craven fear. And I said, rather roughly, "No, it most certainly isn't. Sarah should have gone out and found herself a job."

That raised a laugh or two. So I quickly wrapped it up. "Thank you for your attention," I said. "Good luck on your exams. Goodbye."

And I fled the classroom like a thing pursued.

In my office, I took down my copy of the *Commedia* and flipped through Purgatory till I came to Canto XI, Pride of Birth, Artistic Talent and Power.

I read:

Oh, the vainglory of human talent!
how short a time the greenness of its leaves
lasts, unless barbarous ages follow!...

Worldly fame is nothing but a breath of wind
which moves this way and that,
and changes name when it changes its direction.

and found nothing there to console me. I put the book down, and thought about two things.

First of all, that blond boy. The look in his eye has me convinced he harbours within his tremulous soul a rare and wondrous sensibility. I am sure the kid has been given some great gift, some mastery, that comes to him as easily as breathing, like Mozart at the harpsichord, or Picasso with his pencil. But because his music, his drawing, his easy way with words, has somewhere along the line appeared to him as evil—distracting him from the world and all its sorrows, perhaps, tempting him with glory—he has sought to crush it, to excise it from his flesh or, at the very least, to suffer it like Paul tormented by his thorn.

Secondly, my heartfelt conviction about the triviality of art. I believe, like Oscar Wilde, that art is quite useless. *Poetry*, wrote Auden, *makes nothing happen*. And I know in the very marrow of my bones that its practitioners are an effete lot. They inhabit a rarefied atmosphere that thrives on exquisite anguish, sublime egoism and exalting spleen, and these men, these women, these poets, damned though they may be, belong to a most blessed race. Of what value paint, as opposed to blood, notes compared to tears, words to selfless love? Of what significance, these frivolous markers of time? I blush for them, for me, at our guilty good fortune, at our contemptible irrelevance.

But if that is the truth, why does my heart wrench so in the face of that blond boy's self-denial? Why do I feel such loss at the thought of squandered light?

Tuesday 12 March

At the end of the day, looked up to see Magda standing in my office doorway and felt a smile pour through me like wine. She'd had an errand to run at this end of town and wondered if I'd be in. We went to a Thai place she knows in Osborne Village and then to her house to take a look at some very rare books on the quattrocento. She lives on a secluded street facing the Red, a brisk walk away from the university. Set among the oaks and the spruce of the river lot, the house is a stark piece of architectural design—glass and corrugated steel slicing through the organic asymmetry of the landscape like a blade among petals. I paused on the threshold, snagged for a second on the pinpoint of guilt, skewered by the sudden fear of being caught. (I felt my heart clench, Christie, when I remembered you are beyond the reach, not only of lies and betrayal, but also of my faithfulness.) Magda saw me hesitate, and smiled a little sadly.

"I know," she said. "The place still reeks of him. It's a fucking shrine, icons, incense and all. But you'll see, he's amazingly easy to forget."

The house is a showcase for his art. Magda says she destroyed most of it—the clay, the stone, the marble—when she kicked him out. All that's left are the unbreakables—the bronzes and the stainless steel. And a few kinetic pieces floating like cirrus clouds beneath the vault of the living room ceiling. When I smilingly asked if, after the storm, there'd been anything left for him to take, she gave me one of those heavy, significant glances.

"Nah," she said. "Geoffrey doesn't keep anything. He has no memory and no heart, and doesn't know the worth of any dead or living thing. He'd make a mobile of his mother's bones if he thought they'd move right in the wind."

She changed out of her teaching clothes into jeans and a sweater, poured us a drink and brought out her books. I spent the next two hours immersed in images gifted hands immortalized in fresco six hundred years ago, and gradually came to a clear understanding, with Magda's patient guidance, of Masaccio's pre-eminent place in the history of art. She quoted Stendhal: as antiquity has left us nothing, in terms of chiaroscuro, of colour, of perspective and of expression, Masaccio, rather than the *renovator*, is to be considered the *creator* of painting.

She placed reproductions of frescoes by Giotto and Masolino side by side with Masaccio's paintings so I could appreciate how dramatically he had broken with tradition, how categorically he had refused to make concessions to the past. Even my untrained eye could see the superiority of the sober, sculptural realism of Masaccio's figures, and of his grave, unornamented style. Magda told me that Masaccio has the status of a holy figure among painters and that the Brancacci Chapel is his shrine.

Then she showed me a handful of drawings by sixteenth-century artists, including Michelangelo, that illustrate the crowds pausing to gaze in reverence and astonishment—as Vasari writes—at the Masaccio masterpieces in the Carmine. And, she said, as unbelievable as it seems in the jaded times we live in, the paintings have the same effect today.

Feeling very much the infatuated schoolboy, I expressed, once again, my ardent desire to one day see them for myself. So she said, "The lecture I'm preparing is for a symposium that's being held in San Giovanni Valdarno this May. I'll be leaving as soon as my marking is done and I won't be back till the middle of June. A few colleagues and I have rented a house, there, in the hills south of Florence—a big house, with lots of rooms. One of them could be yours, if you like.... Why don't you come along?"

Still seated beside me, her hands resting on the books piled in front of her, she calmly lifted her sea-green eyes to mine. I looked right back at her, my gaze steady despite the wild knocking of my heart, and said, "Oh God. Florence, Siena, the wine, the sun.... It's very, very tempting, Magda, but no. No, I don't think so."

"And why not? Have you got other plans for the spring?"

"Not really. Other than a canoe trip or two with Nick and Alex. But you're going there to do some serious work. I'd just be in the way."

"You'd be doing some serious work, too, I imagine. And think of the inspiration you'd be able to draw out of the Pratomagno Mountains, and the yellow waters of the Arno."

"Yes, but...."

I hesitated before confiding this to her. She is, after all, a dozen or so years younger than I, and still restless enough to hunger after change. How could I confess to her that at the venerable age of fifty-two, I am terribly settled in my ways and cannot envision a break in my habits as anything less than wrenching? But I did it.

I admitted, with a catch in my throat, that I would find it difficult to trade the comfort of the high, white space of my quiet Canadian prairie home for the harsh unfamiliarity of a foreign villa, to give up, for a time, the solace of routine and small, customary ceremony for the jarring surprise of strangeness, to uproot myself from the usual landscape of my life to enter another, more curious, more alien country.

(To my immense relief, Christie, she did not laugh at me. You, my love, will never suffer the indignity of growing old and sedentary and fearful of the smirking young. But I, I will be spared nothing, it seems. For you have gone, and left me undefended.)

I also confessed that I am not at my best in crowds.

"Really," she said, with unnecessary emphasis. "Now, why doesn't that surprise me?"

"To be perfectly honest," I insisted, "I go out of my way to avoid them."

Magda looked at me and smiled, tossed off the last of her drink and said, "So you might have to mingle a little, make a bit of small talk. A small sacrifice, don't you think? If the words you use to conjure time and place are bright with Tuscan light?"

And so, tonight, as I sit with the pages of the manuscript laid out before me, I think about Masaccio and the chapel of the Carmine, I think about the dusky seduction of Italian beauty and the simmering umber of Italian inflection, and feel myself sway, and vacillate, and finally yield.

At the same time, I am aware of resistance growing deep inside me, building with the warmth and the rush of tears, endangering my heart.

Saturday 16 March

Voilà longtemps que celle avec qui j'ai dormi
O Seigneur, a quitté ma couche pour la vôtre
Et nous sommes encor tout mêlés l'un à l'autre
Elle a demi vivante et moi mort à demi.

Thursday 21 March
Opened the door to Nick's stage voice reciting Shakespeare—a few lines about a constant lover—and I felt winded by the words, like after a fall, or a sudden blow. Breathing carefully, I dropped my briefcase to the floor, slowly peeled off my winter woollens, poured myself a drink and went to join him in the family room. He glanced up at me but apparently did not notice my blanched face, or the skittering ice cubes in my glass. His audition—the role of Orsino in *Twelfth Night*—is coming up fast and he still has quite a few scenes to memorize. We've talked a lot about the play lately, about the lovesick Duke and the courtly artifice of the Petrarchan wooer, and he seems to have grasped the notion of an unreal and fantastical passion that has nothing to do with the object of desire. Today, as he recited Orsino's lines, I heard exactly the right degree of self-pity in his voice.

But while I talk with him about all these things—posturing, and the charade of courtship, and the degradation of the rejected suitor—what keeps distracting me and calling to mind so many other examples of *quiproquo* is the play's device of mistaken identity. Aside from the vaudeville humour generated by the mix-up, it's hard to explain the appeal of such confusion, except insofar as it presumes a tacit complicity between the writer and the reader. It is precisely the connivance, the secret sympathy such a stratagem evokes, that attracts me and tempts me to write it into Masaccio's story. Also, for the comedy that will arise in watching the hapless artist—*le grand naïf*—grapple with forces much larger than himself, and for the tragic implications of such bewilderment.

I am reminded of a film I saw in the early eighties, *Le retour de Martin Guerre,* with a very young Gerard Depardieu. If memory serves, a soldier returns from war and, pretending to be someone he is not, insinuates himself into another man's life. I remember very few details of the story—have retained only a sense of pervading doom, and images of dark, mediaeval interiors and of doubt-shadowed eyes—and would like to see it again.

And I wonder now if Magda would be interested in watching it with me some evening. I could try to dig it up somewhere and then invite her over for popcorn and beer. And introduce her to the boys, have her sit beside me on the family room couch, surrounded by Christie's cushions, and her prints and watercolours, her books and her CDs.

I don't think I can do it.

At the thought of bringing another woman into Christie's house, something gives in my heart, some walled and well-defended place feels suddenly besieged, and grievously threatened. And I know Sheila is right, I know Shakespeare is right—What a plague means that Clevenger, to take the death of his wife thus?—my practice of mourning is ritually lifeless. But it is not time, yet, for the walls to come down.

Forsaking Christie now would feel like death. A second death. More bitter, even, than the first.

Wednesday 27 March
Received a packet of info on the Masasccio symposium in the mail today. Pinned to the pamphlets and prospectuses, one piece of paper with a handwritten note:

HAVE RESERVED YOUR ROOM AND YOUR AIRLINE TICKET. IN ONE MORE MONTH, DANIEL, THE QUATTROCENTO!

Six small words, and I am transported. To 1404, and the cobblestoned streets of San Giovanni Valdarno, and the house at No. 83 Corso Italia. And for a second, I am convinced I will see him there and in the *bottega* of beautiful, scarlet Florence, where he bends over shields and coats of arms while, beyond the door, rise the concentric rings of Brunelleschi's great dome. Yes, for a fleeting second, I believe in the possibility of conquering time and mortality, I believe in the triumph of the eternal moment.

But then I remember Borges: *Time is the substance I am made of. Time is a river which sweeps me along but I am the river; it is a tiger which destroys me but I am the tiger; it is a fire which consumes me, but I am the fire. The world, unfortunately, is real; I, unfortunately, am Borges.*

So, once again, it is to art that I will look for consolation.

(Do you remember, Christie, the hours we spent slowly spinning through the dark halls of the Uffizi, and the Pitti Palace and the Galleria dell'Accademia, our hands locked together and our hearts set adrift? When I will go to gaze once more upon the masterworks of the imagination, though you will not be standing there beside me, I will feel your breath upon my cheek and, soft against my own, the beating of your quickening heart. And I will learn again that in the timelessness of art lies the promise of everlasting life.

With transfigured eyes, Christie, in the infinite hours of a long, long day, I will see you again.)

Saturday 30 March

I know a thing or two about absent-mindedness. In Academe, these distracted types abound. And, like Saul Bellow, I take a rather skeptical view of the apparently overly preoccupied mind. *The secret motive of the absent-minded,* he says, *is to be innocent while guilty.* And again: *Absent-mindedness is a spurious innocence.*

I have yet to determine whether my Masaccio will be of this persuasion—concealing less than honourable intentions beneath the guise of forgetfulness. Does he leave the inn at dawn, for example, to avoid paying the bill, does he *forget* his offer to the serving wench to avoid a potentially awkward entanglement, does he *overlook* the other masterpieces of Siena in a fit of professional jealousy?

And what about in love? Will he forget promises and anniversaries, confuse two lovers or two beds, absent-mindedly be led astray? In the area of sexual politics, the cultivation of distractedness can certainly prove convenient. A man or a woman who has a history of self-absorption can easily be forgiven the occasional lapse or thoughtless word. The small offence will be dismissed with a smile of amused indulgence, the one we reserve for children, idiots and the charmingly ingenuous.

Absent-mindedness can also be a cover for a thousand petty larcenies. Feigning distraction, the artisan walks out of the fruit market with a stolen persimmon in his hand, he picks up the wrong cloak at the end of the working day, he incurs a hefty debt and forgets to repay it, he steals a new idea from a younger rival's sketch. Is he laughing in his beard as he cheats on his mistress and robs his friends, or does he in fact move blunderingly through the world, oblivious to the wreckage in his wake?

Was he a true *grand distrait*, this Masaccio, or simply duplicitous, in love, in life and in art?

Because I like the guy so much, I want to believe him blameless. Want to believe his transgressions were committed unconsciously and very much in spite of himself. I am coming to see him, more and more, as a true innocent who, with his eyes fixed on another reality, could not help but stumble in this one.

The fact is, a distracted Masaccio suits my narrative purposes well. I am beginning to discern a possible explanation for the source of his inspiration, an answer to the question: why him? And it has to do with a convergence of worlds, an intermingling of time and the eternal, of the past and the present. A man too caught in the clutter and confusion of the here and now would not have been open to the gift of a moment of grace. Because Masaccio inhabited two worlds, and moved distractedly between them, it was to him that was given a glimpse of an unearthly sun. Like a new Prometheus, he borrowed light from the gods and painted it on a chapel wall.

III

IT WAS LATE AFTERNOON WHEN HE AWOKE, ALONE, IN THE SHADE of a plane tree. The mare was off grazing at the edge of a field, the grape-pickers had gone back to their baskets and shears. Their song rose in the misty air of the valley and everywhere was the pungent smell of yellowing vine leaves. For a brief blissful moment, Masaccio thought he was back in the Valdarno, in his uncle's vineyard, and he looked about, searching for Francesca. She used to leave him like this, when he'd fall asleep in the afternoon sunshine after they'd made childish love, and, bunching her skirt against her pale thighs to keep it from rustling, would go hide among the vines till he'd come find her again. Then, while the sun heaved its lazy round bulk into the sea, he'd catch her once more, sneaking up behind her between the shady rows and, burying his face in the small breasts that pressed against the laces of her bodice, he'd fall with her to the sandy earth and love her once again. But the song the grape-pickers sang was unfamiliar to him, and even the lingering taste of the fruit they'd given him to eat left a strange tang upon his tongue. He was nowhere near the

Valdarno, night was nearly upon him, and Bolsena was still many miles away.

The village lay beyond the first reaches of Lago di Bolsena. But when the smell and rustle of marsh grass floated up to him on the night breeze, he left the road and turned the mare's head toward the water. He would let her drink, he'd admire the moon's reflection on the surface of the lake, then he'd travel on to town and to the nearest inn.

He knew the lake edge was a dangerous place to stop. Brigands willing to slash a traveller's throat for a few centisimi often camped by the water in makeshift shelters made of reeds at the hour when pilgrims traded the dark roads for the safety of the hostels. But the night was so bright, and the vision of moonlight spread on black water so appealing, he forgot to be afraid and let the mare have her way. They blundered through coppices and bunches of pine, the horse's hoofs by turns sank in fen and clattered on rock, and all the while Masaccio watched the shadows cast by tree and shrub and cloud move across the ground. By the time they reached the lake, a velvet pocket for the bright opal of the moon, he did not know how they'd come upon that place or how they'd go from it again. He eased himself down from the mare's back and, as she drank in noisy draughts, he walked here and there at the water's edge and felt the marshy earth suck at his shoes. It was chilly by the lake, of an autumn's night. He hugged his cloak tighter to his chest and turned his back on the cold cheek of the moon.

Up along the bank from where he stood, there was a clearing amid the low trees and he could see a shape there, shifting among the shadows like wind in a wood. A deer, he thought, foraging for food by the light of the moon. But then the creature straightened and stepped into a pool of light, and Masaccio saw that it was a man. His heart began to beat wildly. He'd heard of the ways these desperate men dispatched their victims after stripping them of all their worldly goods, leaving them impaled by the roadside, a stick through the belly and a toad in the mouth. Moving stealthily, he raised a hand behind him to touch the horse's reassuring flank. The mare whinnied, a soft cry that carried cleanly across the water, and the man in the clearing raised his head. In the moonlight, his hood and the long white beard that hung in the shadows around his legs were clearly visible, and Masaccio breathed a sigh of relief. It was no brigand who haunted this lonely place, but a hermit, a harmless, silent beadsman, as reluctant as Masaccio himself to meet another in these woods. Masaccio would not disturb his peace.

Tugging at the mare's bridle, he led her back the way they'd come, then he swung into the saddle and let her have free rein. With fine animal instinct, she would find her way back to the road, and in the meantime Masaccio could let his thoughts wander on to Rome.

In his summons, Masolino had not given the faintest inkling of what decoration Cardinal Branda da Castiglione wanted on his chapel walls. If only Maso had written a few words about what he was working on in San Clemente—already, Masaccio could be painting in his mind, or sifting through the Gospels and *The Golden Legend*, hoping to fall on some little-known, anecdotal scene that might please the Cardinal, just as the images of Saint Peter had pleased Felice di Michele Brancacci. A flush of embarrassment rose up in Masaccio as he recalled his patron's words of praise. *Signore* Brancacci had turned to Masolino and said, "You have taught him well, Master. Soon, if you are not vigilant, the pupil shall outdo the teacher."

And to Masaccio's everlasting confusion, Masolino had replied, "*Signore*, I stand before you, utterly outdone. What could I presume to teach the painter who, without any man's help, has conquered the world of light?"

Made quite dizzy by these perplexing recollections, Masaccio now tried to make sense of the burnished glow that lit up the low brush spread before him. There was no road anywhere in sight and the dopey face of the moon, it seemed to him, shone down from the wrong corner of the sky. He had a sinking feeling that while he'd lost himself in memories, the horse had made big, stupid circles in the wood. So much for animal instinct, he thought, and squeezed the mare's flanks with impatient heels. He caught a whiff of woodsmoke then, and through the shrubs and the low trees, he saw what could only be the hermit's fire. Against all desire—Masaccio was not curious about any other man's life; the muddle and mystery of his own seemed to him to be quite enough—he made for the light. Stopping within sight of the beadsman's hut, he slipped off the horse and, with a great sigh and greater reluctance, looped its reins through the branches of a willow. The Lord knew he did not want to disturb the man or, much much worse, be subjected to his mad and endless ravings, but it couldn't be helped. He was cold to the bone and resolutely lost. He waited in silence at the edge of the wood for the man to acknowledge his presence. But the hermit did not look up from the mushrooms and nuts he sorted by the fire.

Masaccio stood in the shadows for a moment and watched the fire paint wide swatches of light against the dark tangle of the wood. With a sinking heart, he remembered the long-winded tales of Blessed Tommasuolo, a hermit of the *Sacco*, who was known far and wide for the mystical mirror he carried about in which he claimed he could see the Passion of Jesus Christ. Masaccio wondered what gift this forest hermit would pretend to have, what grace had befallen him in the middle of this dark wood. At the thought that he would have to listen to the man's long and tedious story in exchange for warmth and shelter, Masaccio almost turned to go. But the night was so cold. He could feel the dampness rise from the earth, seep through his flesh like oil through a wick and settle along the edges of his bones.

Before he knew what he had done, he found himself seated by the fire, his chilled feet stretched towards the flame. Beside him, the old man worked in silence. Masaccio could see his hands, weathered and worn, more wood or stone than flesh. He could see the length of the man's fingers, the ragged black crescents of his nails, the thick slabbed cup of his palm—the instruments of toil. Drawing his own hands then, from beneath the wings of his cloak, he spread them before the fire and gazed upon them as though they belonged to another. They, too, were thick with muscle, rough tools bent by the brush, and chapped and reddened by lime. So what is the difference, thought Masaccio, between this man and myself, between his hands and my own?

The beadsman had put aside his work for a moment, had poured Masaccio a cup of hot tea. His feet were beginning to feel warm at last and his back had ceased to shudder with cold. He looked on the old man with grateful eyes and, watching him turn to his work again, he wondered what had driven him away from the company of men. Some great thing, he decided, some huge upheaval in the rolling level of his life. Though he thought hard for a moment, Masaccio could not imagine a disappointment or betrayal big enough to cast him from the smooth, sweet roundness of his days into the bleak and lonely struggle for survival that was the hermit's lot.

Watching him tip the cup to his narrow lips, Masaccio decided that what marked this man out was the absence of hunger. His own hands, he knew, were avid ones. His ambition was greedy, his passion for excellence a famished, ravenous thing. But he knew, too, that he would not trade his insatiable soul for this man's stubborn peace. Settling into the heat that welled up beneath his cloak, Masaccio gave thanks for the hermit's trusting, generous heart and, as the silence between them grew deeper, he felt relief nudge his sleepy brain at the thought that no pious rantings would break it.

The old man rose to light a candle at the fire and turned towards the hut. Masaccio, following close behind him, stumbled with a drowsiness induced at once by the heat and by the strange infusion of herbs the monkish man had given him to drink. Masaccio hoped it would give him dreams as bright as the scarlet robes of Florence.

As they stood together, the hermit and the painter, by the bed of husks that lay lumpily at their feet, Masaccio looked into the old man's eyes, then bowed his head and, in the quiet of his tired heart, wished him away. But he did not go. His candle held high and shining into Masaccio's face, he rummaged about in some fold of the rags around his hips and fished out a rosary—pieces of clam shell strung on a leather thong and worn to dull nacre. First the prayer, then the warning. Masaccio felt his heart tighten with dread. The admonition the old man felt compelled to impart was without a doubt the very one Masaccio did not wish to heed. He ran his thick paint-lined hand across his eyes and waited with clenched jaw. In a voice as hollow as the broken trunks that littered the forest floor, the old man spoke. "You go to Rome?"

Masaccio nodded.

"To sell your soul."

Masaccio felt his teeth begin to ache. The hermit took the painter's hands in both his own and said, "The work of these hands is meant for God's glory, not your own. You chase fame. You chase the death of your soul."

Masaccio stifled a yawn. The old man had it wrong. Fame, honour and repute meant nothing to the painter. He knew man's praise for what it was—as empty as a breath of wind. He also knew his Dante: *Fame is like the color of the grass which comes and goes, and He who causes it to sprout withers it.* With a movement of annoyance, he bent towards the pallet, gave it a few pushes with an impatient hand. But the hermit had not finished. At his next words, Masaccio straightened and felt despair grip his heart once again.

"Beware," the old man gasped, "beware the temptation of excellence."

There it was, he had spoken it. The one sin that left a dark blot on Masaccio's soul. He did not care for *gloria, grido, fama, rumore, nominanza* or *onore.* Shunned by men, even condemned and despised by them, he knew he would continue to paint. Driven, always, by the desire for excellence. *Lo gran disio dell'eccellenza.* The hermit reproached him (Dante reproved him). He knelt by the mat with bowed head and knew himself justly accused.

Lying sleepless beneath the hermit's rough blanket, Masaccio imagined himself travelling to Rome in the morning with the intention of explaining everything to Masolino. He would seek him out among the workmen and *garzoni* in the chapel and tell him that he was renouncing painting forever. Then, he would return to the Valdarno, find a piece of land there and spend the rest of his life working God's earth with calm and satisfied hands, reaping its fruit and knowing contentment. He would live like the humble beadsman who now snored beside him in the dark, in peace and simplicity, emptied of desire.

As sleep began to wind him in its dark shroud, he was suddenly filled with the marvellous conviction that, in the quiet and the solitude of the fields of home, Francesca would come to him once more.

IV

In spite of himself, Masaccio felt a rush of excitement as the Aurelian wall rose up before him. Riding slowly down the Via Nomentana, he had followed the road through the northern hills and now loped along, a singular nubble in the flat patchwork of fields. Sunset was approaching, workers had hung up their scythes for the evening meal. And yet, at the gates of the city, a throng of people were gathered in an animated knot. It struck Masaccio as odd. It was too late in the day for the market and, as far as he knew, it was not an important feast day. Hoping they would have dispersed by the time he reached the wall, he turned his attention to the long shadows cast by the bound sheaves in the fields. Then, swivelling in the saddle, he gazed upon the hills he had travelled through and marvelled at their softness in the dying light. It was in this way, his back to Rome, his face to Florence, that he entered the city of popes.

As he swung around again, he found himself surrounded by a clamouring crowd, their hands reaching up to touch him, to take the mare's reins from him and lead her away. Greetings flowed up to him upon waves of laughter. He looked down into smiling faces, saw swaying shoulders and garlanded hair. Casting about for a glimpse of Masolino, or perhaps even Miuccia, he felt his eyes light up in anticipation, and his smile, falling upon strangers' faces, was like a spark running wild. How good of him to come meet me at the city gates, he thought, and what extraordinary numbers of friends he has made here in Rome. Still he searched, and still found no Masolino, while choruses of "Gian, Gian, Gianlucido!!" broke around his ears. Dazed but undaunted, he let the gay crowd lead him through the streets of the city and down a stately avenue to the steps of a grand house. The Cardinal's residence, thought Masaccio, where Masolino, a huge foolish grin on his face, patiently waits. His own face still wreathed in smiles, he let himself be pushed toward the house by giggling women. He cowered a little as he slipped into the shadow of the portico, then, as his wooden shoes beat out an embarrassing tattoo on the marble of the wide floor, he came to an awkward stop. Looking about then, he saw nothing and no one to reassure him. He turned back towards the people pushing in behind him, a questioning look upon his face, and the place resounded with the noise of their merriment. That's when he saw them, really saw them, these women and young girls, the sons and the old uncles, dressed in silk and damask, with gold on their arms and flowers in their hair. Wedding guests all of them, and from their midst, the sound of wedding songs. He shook his head, making his long grimy locks fly, then, facing the crowd, he tried to explain. "I am Masaccio," he said, pressing the tips of his long fingers to his chest.

The guests fell silent for a moment, then broke out in a roar of laughter.

"There must be a mistake," he tried to say above the noise. "You have taken me for someone else."

No one bothered to answer him, but a young girl detached herself from the crowd, took Masaccio by the hand and led him to the arched opening at the end of the hall. Behind them, the guests spread through the great room, while music flared warm, like fire. Masaccio suddenly became aware of the weight of his cloak and the clumsiness of his shoes. He felt like dancing and drinking wine and burying his face in some young thing's fragrant neck. But first, he would go find Masolino.

At the entrance to the chamber, the child disappeared, letting a curtain fall behind her. Intent upon finding Masolino, Masaccio did not notice at first the young woman seated by a window. Moving into the centre of the room, craning his neck around pillars and great wooden chests, he searched the place for his old mentor and friend. His eyes finally fell upon the woman. She was watching him, her face awash in tears. She rose to meet him, then, reaching out one long, bare arm, she grasped his hand in hers. "Is it you, my love, come home to me at last?"

Speechless and utterly confused, Masaccio looked at her with his mouth agape. She was a pretty girl, small and fine-boned with olive skin smooth and rich enough to drink, her ears tiny conch shells in the dark sea of her hair. Maso's model, Masaccio thought. He likes them exactly like this, the mouth a sensual slash, the eyes a smouldering Roman fire. Masaccio laughed an easy laugh, then glanced about him once again. "Where is he hiding?"

"No one is hiding, Gian. We are alone here, and three years have in this instant disappeared."

"I am not Gian."

"Then I am not Eloisa."

At that moment, the curtain to the chamber spread wide and three men burst in, carrying new robes, leather slippers and gold. They whisked Masaccio off to the baths, scrubbed him to rawness and, wielding flashing blades, threatened to shave off his beard. As his relative ugliness, with or without whiskers, was hotly debated among the three, he managed to pick up a few facts. These men, he learned, were Eloisa's brothers, this was a wedding day and he himself the truant bridegroom, who, three years ago to the day, had absconded at the very hour he was to bed his virgin bride.

"Your sister is very beautiful," he managed to tell them as they tightened the robe's cord around his waist.

"She is a woman any man would be proud to have as a wife," he declared as they draped chains of gold around his neck.

"But you have made a mistake. I am not Gianlucido, the man who left your sister on their wedding day three years ago. I am Masaccio, a painter from Florence, who comes now to Rome to work."

At that, the three brothers grew angry. One of them, the largest and the darkest, approached Masaccio with glowering eyes and spoke between gritted teeth. "Enough of your games, Gianlucido Villani. Know that if it were not for Eloisa, you would be drinking a poisoned cup today instead of the fruit of my father's vine."

And pushing poor Masaccio in front of him, he led him into the great hall where a feast had been laid and minstrels sang to lute and dulcimer.

Eloisa took him by the hand and, as she led him through the crowd, Masaccio felt the searing heat of curious eyes upon him and wondered how *in nome di Dio* he had blundered into all this and how, *Dio mio,* he would ever get out. Fear tugged at his guts and despair settled like an ache upon his heart but soon his whole mind and body and soul were seething with nothing but confusion. With each new guest he met, and with every question that was put to him, he felt his perplexity grow. "And how goes the painting, Master?" "And were the Florentines kind to you?" "And the frescoes, are you planning to finish the frescoes?" He walked about in a kind of dream, seeing nothing before him but Eloisa's white perfumed shoulders, hearing nothing but the hum of the cithern, a high, singing stridulation that bored into his brain like a shard of glass. The fragrance blossomed to a rich, ripe head, the music swelled and split the air, and suddenly, before him, the crowd parted to reveal a man standing alone.

He had a smirk upon his face and in the fat hands he held crossed upon his belly, he grasped a sheet of parchment. Masaccio blinked furiously, trying to clear his mind of scent and song, desperate, even now, to find in the flaccid countenance before him the beloved lines of Masolino's face. But this man was large. His hands were big as spades and his immense jowls hung, full as wineskins. Even his voice, when he finally spoke, was big and bullish. "Gian, Gian." He shook his great, sad, fat head. "First, you desecrate the holiness of your wedding day. Then, you deny yourself the pleasure of your wedding night. And now, at last, when you come back to set it all aright, you spoil the surprise of your unexpected return."

Masaccio gazed upon him with uncomprehending eyes.

"We knew you were coming, Gian. You betrayed yourself along the way."

The man held out the square of parchment, nodded his head and dropped his heavy lids. Masaccio lifted an arm, weighted like the leaden limbs of dreams, and reached out a fearful hand to take it. It was the drawing he'd made of the innkeeper's daughter, a long-ago night in Siena, when he was still Masaccio, and Rome and its madness lay far down a dusty red road. He felt foolish tears rise up in him at the sight of the sketch, this familiar thing in a world gone suddenly strange. He could hear the big voice laughing now, full of disbelief at having found the drawing on a wash-room floor. "It lay there, miraculously dry among the puddles of water, and, as soon as I lay eyes on it, I knew it to be of Gianlucido's hand. When the serving wench told me that the traveller who had left it was a famous painter, when she said that after many years' journeying, he was eagerly awaited in Rome, I had no doubt that the man who had painted this ..." he held the drawing between two plump digits for all to see "... could only be my brother's daughter's truant husband."

As the guests pressed round the piece of parchment, Masaccio felt himself be drawn away, guided through the crowd of tipsy revellers by Eloisa's hand. She led him through the hall and beyond the kitchens, into a garden laden in the moisture of the evening with the musk of ripe fruit. It was fresh and moonbright there in the orchard and Masaccio, breathing freely for the first time that night, felt a weight lift off him and beat away on silent wings. Then, looking into the girl's lovestricken eyes, he felt it settle on his shoulders once again, a dark, ungainly bird, its talons dug firmly into his flesh. She was a small, hurt thing, and he knew that he was powerless to do anything but hurt her more. He looked hard at the girl, willing her to see the stranger in his eyes. She gazed up at him, searched his face, his mouth, his eyes, lifted a hesitant hand to his cheek. Then, startled by something in his expression, she quickly moved away. Masaccio felt relief flood through him like warm wine. She had understood her mistake. He would be free to slip away from her (and her dark brothers) into the sympathetic night. He waited for her to speak. But at her first words, he realized she was perfectly blinded by love and hope, and a deep and yearning despair. "You are full of fear, Gian. I see it in your eyes. What, do you believe I have betrayed you? How can you doubt me so?"

"Eloisa, I ..."

"I have not forgotten the last words you spoke to me on this night three long years ago. I have waited for you, Gian. I have gone with no other."

So, thought Masaccio, the scoundrel had enjoined his bride to wait for him, while he slouched off in the moonlight, leaving her alone in an empty marriage bed. In his unhappiness, Masaccio wished him dead, laid out in a ditch somewhere, fungus growing between his toes. Even if he were a painter.

He looked deeply into her eyes and said, "*Look* at me, Eloisa. I am not Gianlucido Villani. I am not the man you married. I come to Rome for the very first time ..."

"In many long years. I know. You have been to many places. Studying, working diligently, decorating the walls of every city you have gone to. In Pisa, in Siena and in Florence, my father and his brothers have seen your work and have heard men sing your praises."

Masaccio looked up through the lattice of citron tree leaves at the spangle of stars in the purple sky. They shone, bright, hard, perfectly indifferent. He bit his lip, tasted blood and felt weariness soften his bones. His head bowed down upon his chest, he turned to the girl and moaned, "Please let me go. Please. I am not your husband. I am a painter. I have come here to paint."

At that, Eloisa shook the stars from her eyes and grabbed Masaccio by the hand again. She led him to a rear entrance, then stole with him through arched colonnades while the sound of revelry resounded in distant halls, and took him once again to the chamber in which he had first set eyes upon her. The pillars shone white in the moonlight, the huge *cassone* squatted in shadow.

"These walls," she said, "await your brush. My father has often in these three years threatened to have them painted by some other. But I begged him to wait."

She turned up her face to him, and in the dim light, Masaccio saw her eyes fill with mischief as she said, "And he must wait still, until you have finished the paintings you promised to me."

Pushing aside a curtain then, she led Masaccio into a bedroom. A folding screen stood before a tall window. As she moved it aside, moonlight fell from the sky and cast a ghostly glow on walls covered in fresco. Slipping across the floor on leather soles, Masaccio moved slowly toward the paintings. His heart beating crazily, as though he really were going to look upon the work of his own hands, he brought his face up close against the wall and tried to read colour and shape in the obscurity of the room.

"Candles," he begged. "Please bring me candles."

He heard Eloisa step away from him, heard the hush of the curtain as it fell behind her. Moving back from the wall, he cast his eyes around him, and, even in the darkness, knew that there were no figures in these frescoes, no story being told. Nothing but wide sweeps of colour, like ripe summer fields. He breathed deeply, felt inexplicable peace descend upon him, falling like warm August rain. Despite the shadows, he could see that halfway down one wall, all colour ceased, and the faint red ochre lines of the *sinopie* stood out against the whiteness of the *arricio*. There, too, was nothing but long, smooth curves, low horizons and soft hills, wide open meadow, and plain, and lea.

Eloisa slipped into the room, her arms full of yellow tapers, a lit candle in one hand. She laughed softly as he took two of them from her, lit their wicks at her flame, and raised them high above his head. That's when he felt a tightening at his heart. For all around him, in the luminous tones of true fresco, lay the fields of his youth. This unknown, cowardly, craven painter had captured in simple plaster, pigment and lime water the timeless expanses of summer. Moments, full of expectancy, caught and everlastingly held, like in the pause before breath or heartbeat. Every scene waiting upon someone, calling for a presence, open like a cupped hand. Masaccio knew at once that it was for young lovers these wide spaces had been painted. The pastures beckoned to their bare feet, and the fields of crocuses and lilies were beds for their young bodies. Masaccio stood before these landscapes, more alive in their emptiness than the crowded streets of Rome, and felt himself grow weak with yearning. For something sweet and tender and long ago, and he longed for it now, as hungrily as night craves the dawn.

Eloisa had made a circle of the lighted tapers. She'd brought wine and cheese, melons and bread, had spread them out on the woven rug she sat upon. With his heart reeling with nostalgia, Masaccio wrenched himself away from the wall and settled in among the cushions at her feet. She fed him dark bread and fruit, wiped the juices from his beard on the edge of her gown, filled his cup with her father's wine, while all around them shadows leapt. She took his head upon her lap then, and, running her fingers through the tangle of his hair, she told him a tale in a voice as soft as memory itself. "Night had come at last. In the garden, the lemons shone like fallen stars among the dark leaves, and the shadows of the trees lay like lovers upon the ground. The child-bride stood by the open window, her face touched by the light of the moon. Her plaited hair lay in a thick rope upon her breast. Taking up the dark tress in his hand, her young husband coiled it around his fingers and, pulling softly, drew her gently to him. She let her head fall upon his chest, felt against her cheek the beating of his heart and the stirring heat of his flesh. He enclosed her in the safe embrace of his arms, and bent his face to her warm neck. And as they stood thus, wrapped one in the other, a world apart and unto themselves, bird-song came in upon the night and, sharp and neat as sword blade, cleaved them apart. The young husband at once drew away from his bride and, touched to his very soul, bade her wait a moment while he went in search of the bird. Tearing himself from his love's arms, he slipped into the darkness beneath the trees, drawn on by the thrush's song, while his young bride waited at the window for dawn and his return."

Eloisa fell silent, and Masaccio, moving uneasily beneath her hand, glanced nervously up at the windows. Thrush's song, my ass, he thought. This lovely Eloisa has a jealous lover somewhere, who takes delight in killing off her husbands on their wedding night. Poor Gian, sweet, sensitive artist that he was, tricked into death by some murderer's bird call. He rose up on one elbow to cast a wary eye into the garden and found himself enfolded in Eloisa's long hair. She had unpinned it, and it flowed now down her breast, covering Masaccio's face, stroking his lips, catching in the whiskers of his beard. He felt like he was drowning, a wall within him had yielded and he was being carried off in a warm rush, his blood thrumming in his skull, his breath thick and wet with tears. He closed his eyes, felt Eloisa's mouth on his, and the room at once was full of sun and the smell of meadowsweet. She brushed her cheek against his and whispered in his ear, "When the spell was broken at last, and the young husband left the garden to return to his bride, he found to his surprise that three years had flown by while he listened, entranced, to the thrush's song. But nothing had changed. Nothing aged or withered or grown cold. His lover, with still and patient heart, waited by the window, her desire a warm fruit in her mouth."

Eloisa fell silent once again and, bending over him, bid him taste of her to see if he were home. Losing himself in her flowing hair, stroking with his tongue the tips of her breasts, breathing summer and lilies and jonquils in the fragrance of her skin, he forgot about the murderer in the garden, forgot about Rome, forgot about Eloisa, as Francesca came to life once again in his arms.

Tuesday 2 April
So, it has been decided. Masaccio's muse will be a woman or, more precisely, a young girl. It could easily have been otherwise. After all we have learned of Renaissance masters and their *discepolo*, it would not have been a stretch to imagine Masaccio in love with a young boy. In the fifteenth century, the civic authorities of Florence had opened a brothel—it lay near the wine market between the tavern and the hot baths—in order to discourage homosexuality. The truth is, I chose Francesca as the source of his inspiration not out of some bourgeois sense of propriety, but because I wanted to be reminded of Christie.

(You, Christie, are more real to me than the women of flesh and blood whose paths I cross every day of my life. And I am convinced a man like I imagine Masaccio to be would be more faithful to a vision than to some mere incarnation. It pleases me to think that if he came to a sudden understanding of the eloquence of light, it is because of Francesca, a lost and longed-for love. And though I know it will make me ache with envy, I will give to him the very thing I want most in the world.

For months and months after you left us, Christie—I'm sure you remember this—I moved constantly between two states of being. If I was not bent over, prostrate with grief, then I was morbidly alert, vigilant as a hawk. I believed with a lover's blind faith that if only I could watch carefully enough, you would appear to me somehow, in some form, and give comfort to my heart.

And I was not content with evocations—your voice in a young girl's laughter, your scent in the dusky breath of evening, your silhouette, your small blonde head in the press of a crowded street—but wanted, expected, demanded to see you with my very human eyes, exactly as you were when you walked upon the earth.

It was when I was alone that I waited most intensely. In the forest, in the garden, in the darkness of my room. Willing you to appear, to turn your face towards me, to leave upon my skin the shimmer of your heat.

But my senses are too dull, and the world too thick a place. You did not appear to me in dream or fever or vision.

I still wait, but differently. The way one waits for fields to ripen and for fruit to fall. In the fullness of time.)

But to Masaccio, he of the sharp eye and the wise heart, will be granted the gift of revelation. And it is in his uncle's vineyard, where he and Francesca first loved, that she will appear to him, haloed in unearthly light.

The question will not be asked again. If Masaccio was in fact the first artist to paint with light, he did so through the grace of a divine apparition, a radiant vision, but mostly, through the grace of love.

Wednesday 3 April

A message from Gavin on my voice mail this morning, asking me to join him for lunch at the faculty club. I'd heard rumours about his latest entanglement and, all through my first class, I could feel worry building in the pit of my stomach. So many times in the past, I've had to helplessly stand by and watch him go crashing into disaster. In love, Gavin is like the fictional Benn Crader, *the kind of hemophiliac who would shave in the dark with a straight razor*. And who am I to counsel him, me, the recluse, the old stick, desperately in love with a memory?

When I arrived, I saw Clara's slight shoulders lifting in excitement as she moved in beside him. (And no, Christie, nothing has changed in her life. Still Chair of the German department, she's older, of course, and deafer, but still on the lookout for a life partner. The last time I bumped into her, I noticed her attitude towards me had changed in some undefinable way and I had the uneasy impression she'd maybe set her sights on me.

Three years have gone by, the world thinks: he must be ready to start again.

She asked me what my plans were for the summer. I told her, not very much. A few trips up north, maybe, a little canoeing and camping.

"Where exactly do you go, up north?"

The question struck me as being nosy, a bit too specific. I didn't answer right away, distracted by a sudden vision of Clara Reichmann, in pith helmet and mosquito netting, her knobby red knees knocking together above brand-new, high-topped hiking boots, smashing through the undergrowth and bursting into my campsite. I told her, "Oh, I don't know, on the Bloodvein, maybe, or up along the Berens River."

And she said, "What do you do up there?"

"Well, we paddle a lot, fish a bit, set up camp and watch the sunset and the northern lights, take a few runs on a little white water and occasionally shoot some rapids."

She didn't say a word, then. Just looked at me with an arch look in her eyes. After a moment, she asked, "And do you cook them on an open fire?"

I didn't get it at first, but when I did, I grinned like a fool. I stood there, shaking my head and grinning my face off. Rabbits! She thought we went up north to shoot rabbits! And I thought of how you'd laugh when I got home and told you....

I still do that, you know, at least a dozen times a day.)

So the three of us sat together around our clubhouse sandwiches, our pickles and our chips, the bachelorette, the widower and the divorcé. As we talked rather stiffly about selection committees and the new VP, I could feel the real topic of conversation lurking in the background, waiting for the right moment to pounce. There was a palpable tension in the air, so thick, so blinding, that for a moment I began to imagine some spark had recently caught fire between those two. But I should have known better. Gavin's incredibly robust libido was producing the smoke all on its own. He's found a new lady friend, a ballet dancer—I winced at the thought of those rock-hard calves and massacred black toes—and he is positively enthralled by the woman's asceticism. He, too, has begun a strict diet of green apples and mineral water, and is thinking of joining a dance class for beginners this summer. It is, he says, so very exciting.

I stared at the pickle juice inching towards the crust of my rye bread. And thought of the hundred and one metamorphoses my friend has undergone in vain attempts to please. The women he sees now are all much younger than he and the contortions he must impose on his body and his mind in order to adapt to their nimbleness—and I'm not even referring, here, to sexual performance—will, I believe, eventually kill him or, at the very least, fill him with a very lethal dose of self-derision. How do I protect him from ridicule and heartbreak once more?

Then, Clara quietly informed us of *her* new friend—someone to whom she had been introduced on the Internet. At her age, she very demurely stated, she had to use all the means at her disposal to broaden her circle of acquaintances and increase the chances of *fruitful* contact. She'd had the pleasure of being wined and dined by several amiable gentlemen—trial balloons, if you will—but there was one in particular who had caught her very discerning eye.

My sense of relief was so great I overdid the congratulations a little. Her blanched face blushed pink for a second, she wiped her mouth with the corner of her napkin, then leaned in to touch my hand. "Daniel," she said, "I urge you to try it. We're not getting any younger, you know, life is passing us by."

She squeezed my fingers and promised to e-mail me some addresses on the Web.

When she finally left us, Gavin lit a cigarette, then immediately stubbed it out. "Have to quit," he said. "Alyssa won't stand for it."

And then, "Did some shopping this morning." He picked up the bag at his feet, opened it up and proceeded to spread its contents on the table. "Got that new book by Godin, on the end of humanity."

He lined up a couple of new CDs—the top one was Scarlatti, sung by the boys' choir of King's College—a bale of handkerchiefs of Egyptian cotton, the book, and a bottle of sesame body oil. When he caught me staring at it, he grabbed it, popped the lid open and stuck it under my nose. "Good enough to eat, wouldn't you say?"

I looked at him and rolled my eyes. The bloody braggart.

But I just said, "Yeah, you're right. That's what *I'd* do. Cook with it—a chicken stir-fry, or salmon steaks. The boys are very fond of salmon."

He came down hard from the lusty heights he'd been scaling. A severe look on his face, he said, "Clara's right, you know, Daniel. It's high time you woke up, man, and found yourself a nice girl. I've offered to introduce you time and again to dozens of pleasant women. I'm not talking love here, Danny, I know how you feel about that, but simple warm companionship, you know, like in the Bible. *Better two than one by himself, since thus their work is really profitable. If one should fall, the other helps him up; but woe to the man by himself with no one to help him up when he falls down. Again: they keep warm who sleep two together, but how can a man keep warm alone?*"

As he recited Ecclesiastes to me, my brain glazed over and, in my heart, I felt a sudden squeeze of pity. For all those, like Gavin and Clara, who spend their lives searching for lasting love. Despite the evidence of the senses, despite failure and conflict and endless sorrow, they keep crawling out from under the heel of love, shaking themselves off and looking around for more. Love that banishes loneliness, love that fills our empty days, love that gives meaning to our lives. Men and women all over the world, driven by their great thirst, throw themselves headlong into strange and troubled waters only to find, again and again, their craving is not slaked. It's the thought of their unending disappointment that catches in my throat, of the hope that lives unwithered in the desert of the heart.

"Thanks, Gavin," I said. "But I'd rather take up a foreign language."

As I prepared to leave, I added, "Italian, maybe. Yeah, I think I'd like to learn Italian."

And I told him about Valdarno.

(Am I cynical about love, Christie? Is that what losing you has done to me?

I think not. I think that having shared with you a singular, most extraordinary passion, I see too clearly now, I understand, perhaps better than most, how rare real love is, and how ephemeral. Clara's love and, most certainly, Gavin's, will be a compromise at best and, at worst, a desperate, blind embrace against the terrors of the night. Finite loves, temporal loves. Because, unlike ours or Masaccio's, theirs is only human.)

Thursday 4 April

Caught it in the air this morning, when I opened the front door. The first faint stirrings of spring, a balmy edge to the dodgy wind. And I felt a rush of regret at the thought I would be missing it. May and June spent beneath a foreign sun, far, far away from the incandescence of the boreal sky. I already know how nostalgia will grab me in the guts when I'll gaze out over rows of vines and olive trees and poplars shimmering silver in the unfamiliar light and think of the cool green of the birch and the trembling aspen of home. I remember it well, that pinch of homesickness, that sense of loss. I felt it, at five o'clock each afternoon in Rome, when the starlings lifted up in great rafts above the trees and made me long for the tumbling of snow geese in a Canadian October sky. I felt it, that summer in London, when I stepped into the murky shallows of the Serpentine and imagined I could smell and taste the fresh, clear waters of Simonhouse Lake. I felt it, at six p.m. at Playa Uvita, when I watched the sun fall like a stone beneath the horizon and knew that far away, in the north, a long, long twilight was spreading its wings across the sky.

But, I keep reminding myself, it's only for six weeks. First, I'll have April, the best month of the year, and then the whole of the summer, too. There'll be time enough to shake that old world dust off my feet and, out of my bones, the cold grey clamminess of ancient stone.

Attended the theatre class's year-end production tonight. Nick played a wonderful Joxer in *Juno and the Paycock*. Smarmy to a fault, the charming Irish rogue, he moved from slavering sycophancy to bitter, hypocritical opportunism without missing a beat. And though I laughed as loudly as the others, I couldn't help but feel the shame—oh, the vanities and the violence of the world of men. I don't suppose poor old O'Casey would be surprised to learn nothing much has changed. Seventy-five years later, we are still maiming and killing, traitors still abound, and our heroes are, more often than not, an equivocal lot. The imagination, too, fails in very much the same way it did then. There is, now as ever, a falling short in each of us of the sense of other peoples' tragedy. *The whole worl,* Captain Boyle, *is*, indeed, *in a terrible state o' chassis.*

(There are only crows in the city, now, crows and blue jays—the orioles that used to come and eat the high-bush cranberries in your garden are gone now, even robins are in short supply, and it's a rare thing to hear the warbler's song in the stillness of the morning. City trucks still ply the back alleys of the suburbs, spraying poison to kill off the mosquitoes, men in moon-shoes walk around the well-kept beds of landscaped lawns with hoses full of herbicide and fertilizer to keep the grass a neon green, jumbo jets fill the sky with noise and turbofuel, neighbours' air conditioners drone on with a maddening steadiness in the vacant heat of summer afternoons, cars multiply like cancer cells, speeding down the city streets or idling at the curbside like squat, malignant beasts. And the rivers, Christie, and the lakes are dying, the sun grows hotter, the murderous oceans rise and the wild winds blow with biblical wrath.

In the darkness over the deep, an ungodly spirit hovers over the water.

Sometimes—only sometimes—I am grateful you are no longer here to witness the desecration of the world. At other times, when alien storms unleash their unnatural anger, I know that you watch with me, and smile, as a furious planet builds towards apocalypse. The day is not far off now, when, in a paroxysm of rage, it will shrug us off its face, dust off its mountains and its hills, and begin again without us.)

Today was the last day of classes. I feel time open up before me like a forest into field, like a river into ocean, like a fistful of light in a dark bruise of sky.

Saturday 6 April

I can see it in my mind's eye. These men, these rough artisans, sitting around Paolo Uccello's house at dusk in a Florentine autumn, drinking new wine, tearing at bread and bunches of grapes, listening to blunt-nosed Brunelleschi talk about Rome. Their hands are broad, their jaws are blue with a few days' growth, their cloaks and gowns are threadbare and torn. Brunelleschi has a piece of charcoal in his hand and, with short masterful strokes, he covers Uccello's walls with sketches of ribbing, arches and vaults, with drawings of intersecting lines that pull the eye to a diminishing point. With the sleight of hand of the magician, he creates for them the illusion of depth and distance. The men—and perhaps the women, the wives and the young concubines—ooh and aah over the mathematical formulae he prints upon the wall, but turn again and again to gaze upon the scenes he has brought to life through the artifice of perspective. There is a hum of excitement in the air, and much boisterous discussion, the women and the wine are all but forgotten till night falls, and the lamps are lit, and shadows leap along the walls. Then the young girls and the wives snuggle close and tip cups of red Chianti to their men's lips and, with their small hands and their small mouths, stoke a fire in their men's blood.

Later, when they have all returned to their homes, Masaccio

will lie awake in his bed, his arms beneath his head, and dream up compositions in which everything bends to the iron rule of relative distance. While, in imagination, he places his Madonna and Child, his saints and his angels squarely in space, Uccello stands in front of yet another wall of his house, drawing lines over and over again, sketching landscapes that recede like magic into the distance.

These are men who have nothing. According to Vincent Cronin, their lowly position in society dates from the Dark and the Middle Ages, during which painting, sculpture and architecture were not ranked among the seven liberal arts. Their practitioners were counted as manual or servile workers—in Rome, painters were lumped together with carters and grooms, with whom they had to take their meals—and the word *artist* did not even exist. The architect belonged to the Guild of Masons and Joiners but, since 1378, the painter had no *arti*, except in Florence where he had a social guild of his own, The Company of St. Luke, and had to enroll in a subsection of the *Arte dei Medici e Speziali*, the Guild of Apothecaries and Doctors. So it was at the druggist's, among the bunches of dried medicinal herbs, the simples, the sapphires and the celandines, the "cures" for gout, influenza and bubonic plague, that Masaccio and his friends had to buy their pigments and their brushes.

What was it they hoped to gain, these humble, debt-ridden men, from the possibilities perspective afforded? As Uccello stayed awake at night, drawing converging lines among the paintings of birds, cats, dogs, serpents and lions adorning his walls, did he once imagine the illusions he created could make him rich? Or attract women? Or make his name immortal? Or was his fascination a more disinterested thing?

It is difficult to explain the artist's devotion. We have seen it portrayed again and again in film and in literature—the beautiful obsession that keeps men poor and distracted, that uses them and spends them and leaves them now crushed and now exalted—and think we understand. It is the freedom of the artistic life that attracts them, and the desire to be marked out among men, it is the pursuit, the chase, perchance the capture, of the elusive prey of the imagination, it's the passion for excellence, the thirst for beauty, the compulsion to express. It is also the sheer, guilty extravagance of giving over one's life to the superfluous and the inessential. And it is, most of all, obedience. To some mysterious, innate injunction that some call madness, and others, divinity.

But perhaps it was simpler than that in Masaccio's case. Drawn to the trade because of a certain affinity for its instruments and science, he went to his paints and plaster the way the mason goes to his mortar and the carpenter to his plane. And it was nothing more than his pride as a craftsman, his love of the work of his hands, that brought him to the edge of discovery. Perhaps.

I prefer to see him otherwise. I want him, and I shall make him, intense, passionate and inspired.

Sunday 7 April

Alex and Stephanie took time out from studying for finals to prepare us a fine dinner. The first barbecue of the year, grilled halibut with lemon vermouth butter, eggplant parmigiana and roasted sweet potatoes. I brought the wine and Maggy, Nick's newest friend, brought her mother's apple pie for dessert.

(I never feel your absence more, Christie, than on these evenings when the boys have their girlfriends over. I stand before them, truncated, as though I had an arm or a leg missing, as though my left side, my heart side, were gouged out and bleeding. They look at me, these pretty young things, with guarded, questioning eyes, wondering at my incompleteness.

You would have been so happy to sit surrounded by your boys and the girls who've fallen in love with them. I can imagine your laughter and the affectionate way you would have placed your hand upon an arm, or straightened a lock of hair upon a forehead. And the talk around the table would have been easy and light, and I would have caught you, again and again, gazing with undisguised love at these children of your heart.

You would be proud of your men, Christie. They are warm and affectionate and they treat their friends with gentle respect. And they love us still, you and me. I can see it in the devastation in their eyes.)

I told the kids about my plans for the spring, and a little about Massacio, so we eventually found ourselves talking about the Italian Renaissance and all the great masters whose names have come down to us over the centuries. We tried to recall the most famous ones, men one and all, and then Maggy said, in a petulant voice, "So were there no women in Florence of the fifteenth century?"

I assured her there were, quite notorious ones, even. Duchesses and mistresses and the powerful Medici women—Catherine and Marie—who became the queens of France.

"But were there no women *artists*? No fresco painters, or sculptresses, no weavers of tapestries or makers of stained glass?"

I couldn't answer her except to say I was sure there had been, but that unfortunately, few names, if any, had survived to this day.

Then Nick pointed out that, even in more recent times, women do not figure prominently in the ranks of illustrious artists. Let's see, he challenged us, how many we can come up with.

"Emily Carr," Stephanie said.

"Mary Pratt," I said.

"Frida Kahlo," Maggy said. But the list was short. We all looked at each other, a little ashamed.

I tried to make excuses. You have to remember, I said, that fresco painting was an extremely labour-intensive process. You had to be very strong to work the several coats of plaster—heavy work for a woman. And besides, painting was considered menial. It was difficult, messy and underpaid. No woman would have wanted to sit among the poor, dirty men she saw eating cheese soup in the back rooms of the inns, or hauling scaffolding and olive planks through the side doors of churches. Painting fresco, even at the request of princes and popes, was not prestigious, and certainly not romantic.

"Okay," Maggy said. "So they didn't want to *be* artists. But at some point in time, their perception of art and artists must have changed. I mean, they wanted to pose for them, didn't they, and become their mistresses and their muses. When did that happen?"

"When the poor, hungry buggers started getting huge commissions and being paid big bucks, of course." This, from Alex, with a gentle nudge.

And then Maggy said, "I don't think so. Some of those women put up with a lot of heartache from those guys. It couldn't have been only for money."

"Imagine trying to live with an emotional dwarf like Jackson Pollock."

"Or with Picasso and his endless series of women."

"Yeah," Nick said, "but it's cool to hang around an artist's studio. Things are happening, man, there's lots of booze and ganja and sex, it's kind of messy and easygoing, it's the whole bohemian lifestyle that's so appealing to the daughters of the bourgeoisie."

"Hang around long enough," Alex said, "and somebody's bound to ask you to take off your clothes and sit for a portrait."

"Ah! Immortality! Reason enough, maybe, to run with the wolves."

But Maggy said no, again.

(I like this girl, Christie, she's a bit rough around the edges—you know, a lot of body piercing and a few tattoos, her hair is spiky and dyed that Gothic black, but her eyes are suffused with light and, when she looks at me, with a gaze direct and candid as a summer sky, I feel my breath catch in my throat. Such vulnerability, I think, but at the same time, such incorruptible lucidity. The clear-sightedness of all those to whom life has shown its cruellest face. If they were drawn to each other, these two, in friendship or in love, I believe it's because each heard in the other's voice the sad song of a severed heart-string. They are children of loss, Maggy and Nick, and they carry a burden of knowledge too great for their years.)

Maggy said she believed that it's the feminine side of these artists that draws in the women. They are attracted, she said, to men who are easily moved by colour, music, shape and texture. Who are on intimate terms with emotion. Who feel no shame in the face of tears. Who respond to tenderness. Who delight, she said, in beauty.

Around the table, amid the crumbs of a most delicious apple pie, in the warm aroma of coffee and Drambuie and candlewax, we all fell silent.

And, as usual, let beauty have the final word.

Monday 8 April

I have a postcard from Florence that Magda gave me. It is of *La Cacciata*, *The Expulsion of Adam and Eve*, painted by Masaccio on the walls of the Brancacci Chapel. I take it in my hands three or four times a day, turning it this way and that to catch the light, reading the details with an aching, anguished heart.

It is a portrait of violent despair. As Ladis and Procacci describe it, "Adam hides his face but every part of him betrays his grief—the short arms brought up to cover his eyes, the bent shoulders and the large head form a compact mass over the long, tormented lines of his body. And in the distorted features of Eve's face, there is nothing but torment and unrestrained agony. Light gives her foreshortened profile an alarming shape, her eyes are violently applied strokes of dark and in the skull-like features of her face, the meaning of the expulsion is made explicit. The two sinners burst into the shocking glare of a pitiless, searing light, so strong it seems to bleach the flesh of Adam's fingers and thigh."

I study the postcard, am surprised at the sharp stab of despair I feel and immediately understand why. *One man's deeds*, writes Borges, *are like the deeds of all mankind. This is why,* he says, *it is not unfair that one disobedience in a garden should contaminate the human race; this is why the crucifixion of a single Jew should suffice to save it. Perhaps Schopenhauer is right,* Borges goes on to say: *I am others, any man is all men. Yo soy los otros, cualquier hombre es todos los hombres.*

If a mediocre reproduction on a postcard can draw me into its universe so completely, I can imagine how I'll feel when I stand within the walls of the Chapel of the Carmine, raise my eyes to the figures painted there by Masaccio and know them *in the flesh*. (Because of you, because the whole of my being is infected with the desire to be with you again, the drama of sin, redemption and the hope of eternal life speaks to my heart with a terrible urgency.) I know that I, too, will be torn by convulsive sorrow, by a sense of loss so great that nothing merely human can ease the pain. I will enter, like Masaccio did, into a landscape not yet touched by the sun of Easter morning.

And isn't that the wonder of his *La Cacciata*? In the tortured physiognomies of his fallen gods, there is not a trace of hope. In order to paint an image of such infinite and unmitigated despair, Masaccio had to travel back through time to a place of unknowingness. He had to ignore the gifts of faith and love. And forget he'd ever heard the amazing piece of news that though one world is lost, another world awaits.

Wednesday 10 April

It is time to remove Beckett from the syllabus. The students either do not understand him—witness the confusion in these examination essays—fail to appreciate his humour, or are stricken to the soul by the bleakness of his vision. For these are not war children. They are the generation born to the smug acquirers of the eighties whose faith in the fat gods was unshakeable and deep. They grew up believing the world was a benign place, quite unhostile to their pillaging hands. When things began to go sour, when planes flew into towers and snipers shot their friends, when the seas and forests began to revolt, these children—hard-wired as they are for happiness—were not equipped to handle despair. They need to be bolstered, now, by messages of hope and promises of regeneration. Though they have guessed the truth, they need to be confirmed in their illusions.

I will save Beckett for a less dangerous time.

As the pile of marked exams grows taller on my office floor, I feel slow deliverance gaining on me, like a disturbance of the blood, a loosening in my bones. Soon, I will be putting the dislocation and the angst of the twentieth century behind me, parting company with Faulkner, Beckett, Eliot and Woolf, and embracing, for a time, the quiet certainties of the quattrocento. This, I believe, is a very good thing. But now and then, when the moment of departure seems frighteningly imminent, I become aware of some largish thing, with wide shoulders and a beastly big head, stirring to life suddenly in a dark womb within me, thrashing about, struggling to be born. I refuse to yield it passage, refuse to look upon its face, ancient as it is, and undying, with its eyes rimed with fear and its mouth tremulous with guilt.

I am leaving my boys alone for six long weeks. We are still vulnerable, the three of us, and easily shaken by change. Absence, even temporary, has all the markings of death, and goodbyes, now, are touched with unspeakable terror. Were I to go and never return, the trust time has replanted in them with slow and patient hands would be torn out by the roots and all its budding fruit laid waste. A second betrayal would damage the boys beyond reckoning. And still, I risk it.

There was a time when the very thought of departure left me

queasy with dread. I would spend the night before an early flight, watching. I did not want to be taken unawares, or be surprised by morning. I sensed extinction very near—could see with premonitory clarity the ball of fire, the collision, the crush of glass and metal that would end my life.

But all that has changed now. I go now with a much lighter heart. On easy terms with infinity, I walk even here among angels.

Life is exile, and death is the door that leads me back home.

V

HE WAS PULLED FROM SLEEP AT COCK-CROW, DRAWN EVEN IN HIS dreams to the wonder of Gian's frescoes. These paintings were like nothing he had ever seen before. Their colours were luminous, the perspective perfect, and the light seeping out of the blue of the sky made every flower in the summer fields glow. Masaccio recalled the bare mountains of his own landscapes, the alien tracts of dust and barren rock he had painted as backdrop for his figures, and he wondered now at the narrowness of his vision. As difficult as it was to admit it, he saw now that his physical worlds were barely more real than Giotto's. Compared to these meadows that moved with the wind and shimmered in the sunlight, his landscapes were dreary, abstract, symbolic conceptions. But he could change that. In the Chapel of Cardinal Branda da Castiglione, if God were willing, he would paint the world as it was. And Masolino would say, shaking his small hands in front of his face, No, no, Masaccio, it is man you must extol, not the trees and mountains and sky. But Masaccio, unheeding, would continue to paint the beautiful anarchy of the world, the power for which above all else he gave unceasing thanks to God, coursing through him like a river in spring.

Eloisa stirred beside him and he watched as the morning sun played long, golden fingers across her face and teased her out of sleep. He knew she would turn to him at once, call him Gian, and press her body to his. Then, as memory slowly woke, she would stiffen and recoil in his arms. But this might take a little time, and he was growing impatient. Her physical presence here in the bed beside him was an unwanted distraction. She had served to evoke Francesca, the smooth matte feel of her skin, its sweet summer smell, but now she lay like a cloud upon the sun, or a dusky veil across a vision. Masaccio lifted a hand to his face as though to clear the blurring of his eyes, and, summoning her with all his strength, he willed his beautiful Tuscan angel to appear before him once again.

In the night, when he'd lost himself in the musky tangle of desire, she had come to him and touched him with her light. He had seen her as she had appeared to him in the fields of Valdarno in the months following upon her death. A bright phantom, a ghostly radiance, that had set his heart to pounding and his wild blood on fire. He had stood transfixed amongst the vines, watching her move like sunlight, and had been filled with perfect love. Years later, with the memory of the vision still vivid in his brain, he had striven to recapture in paint and plaster the light that had enveloped his bright angel like the nimbus of a saint. He had worked, then, like a man possessed and the exalted expression upon his face had struck his assistants dumb with awe.

When, in the night, Masaccio had pulled away from her and, his body stilled and waiting, had opened wide eyes upon the dark, Eloisa had understood that her Gian had changed. When he had at last closed his eyes and begun to speak of a love he had known in summers long ago, she'd understood he'd never been her Gian. At first frightened, then full of tearful grief, she'd grown quiet as Masaccio's voice rose and hovered above them, filling the room with the softly beating wings of memory. He evoked for her the figure of his young cousin, a round baby girl, with dusky cheeks and chubby hands, at play in the fragrant wood curls of their grandfather's workshop. Even then, Masaccio assured Eloisa, an unearthly light had shone in the depths of her dark eyes and when she'd looked upon him, he'd felt his heart lift with strange rapture. When still a very young thing, she'd held her head in a curious way, averted, as though listening to some faraway music only she could hear. And it had struck Masaccio, when recalling it afterwards, that towards the end of her brief life, she had taken to withdrawing in this way again, cocking her beautiful bright head, turning inwards to the summons of a compelling sound. He'd understood after her death that it was God's voice she had listened to, God's voice speaking clearly in her heart that had called her back into His light.

"I was a boy of five," Masaccio said to Eloisa, "when my father died and my mother remarried. I had to leave my cousins, my uncles and my grandfather's beautiful chest-maker's hands, and go live in Tedesco del Maestro Fe's house. He was a rich old apothecary who was very good to my mother and me and he did not mind that I spent all my time running back and forth between my grandfather's house and ours. I could not leave Francesca, you see. When I was away from her, nothing was bright enough or sweet enough, and in some strange way, I ceased to exist. It was only while watching her eat a cluster of blue grapes, or weave the thick stems of yellow crocuses into her dark hair, or bare her long legs to the sun that I knew I was alive. I loved everything about her, her mouth, her tiny white teeth, the specks of gold in her brown eyes. I loved her with every bit of strength in my body, and with all of my soul, passionately, completely and forever."

In the darkness, listening to Masaccio's quiet voice, Eloisa had struggled with the knowledge that she had lost Gian a second time. And as she'd wrapped her arms around the emptiness within, she'd understood with a clear and piercing light that no Gian would ever come to fill it. She was just like this Masaccio beside her, then, this stranger in her bed. Lovers bereft, the two of them, their love a grieving, unrequited thing cowering within their breasts.

Beneath the blankets, she'd stretched out a timid hand and searched for his. Enclosing his long bent fingers in hers, she had held on tight while he'd continued to speak. And when he'd finished telling her of Francesca's last autumn, of the harvest of grapes they'd gathered together and crushed, their feet turning violet as they danced in their uncle's great vats, when he'd described how she'd suddenly weakened beneath the winter sun, her blood thinning and turning pale as holy wine, when he'd recalled the terrible pallor of Francesca's skin and the ashy dullness of her eyes, when he'd remembered her body limp and blue in his arms, twilight imperceptibly fading into deepest night, Eloisa had turned to him and, pressing her face into the wild nest of his hair, had called him Masaccio.

This morning there would be more tears, he supposed, and just the thought of all that wretched grief filled him with unspeakable weariness. She would want to be comforted and consoled, she would seek the dark and haunt the shadows and expect him to follow her there, when all he wanted was to bask in light.

He felt her eyes upon him then, so, setting his mouth and furrowing his brow—a scowling kind of sympathy—he slowly turned to face her. To his surprise, he found that her cheeks were dry and that a shy smile played around her lips. And as he watched, the memory of their night together rose up in her, a blush spreading through her dark skin like spilt vermilion. She lifted one hand beneath the blankets and tucked her fingers into the black hair on his chest. Pulling hard on the coarse curls, she said, "My brothers will kill you when they discover the truth."

Masaccio groaned and, easing away from her grip, turned desperate eyes to the garden window. "Let me slip away," he said. "I did not mean to harm you."

Eloisa simply smiled and said, "Now that I look upon your face in the morning light, I see you are nothing like Gianlucido. But you are more my husband, dark stranger, than ever he was. And so shall you remain."

Taking her hand from his chest, she let her fingers travel the length of his body, across his belly and down his thigh, and felt his skin thrill to her touch. Then, pushing away the blankets, she rose and, with uplifted arms, coiled her heavy hair at the nape of her neck, letting the sun kiss her breasts and flick its tongue at her young flesh. Watching her stoop to pick up her gown on her way out of the room, Masaccio let his eyes wander over her body, saw the fine bones beneath her skin, the unblemished line of her limbs, and knew at once that he would draw her. He had no use for a wife, and little time for a lover, but a model as perfect as this one, he knew, was a gift. Masolino would be grateful.

Reaching for his new robe, and idly wondering what the brothers had done with his own tunic and cloak, he noticed a folded scrap of parchment lying on the floor. It had slipped, he supposed, from among Eloisa's things. It fell open as he picked it up and he found himself gazing at the sketch of a face remarkably like his own. A self-portrait of Gianlucido which his faithful wife had worn pressed against her breast three long years. Studying the drawing more closely, Masaccio decided that the deceased Gian was an uncommonly handsome man. A brilliant painter, a romantic and a visionary, his only fault, as far as Masaccio could see, was that he was dead. Carefully folding up the face again, Masaccio placed the sketch upon the bed, then left the room in search of Eloisa.

She had promised to take him that very day to the Church of San Clemente, where at last he would be reunited with Masolino. They would embrace, they would gaze upon the paintings on the chapel walls, and, in his hands, Masaccio would feel once again a thrumming desire as deep and as fragrant as blood. And watching him turn from her, watching the passion flare in his eyes, Eloisa would understand that mere flesh, her flesh, was like a crumb of bread to a starving man.

VI

IN HIS METICULOUS DESCRIPTIONS OF ROME, BRUNELLESCHI HAD touched upon the essential but, somehow, had neglected to mention the grey. As Masaccio moved through the wrecked streets of the city, a completely forgotten Eloisa tripping along at his elbow, he felt his spirits sink. The whole place was the colour of stone. Even the savage green of the bushes flourishing in the crushed rock was dulled by white dust. The shapeless sacks people wore had been cut from coarse dun-coloured cloth and Masaccio, recalling the bright robes of Florence, felt a giddy wave of homesickness wash over him. There was nothing here to please the senses.

Casting a starved eye about him, he caught a glance of Eloisa. Even she was robed in white beneath her grey cloak. Looking down at her, a cross, unhappy look upon his face, he noticed she was having difficulty keeping up with him. The small vein at her temple was a hot throb of purple and her breath came short and fast. He felt annoyance surge up in him, and he felt his tongue grow sharp. He wanted to tell her to go, that he had no use for a dog, even a pretty one, at his heels, but he knew she would not let him out of her sight.

He would have had no trouble finding the church on his own. San Clemente, he had been told, was on the Via San Giovanni in Laterano, between the Flavian amphitheatre and the Lateran Basilica. But it was far from the Rienzi's villa, and the ruins of arches and colonnades, half hidden in plane trees, laurels, cypresses and brushwood, kept catching his eye and taking him off course.

Gazing upon the heaps of rubble and the fluted columns lying like giant bones among the wild shrubs, he tried to remember what Brunelleschi had told him about the monuments of Rome—Pippo had spent twelve years studying the architecture of the city—and attempted, in vain, to re-awaken the sense of excitement he'd felt while sitting around the fire in Masolino's *bottega*, listening to the master tell them of his discoveries.

Brunelleschi had systematically inspected all the ruins of Rome. When he had wanted to study a building from its base, he had hired labourers to excavate or he had dug and searched himself, with the help of his friend Donatello. They had found an occasional coin or cameo, an *intaglio* of cornelian or chalcedony, and, watching them root around in the dirt, the Romans had laughed at them and called them treasure seekers. Wanting to learn exactly how the ancients had constructed their colossal buildings, Brunelleschi had measured the thickness of walls, he'd studied fragments of columns and arches, the size and shape of bricks, the dovetailing of blocks of marble. He had written down all his notes and calculations on strips of parchment (cut off when squaring sheets for design in the goldsmith's shop in Florence where he worked). He had even climbed onto the roof of the Pantheon and removed some of its tiles in order to study the ribbing of the shallow cupola of the temple. The knowledge he had gained there, high up on the temple's dome, had held him in good stead. For some eight years now, he had been hard at work on the vault of Arnolfo di Cambio's cathedral in Florence, where every day all his knowledge and expertise were put to the test.

Many times during the course of construction, Masaccio had wandered over to the building site, had watched workmen climb the four hundred steps to the dome, had listened to Brunelleschi explain a difficult turning or an awkward joint by picking up a knife and cutting a model in a turnip. He had greatly admired

Brunelleschi's science and his art, and had looked forward to the day when he could discover Rome for himself and study the colour and design of the remnants of its gloried frescoes and mosaics. But now that he was there, and he saw all around him the shattered remains of temples and statuary, their bleak bony stones, he felt nothing but weariness.

His eye caught by a coloured shard half-concealed in the long grasses by his feet, he stopped suddenly and Eloisa, who trotted behind him with lowered head, piled into his back, catching him squarely between the shoulder blades. Masaccio swore under his breath, then, reaching one rough arm behind him, he drew her level with him on the path. Looking down at her, he saw her fluttering breast and the wild wisps of hair curling like seaweed around her small ears and it was all he could do to resist taking one of them between his angry teeth and biting it cleanly off. It would appease him, he thought, to have the taste of blood in his mouth. Instead, he cast upon her all the weight of his disappointment. "Can you tell me, *Signorina Rienzi*, why it is that even the simplest, most boorish ploughman of Tuscany will hang the neck of his white oxen with red tassels, just to delight his eye with colour and contrast, while these learned and scholarly book-hunting Romans are content to live among ugly, broken stones beneath a dust-filled sky? I see no beauty here, in this ruined city" (at that, the pulse at Eloisa's throat quickened visibly and the shadow of her heavy lashes fell upon her warm cheeks), "and I fail to understand how grace or light or harmony could be born in such a place."

Eloisa raised one hand and touched her fingers to Masaccio's chest. She paused a moment, sighed inwardly at the thought that life as an unmarried woman, safe among her brothers, was undoubtedly simpler than this bizarre union she'd struck up with a childish and awkward man. Then, wondering what it was about these gruff, artisan types that attracted her so, she decided that a meek, placating wife would please him more than a defiant one. In a quiet voice, with a still hand upon his breast, she told him it was true, Rome did lie everywhere in ashes but that, with his help, with the help of the hundreds of artisans Pope Martin v was summoning to Rome, it would be made beautiful again, a great and wondrous city on which all other nations would look with envy and admiration. But Masaccio would not be stilled. In a cranky, tiresome voice, he continued, "Rome is grey. The skin of its people is grey. Their blood runs grey in their veins."

Overtaken by nostalgia, he let himself sink onto a pile of broken columns that rose up along the path and, eyes turned inward to the memory of home, he began to speak in a far-away voice about the colours of Florence.

Eloisa stood before him, and kicked and kicked at a shard of stone that poked its snub nose out of the ground, while she debated the likeliness of a future with this man. She couldn't help being drawn to his kind. Gianlucido, too, had had the rough, strong hands of the tradesman, he'd lived like the poorest of labourers, without decent clothing or food, but he also had been possessed of some ideal, some perfect vision that for him surpassed all earthly riches.

Eloisa heard Masaccio go on about the scarlet dyes of Florence, and how they were made of madder and kermes. Then he made a disgusting reference to the dried bodies of some female insect, and she turned a deaf ear to him once again.

The most amazing thing about these painters, so lowly in social position they did not even have a guild of their own, was their complete indifference to material wealth. The only thing that mattered in their lives was the beautiful obsession that haunted them even in their sleep. This was not totally unfamiliar to Eloisa. Her own father and uncles were driven by a kind of passion, too. They combed the world's cloisters and monasteries in search of illuminated manuscripts and books in Latin and Greek, but it seemed to her a pastime for the idle rich, a means by which they would be immortalized in the libraries and academies erected in their name. If their wealth had not been established, if they had not had a weakness for letters and the arts, they would have looked upon such trivial pursuits with a disdainful eye and, without a doubt, would have forbidden her marriage to Gianlucido. For her betrothed, like this Masaccio ("Bright yellow," he was saying now, "comes from the fields of crocuses at San Gimignano, purplish red from a lichen called 'oricello,' which grows in far-away Majorca, vermilion comes from the Red Sea, carmine, crimson, henna, lake and saffron are all from the east."), had willingly dressed in rags, and incurred debt, and gone without food, in order to be able to paint. And all their brother painters, she knew, were each and every one of them prepared to suffer deprivation for the greater glory of their art. It was this passion she envied, and sometimes despised, this gift for losing oneself in the chase, in the pursuit and capture of an ephemeral image born in some dark chamber of the heart. In some small way, Eloisa wanted to be part of the mystery. Even if she were only the woman in whose arms he would lay his weary, empty bones, even if her body only served to slake his blind desire. She would sit quietly, she would watch, invisible, while this man, this Masaccio, surrendered to the god within.

By the time his eyes had begun to focus again, Eloisa was sending up a prayer to the Virgin Mary to help make him hers.

"Colour," he said, as he looked up into Eloisa's determined face, "is to the people of Florence as necessary as love or food."

Casting doleful eyes about him once again, he muttered in a bleak voice that he felt quite sure he could starve to death in Rome. Then, dismissing her and the forsaken Roman landscape with one scornful wave of the hand, he stood up and strode off in the direction of San Clemente.

Saturday 13 April
For a man who has no use for a wife and little time for a lover, Masaccio seems to have more than his share of women. Francesca, first of all, who lives in him like a small thing nestled in his heart, a gift he bears with careful hands, like a chalice full of light. And then there is Eloisa, across whose threshold he has stumbled, and against whose adamantine will his wiles and his wit shall be measured.

The struggle, I think, will be short-lived. Masaccio will simply become absorbed in his work and forget her, and she, loving the artist more than the man, will resign herself to leaving him at his paints.

I sense in her a generosity of spirit that strikes me as being profoundly mediaeval. She will be, like Chesterton said of St. Francis, *a deep tide driving out to uncharted seas of charity.*

And then there is the mysterious Miuccia who lies in wait for Masaccio with warm breast and unforgiving heart. A casualty, I presume, of *malentendu....*

I know nothing, of course, of the women in the real Masaccio's life. Records speak of his mother, Monna Iacopa, and mention a stepsister, Caterina, whose husband, Mariotto di Cristofano, was a Florentine painter with whom Masaccio might have apprenticed, but none of the documents indicates that he had taken a wife. In his short biographical sketch of the artist, Douglas Preston tells us that, before leaving for Rome, Masasccio filed a tax return on behalf of himself, his mother and his brother, in which he claimed he was dead broke. He said he had no assets and no expected income. He lived in a rented house with his mother and brother on the Via dei Servi in Florence, he shared a *bottega* near the Bargello and he owed forty-four florins to various people. In short, he was the very prototype of the impoverished artist, overlooked and underpaid, having nothing but his talent with which to attract a lover. And so, I gave him three, like the Graces.

Francesca is his Muse. Because of her, he is more at home in the super-sensuous realm of being than in the real world, more at ease with the effigies of Eve, Saint Catherine and the Virgin Mary than with women of flesh and blood. Through her, he is tempted to turn away from reality and live, like those ethereal saints he paints, in heightened communion with the heavenly world, in visionary transcendence. Because of loving and losing Francesca, he is a *pilgrim of eternity,* waiting on the moment of death when, writes Shelley, *the pure spirit shall flow Back to the burning fountain whence it came.*

Eloisa, for her part, represents the temptation of material comfort. It is easy to imagine that he who possesses nothing but a stroke of light in his brain might crave a clean bed or a warmer cloak, might want to trade hunger for a bit of cloy and glut and surfeit. But perhaps he is not inclined to compromise—loath to give up his paint-spattered robes and his irregular hours to become a plump and pleasing husband, *grinding,* as Blake and Milton saw it, *in the mill of an undelighted and servile copulation.* Perhaps he knew how these things went. That sooner or later, when he returned to his disorderly way of life, fed up with playing the attendant lord to her golden-slippered princess, she would scream at him and remind him of his debt to her. Alluding to his shady past, his feckless brother, his conniving mother, she would rub his nose in his ineptness and mock his megalomania, call him lazy and heartless and mad with abstraction.

Depraved by luxury, or shrilly undermined, one way or the other, his gift would have shrivelled. Too great a punishment for the small sin of yielding to Mammon. Besides, he was used, by then, to living on cheese soup.

To my mind, Miuccia represents conflict of a different order. It is the image of her warm breast that lingers longest in my thoughts. She is the sensuous one, whose round limbs and fragrant skin lie in ambush in the corners of Masaccio's life. In a constant state of imaginative arousal, he looks upon all things with the same passionate eye, shifting easily, in a moment of distraction, from matters of the soul to matters of the flesh. And she, waiting there with a purring in the belly and a churning in the heart, reads into every touch and every glance, imbues each tender gesture with sexual significance. Mistakenly. He finds her beautiful, he flirts with her, he might even love her a bit, but he does not want her, or any woman, for his wife—a simple case of Eros being eclipsed by Art. And so, her hunger left unsated by the meagre crumbs he tosses her, she will, like any woman scorned, sink her perfect little teeth into his indifferent hand.

And there is a fourth woman—already forgotten by Masaccio, and almost by me—who may come to complicate his life: Cecilia, the young serving wench in whose comely bosom the absent-minded maestro has wakened an inarticulate hope.

Sunday 14 April

Finalized arrangements for the boys today. Alex starts working on the research project at the university in the first week in May—no summer courses this year, thank God—and so will quickly settle into a routine. He is quite capable of cooking for himself, doing his laundry and keeping the house relatively tidy. Sheila has promised to call—as I will, of course—and maybe have him over for dinner once in a while. As long as he has money to cover housekeeping expenses for the first few weeks, he'll be fine. Nick will be doing Shakespeare in the Ruins all summer—I'll miss the first two plays, but he's okay with that—and living in a rented house by the Red River with a few of the other actors. I know he'll be keeping wild hours but Alex says he'll look in on him to make sure he's eating and sleeping enough. I suggested he bring the kid home now and then to give him a break from some of the high-strung characters he'll be rooming with.

Oh, those man-eating theatre people.

Nick's edges are still soft. He scars pretty easily and often doesn't see the knives until it's too late. I will worry about him in this, his first summer away from home, while I am off on an Italian sojourn, engaged in an enterprise of questionable literary worth with a woman who might prove to be the source of serious distraction.

(While you watch me buy new clothes, dig out my passport and play my Italian tapes, do you shake your head, Christie, and bite your lip and wonder at my selfishness? I can hear you whispering to my heart, making it beat with breathless urgency, admonishing me to be careful. We must still be vigilant, I know.)

And in the quattrocento, I wonder, did parents hover over their children so?

What did Monna Iacopa teach the young Masaccio, what knowledge did she impart to keep him safe in a perilous world? His prayers, for sure, a little right and wrong, a little personal hygiene, then off he went, on his own, to find life. In the Andes, mothers set their babies down on the ground and watch them crawl to the fire with outstretched hand and do not pull them away, even at the last. In Calcutta, beggars put out their children's eyes with bicycle spokes to provide them with a way of making a living. In North America, parents worry their daughter won't like the sandwich they packed for her lunch.

Sometimes, when I think about Alex and Nick out there in the world, a vague uneasiness grips me in the guts. They are children of affluence and education—comfortable in hotel lobbies and fine restaurants, conversant with the main currents of thought of the twentieth century, familiar with the most prominent of our cultural icons. But sometimes I think we should have spent less time in airports, bookstores, cinemas and galleries and more time talking about politics—the politics of power, of sex, of moral ambivalence. With a cringing heart, I see them stumbling into minefields of cynicism—where colleagues plot and managers smile, *where women eat green salad and drink human blood*, where horror waits upon a murmured yes.

(I can still hear you say, in a voice gone husky with hope, that all you wanted was for them to grow up safe. To survive those nights in cars, those rough bars with thick and sudden men. But all our words, Christie, yours and mine, cannot save them from life, like my love could not save you from death. When we brought them into the world, you and I, we had no way of knowing just how much we risked our hearts. The minute we set eyes upon them, those blue-tinged squealing larvae lying between your quaking thighs, we discovered that our love for them laid us open as keenly as a scalpel splits the skin. Love made us the willing prey of a life bent on killing, and love made the risk worthwhile.)

Ah, and sometimes I don't care about the world and its hypocritical cunning. Sometimes I say let them see it for what it is so they can turn, and turn again, to what they know is true: rivers cut like silver foil through tangles of black spruce and tamarack, summer sky curdled with cloud, nights riddled with frogcall and the soft hoot of hungry birds. Sometimes I say let the bloodthirsty women take them and squeeze them and make them howl, let them be cheated and bought and sold, let them sin and feel shame and sin again. As long as the forests stand, and the wind blows and the curve of a paddle feels right in their hands, they will survive.

Wednesday 17 April
I love it when Magda gossips.

We met for lunch today on a terrace at The Forks. I sat in the sunshine, my white face turned to the sky, while all around me over-wintered Winnipeg settled with a sigh into spring. Magda's hair touched her shoulders and shone like burnished copper in the sun. And in the bright light, I could see the tawny flecks in her green eyes and the freckles sprinkled like gold dust beneath her milky skin. Looking into her youthful face, I felt I was twenty again, and April had come for the very first time.

We talked about her presentation, "The revision of Masaccio's taxonomy as seen in the work of Domenico Veneziano and Piero della Francesca"—artists whose work I am not familiar with, we talked about the freshness of Tuscan evenings, and the sweetness of Tuscan wine. The *vino santo,* she told me, a blend of the white fruit of the Trebbiano and the Malvasia vines, is served at the end of the evening meal with biscotti or *cantucci alla mandorla.* And we shall linger, she said, and savour it, as dusk slowly lengthens into night.

"And indulge, please, in amusing anecdotes of private history?" I said.

Naturally, she replied with a gleam in her eye. And to give me an *avant-goût,* she began to speak of Filippo Lippi. Fra, or Brother: a monk. He finally eloped with a nun after years of shameless womanizing. Together they had Filippino, also a noted Renaissance painter.

The great Brunelleschi, she told me, had been imprisoned for unpaid guild dues.

Poor Luca Della Robbia, the Florentine sculptor, kept his feet warm when he worked at night by sticking them in a basket full of wood shavings.

Paolo Uccello's wife could not get him away from his drafting paper and to bed at night, so obsessed was he with the wonders of perspective. Donatello said to him, "Ah Paolo, this perspective of yours leads you to abandon the certain for the uncertain."

"Uccello?" I said. "He of the menagerie painted on his walls?"

"The very one," she said. "His favourite animals were birds. Even his name is derived from the Italian word for bird: *uccelo*."

And then she asked me if I'd come across the expression, "You are *tondo*," meaning, "you are more simple than Giotto's O." When I told her I had not, she proceeded to explain. Vasari tells us that when the Pope was proposing to decorate St. Peter's with some paintings, a courtier was sent from Trevise to Tuscany to see what manner of man Giotto was and to determine the nature of his work. The courtier asked for some small drawing to send to His Holiness. Giotto took a sheet of paper and a red pencil, pressed his arm to his side to make a compass of it and then, with a turn of his hand, produced a circle so perfect in every particular that it was a marvel to see. The word *tondo*, Magda told me, has a twofold significance in Tuscany: it means both a perfect circle and a slowness, a heaviness of mind.

Delighted, I looked at her across the table then, and smiled broadly, a slightly wine-skewed smile, while she gathered her things to go. As I watched her saunter through the sun-stupid, idolatrous crowd, her bare legs gleaming springtime whitely, it occurred to me that the light, the chardonnay, and the pressing warmth of her gaze had conspired with brilliant success to make me quite deliriously happy, and perfectly *tondo*.

Sunday 21 April

There was something about the sky this morning that made me long for the bush.

The boys had friends in last night to celebrate the end of another year of college classes and the house was a mess. There were bodies and empties and grease-stained pizza boxes everywhere underfoot. I saw Mike and Jared and, I think, Tyler, sleeping on various pieces of furniture, trying to keep warm under bath towels, of all things. My sons, good hosts that they are, too pie-eyed to find the blankets. Before leaving the house with my sandwiches and thermos of tea, I dug out the sleeping bags and covered up their thin shoulders—they sighed gratefully, then settled into a long, long sleep. I didn't want to be around when they woke up, all bleary-eyed and dumb.

So I headed out to Rice River.

The poplars had that newly fledged look about them, those downy round heads touched by *spring's green preliminary shiver*. The ditches were full of black water, the fields lay steaming under the sun. Ravens drifted like rags across the landscape, beating dull wings against the sharp blue ceramic of the sky. I was alone on the highway and alone in the closed space of the car. (And it seemed to me that, if I reached out my hand, I would find you sitting there beside me, your skin warm, your face bright with morning light.

But you did not come along on this ride, either, and the highway, the landscape and the whole world felt emptier than ever.

When I reached the river, I pulled off the road and walked to the bridge. As I stood there, listening to the water run crashing over the rocks, I looked deep into the vortices slowly spinning their wide circles at the foot of the falls and caught an image of us, just as we were, on one of our last days together on that beer-brown water. The canoe was full of scrambled camping gear piled *pêle-mêle* between the struts, and you and I were laid out at each end of the boat, our heads cushioned on life jackets, our legs spread wide, our bare heels upon the gunnels. And we lay there, in the late afternoon sun, feeling it hot upon our faces. We were reluctant to leave—the weekend had been so extraordinarily fine—so we stayed there, and let the current wind the canoe round and round in the slowly spinning spirals of the eddy. Our ears were full of water music and our eyes were full of sky, our mouths were brimming with the taste of sun and salt, of fire and smoke, of our flesh, yours and mine. For, the night before, do you remember that night, Christie—in this place where you are now, does memory survive, can nostalgia set your heart afloat upon the sea of love you left behind?—in the searing hot month of July, we had left the fly off the tent to catch whatever wind came breathing off the lake. And as always, in summer heat, with our bodies chafed by the sun, our bellies kissed and stroked and fondled by white hot fingers of light, we turned and reached out to each other with bare-faced, shameless lust. We loved then like it was the first time, like it was the last time, desire licking at our skin with a fiery crimson tongue. We sank so completely into each other, got so lost and went so blind, that when we had eyes again to see the world, we were astonished to discover that day had rolled into night.

And what a night it was. The moon glowed huge and white over the earth, imparting its radiance to stone and leaf and flesh. It was too bright to sleep. And your body, as though lit up from within, shimmered soft and luminescent. I was entranced, I was seduced, I fell into you head first, falling from a great, great height into a moon-kissed pool of light. And we loved again, while all around us milky shadows mingled, and heaven rubbed its cheek against the shoulder of the night.

While I stood there today, on that road by the river, it was not memory that came alive, not simply sweet reminiscence, but the past itself, intermingling with the present, time telescoped and collapsed, ebbing and flowing, like water, like light. By some strange and wonderful alchemy, I had moved between worlds, I had stepped into the slippery stream of timelessness.

When evening fell and the wind grew cool, I watched the water grow dark as *then* gave way to *now*. I felt the worlds fall asunder, riven like a veil of silk, parting with a sad, soft sound. Though I stood with my feet in the gravel of the road, and in the shadow of a hovering wood, the vision lingered still, like a fever or a fragrance, like a slow and sweet intoxication. And I felt my eyes fill up with grateful tears.)

And so, Monsieur Bergson, I suppose I must now admit you are right after all: time is in constant flux, moments of the past and the present can have equal reality, my life, my paltry mortal life, partakes of the eternal.

(Going home again, on that dark road, I dug out The Chieftains and slipped the disc into the player. When Van came on, I opened all the windows, even though the night was cold, and turned it up loud. He was singing *Have I told you lately that I love you*, and I wanted to be sure that you could hear it.)

Wednesday 24 April

This spring, as always, the world beckons. Paris, Prague, Cartagena, Leningrad, the Yucatán and Guatemala. Faculty members are spending their travel allowances with happy profligacy, looking to change, to distance, to the heady joy of dépaysement to bring new vitality to worn and wintry ideas. The whole of the evening—at the Fitzsimmons', the patient hosts, once again, of the staff's end of the year get-together—was spent enumerating the cultural, linguistic, culinary and sexual delights of foreign sojourns. I did not participate in the discussion, but apparently suffered its effects subliminally, while otherwise engaged. It is that background noise, I suspect, that steady and sometimes seditious soundtrack, that has left me reeling tonight with vague romantic yearnings.

Mikkelson and I were talking about fly-fishing. He's going to Scotland in June and plans on catching a few brown trout in a private river in the Highlands. I asked him about flies, told him I'd found a whole box of them one summer on a portage in Nopiming. Wondered if he'd like to have them. Between my question and his answer, bits and pieces of conversation drifted up to us.

"So, after the conference, this linguistics prof from Bologna asks me to join him in his room for an expresso. We're halfway up the residence stairs when he leans into me and whispers in my ear, 'What hurts me most,' he says, 'is the thought that, at the same time as me, in some other room, in some other place, someone else is making love.'"

Mikkelson took lessons at a city pool, standing on the concrete edge with a line and a pole, and casting into chlorine. Not exactly the Coeur d'Alène, he said. Then he spent the winter making his own flies with feathers, hair and plastic—dry flies, wet flies, nymphs, streamers and bucktails.

"... Watching them dance the merengue makes you tense with desire. You feel like a voyeur, staring with sexual envy at a seething intimacy that borders on the obscene."

Fly-fishing lines are woven synthetic strands coated with several thin layers of plastic, according to Mikkelson. The weight and thickness of these coatings create three distinct types of lines: lines that float, lines that sink gradually and lines that sink rapidly. The concept, it seemed to me, had interesting metaphoric potential. We tossed ideas around for a bit, then let them die a natural death.

"... its putrefaction and its flowers, its moist steamy depths, its darkness and its danger."

In 1496, Mikkelson told me, the prioress of an abbey near St. Albans, England, wrote "A Treatyse of Fysshynge wyth an Angle." In it, she describes the construction of hooks and rods for angling.

"Ah, the jungle, and those young grad students, with beads of sweat in the duvet of their *décolleté*."

In 1653, Mikkelson added, a guy called Izaak Walton—a.k.a. John Donne's friend and first biographer—published *The Compleat Angler or The Contemplative Man's Recreation*. Interesting, I said. Hemingway stayed at a hotel called The Compleat Angler when he went blue marlin fishing in Bimini. The setting, apparently, for *Islands in the Stream*.

That's when we heard Dagenais, from Romance Languages, reciting Baudelaire:

Là, tout n'est qu'ordre et beauté,
Luxe, calme et volupté.

And so tonight, I feel it like an ache in my bones: the longing for tenderness and soft, sensuous song, the rapture of willing skin and of wet, perfumed hair.

Oh, this naked, animal heart, lost and pining among shadows.

Saturday 27 April

Came down to breakfast this morning to find Nick and Maggy eating leftover hot and sour soup and moo-shi beef. The smell made me gag—my stomach was all geared up for coffee and toast.

I didn't recognize her at first. Her hair lay flat on her head and her face was full of tiny holes where the studs had been removed. But when she looked up at me with those translucent blue eyes, I knew it was Maggy. She grinned at me a little sheepishly and said, "Sorry for the late hour. Hope I didn't wake you. All my friends were out and by the time I thought of Nick, it was after one."

"Did you get locked out of the house?"

"No. I ran away from Groping Graham."

Nick, with bean-sprout juice and hoisin sauce running down his chin, explained, "Her mother's new live-in."

"My mom's visiting her sister in the States for a few days. So I'm alone in the house with Graham."

"Oh."

"Don't worry. I can handle myself. But he's a creep. I bought a new bathing suit last night and he asked me to try it on for him. I said no, of course, and went to take a shower. When I came out, he was standing there with a towel in his hand."

I made a face and told her she was welcome to stay with us till her mother comes home.

Poured myself a cup of coffee and went to sit in the front room but could still hear what they were saying. They were laughing, the two of them, at the boyfriend's decrepitude. He's running to fat, apparently, and hasn't much left on top, he has jowly cheeks and dark raccoon circles under his eyes, his ears are large, quite detached from the head and full of hairy sprouts, he has short sausage fingers and a rather large ass.

Sitting there in the clear stillness of the morning, I felt my heart wrench for the poor old lecher.

A story as old as mankind. The satyr panting after the nymph. Hades dragging off Persephone. Gauguin and his Tehemana, Edgar Allen Poe and his idiot-child. Aging men trying to bury their years in the forgetfulness of young flesh.

Sipping my coffee, I considered the timing of Maggy's story, this unexpected irruption in our lives. Reflected upon its relevance to my life. And squirmed a little under the scrutiny of its gaze.

They were laughing quite loudly now at Graham's attempts to stay fit. Maggy imitated the noise he makes as he grunts over his barbell set and then launched into a description of the rows of vitamin bottles he keeps lined up on one whole shelf of a kitchen cupboard—they have names like Rejuvenate and Renewal and NRG—say it fast, she told Nick—printed on them and he takes them religiously after every meal.

I tried to shut out the sound of their laughter, but found I couldn't. So I set down my coffee cup, slipped on a jacket and headed out the door.

The morning was cool but I could feel the heat of the sun flexing its muscle. It was going to be one of those intense spring days, the earth spread leafless and vulnerable beneath the merciless onslaught of a cocky, young sun. And in the ground, in Christie's beds, seduced by the heat and long yellow thrust of the light, new life would be stirring, pushing green stems towards a blue sky. I spent some time walking around the back garden, taking an inventory of promise.

The tulips and the daffodils were up, their blades slicing through the loam with green impudence while, deeper in the shade, crocuses huddled in pastel clouds. Along the wall of the house, the black-eyed Susans stretched slender snub-nosed necks out of the hot dark earth and, among the long thin leaves of the iris plants, I could see snaky stems and bulbs split and streaked with purple. The sprouting clematis already betrayed a willowy waywardness and I made a mental note to drive in the trellis before I left. While I am away, the clematis vines will climb and spiral and thicken and, in the dark green shelter of its leaves, white cones with purple hearts will appear like stars against the fabric of the night. Those, I know, will still be blooming when I come home. They are summer flowers, unlike the jonquils and the hyacinths that will break through the earth while I am away, burn brightly in the shadeless light of May, and die a brown and withered death before my return. As I ducked to avoid the spines of the wild plum tree, I realized with a squeezing of the heart that I would miss it, too—the fragrant flowering that puts one in mind of bridal gowns and first communion dresses, those snowy-white blossoms against the leafless gnarl of black and thorny branches.

And all of a sudden, I was overcome with longing. Standing there, in Christie's garden, with the earth at my feet bursting in a green, effulgent riot, I felt the restless spring-time yearning for something that lay forever beyond my reach. Youth, perhaps, and callow hope, and love that burns eternal: December craving May. Winter in love with spring.

Tuesday 30 April

I want to see him at work. Want to watch him apply the *arriccio*, while the rough plaster clots up on his trowel, clings like white mud to the ragged hem of his robe.

I want to see him run his thick, blunt hand across the surface of the plaster, checking it for *tooth*. When he reaches up, spreading his fingers wide, the ample sleeve of his gown crumples in awkward folds beneath his elbow, reveals the thick, black mat of hair on his massive forearms, the wide wrist, the lime-eaten skin on the back of his hand.

I want especially to observe him drawing the *sinopie*, laying out the composition, giving birth to the design, his fingers translating into line and pattern and dimension the coloured vapours of his brain. The charcoal lies in violent streaks against the whiteness of the wall, the red ochre slips in, shadowing the darkness with softer, subtler shade. The coal dust collects on his fingers, and maybe in his eyes, and he stands back, considers with streaked hand upon his brow, hesitates, then moves with quick decision. He spreads a patch of *intonaco*, small enough to paint before the plaster dries.

Then I watch some more, as he dips his brush in pigment and applies it to the wall, the upper left-hand corner, say, of the fresco known to the world as *Il Tributo*, the story of Saint Peter and the tribute money.

I imagine him on the scaffold, his gestures large, his attention a fixed and breathless thing. And his mind races like his hand over the quickly drying *giornate*, touching on Voragine and Senor Brancacci, weighing the relative merits of crimsons and beryl blues, considering the truth and the limits of simple, untutored imagination. He knows that, like the mediaeval playwrights of Christian drama, he is participating in a huge, didactic effort: through his paintings, he must lead the trembling, ignorant masses from the concrete, the everyday, to the hidden and the true.

And the way to do that, he knows, is to be faithful to the truths of vision.

The Florentine humanist Alamanno Rinuccini explained it thus: “In painting, Masaccio expressed the likenesses of all natural things in such a way that we seem to see with our eyes not the images of things but the things themselves.”

The uneducated throngs who passed through the chapel that stands in the right transept of the conventual church of Santa Maria del Carmine looked with amazed eyes upon those stories told in fresco, and immediately felt connected to the men and women painted there: as Ladis has pointed out, “their bodies were true, their gestures were natural, their emotion was strong.” And unconsciously, surreptitiously, exactly as Masaccio intended them to do, they moved from the contemplation of one trivial episode in the life of St. Peter to a larger awareness of the saga of human salvation.

Basking in the light cast upon them by the luminous colours of fresco—the vermilion and the ardent yellow of the antagonists’ robes, the deep blue of the Saviour's gown—the good people of Florence might have felt it steal upon them, then, the sense that something lay beyond the mean and common hours of their earthly existence. As they gazed upon the play of light and dark, saw space measured out and defined by a master's hand, some swelling tide might have risen up deep within them and swept them off to a new conclusion: beyond the endless cycle of time, the dull succession of morning, evening, noontide, night, birth, copulation and death, there was, there could be, there must be, an eternal purpose outside Time. A new faith might have taken root in their hearts, then, a belief that maybe, just maybe, within their bone-numbing labour, their boredom and their daily bread, lay a kernel of sacredness.

And as they shuffled through the chapel, their work-weathered hands folded upon their heaving chests, these men and women might have tasted a sharp, tender, painful nostalgia for something that lasts. Like the disciples on the road to Emmaus, they would have looked upon the works of Masaccio's hand and felt their hearts burn within them. With an old passion, an ancient desire—the love of the finite for the infinite, the human for the divine.

VII

BEFORE SLIPPING THOUGH THE SIDE DOOR OF THE BASILICA, Masaccio glanced up at the late August sky and understood, all at once, why Masolino had urged him to hurry. There were signs there, in the ripe yellow light, in the wind-swept drift of the clouds, that summer was moving inexorably into fall. Now was the season for fresco. In warm, rainless weather, it was easy to predict how colours would dry, and as they dried more quickly, painting could proceed at a lively pace—one whole wall completed in ten *giornate* or less. In his letter, Masolino had explained that much work had yet to be done and that time was running out. Late autumn in Rome, he'd written, could be rotten and wet. Masaccio did not doubt it for an instant.

As soon as he entered the church of San Clemente, he felt himself drawn to the left, out of the shadow of the columned aisle and into the vaulted space of the central nave. Called, as it were, by the golden light spilling from the great mosaic of the apse. He took a step towards it, but, having caught a whiff of plaster and limewater, such an extraordinarily evocative smell, he turned on his heel and found his way to Saint Catherine's chapel, hard by the side door of the church. Eloisa, for her part, moved by the beauty of the golden Christ, walked past the chapel door into the nave of the cathedral and slid into a pew. She had much to reflect upon and was happy to linger a while at Christ's feet with the Virgin and Saint John, with the doves and the drinking deer. And once again, she sent up a prayer for this Masaccio, that he might see his way to loving her between paintings, or if it was not too much too ask, that he might remember her later, when it was time to go.

Masaccio stopped a moment beneath the arch of the chapel door. Breathing deeply, he took in the work that Masolino had done, and smiled at the unmistakable traces of the master's touch. His tender colours, the affected faces and attitudes of his saints, their sumptuous dress and quiet charm. Masolino stood before a painting of the beheading of Saint Catherine (prettily rendered, as usual, martyrdom as courtly tale), deep in conversation with his assistants. Masaccio looked him over with an affectionate eye. His smile broadened as he recognized the delicate smallness of the man and his wild, expressive hands, then faded quickly when he noticed the marked stoop in the maestro's shoulders and the messy smudges beneath his eyes. He felt a tightening at the heart. Masolino seemed whittled down by work and worry, a shrunken version of himself. Moving quickly to dispel the vision, Masaccio broke through the crowd and, flinging wide his arms, wrapped his Maso, *ch'era molto amico suo*, in a warm embrace. After some discussion regarding the unfinished frescoes of the Brancacci chapel, a few inquiries as to the well-being of friends and family in Florence and a quick introduction to his assistants, Masolino spun Masaccio around to face the rear wall of the chapel. "The Cardinal would like you to paint a Crucifixion on this wall, and there," he turned Masaccio towards the door of the chapel, "on the arch above the entrance, he wants an Annunciation. I, myself, must finish the St. Catherine fresco while Giuliano and San Salvi put the last touches to the scenes from the lives of St. Ambroise and St. Christopher."

Masaccio glanced briefly at the expanses of wall Masolino pointed out to him, but let his gaze be drawn back to the martyrdom of Saint Catherine. Now there was a story he would have liked to have been entrusted with. He had Voragine's retelling of it by heart. The images the venerable old *cantambanco* had elicited were full of the kind of detail that spoke at once to the heart and to the senses. He remembered the conversion of the fifty savants, and their preservation, through Catherine's intercession, from the flames of the pyre. Neither their hair nor their clothes had been touched by the fire. He recalled her scourging with a scorpion, and the angels who ministered to her wounds in the ineffable light of her prison cell. Many times he had imagined painting the brightness surrounding Catherine's torn body, and the white dove that fed her, and the brilliant apparition of Christ himself amid the multitude of angels and virgins gathered in the dark dungeon. The cruel instruments of her torture, too, had played a long time upon his imagination. He had pictured wheels, a horrible kind of grist-mill, equipped with iron saws and sharp nails, upon which her body would be impaled and mutilated and broken. But mostly, it was the image of her beheading that had stayed with him. He had seen clearly in his mind's eye the headless body of Saint Catherine of Alexandria pouring forth healing milk instead of blood. Looking up now at Masolino's fresco, highly coloured and refined, he saw there a universe from which all traces of cruelty had been removed. Beauty had transfigured the horrors of torture and torment, had infused the scene with serene grace. In this world, nothing seemed so natural as the miraculous.

A woman's question broke in upon his reverie. "And I suppose he, too, shall be wanting his fruit and wine?"

Delighted, at first, to hear Miuccia's voice again, Masaccio had half turned to greet her before the memory of their botched farewell in Florence filled him with a cringing dread. He had been told she'd wanted to kill him that last, long, hot summer day, and most surely would have done so if Masolino had not bundled her off to Rome. Realizing there was no point in postponing the inevitable, he went to her now with open arms. Her hair fell heavy on her shoulders, her dress was cut low on her beautiful breasts. He felt a wrenching in his heart that nearly drove him to his knees. The mixture of awe and envy and gratitude that smote him whenever he stood in the presence of a god-driven piece of work. She held a large basket of food in her arms, its rim pressed up against her belly. He tried to take it from her to set it down on the chapel floor, so he could hold her close and ask forgiveness. But she would have none of it. Moving away from him, she went instead to Masolino and, speaking in quiet tones, busied herself with setting out his lunch. The men gathered around them, and, sitting on overturned pails and sacks of plaster, held out dusty hands for their cup of wine.

Standing off to the side, as good as dismissed, Masaccio observed her every move. She served everyone with the same haughty grace he'd come to know during his years as a *discepolo* in Masolino's workshop. It was while watching her then that he'd come to understand that beautiful women know no caste, no class, no hierarchy. That no mistake of birth or breeding can take from them what their beauty has laid claim to. Her own origins should have been a source of shame to her, she should have lived in fear of the betrayal of her own flesh, but instead, she rejoiced in her body and its flawless perfection.

She had been born to leper parents. Their eroded hands had caressed her, her perfect face had been pressed to their scaly breasts. But before disease could set upon her its indelible mark, they had entrusted her to Masolino, the *dipintore* who collected beautiful women as models for his portrayals of the Madonna. Maso had indeed painted Miuccia, as saint and virgin and martyr, but, above all, he had loved her as a daughter. And when, over the course of time, he had seen her awaken a different kind of love in Masaccio's callow breast, he had looked forward to the day when the sweet grace of the leper's daughter and the divine gift of the absent-minded apprentice could be united in marriage.

She listened now, face uplifted, as Masolino and his assistants debated the afternoon's work. If the final touches were put to St. Christopher and St. Ambroise before nightfall, could the base coats of plaster be applied to the rear wall before morning? Would Masaccio be able to draw the *sinopie* as early as tomorrow? Was the Cardinal's approval necessary before work was begun? With Masaccio, Masolino informed his collaborators, the Crucifixion would be imbued with all the gravity and solemn vigour the Cardinal expected. No anecdotal pleasantries, no pastel-coloured landscape, no charming detail—only austere, expressive art. At this, Miuccia tossed her fine head and snorted her derision. Masolino looked up at her with a sad and pained expression in his eyes. Ignoring him, she took a melon in her hands, and cleaved it cleanly in two with her long fingernails. She scooped the seeds and filaments out of the pale peach flesh with a quick flick of the wrist before handing one half to Masolino. Then, visibly revelling in the heat of Masaccio's gaze, she began to lick with her pointy pink tongue at the drops of juice beading up on the fruit's torn flesh. She pretended to be totally absorbed by the workmen's discussions, completely oblivious to Masaccio's unease.

Though the look on his face did communicate a certain distress, he was in fact considering the angle of her defiant little head and wondering how long he'd have to play the part of the guilt-stricken lover before being able to turn from her at last and concentrate on his work. It seemed like years had gone by since he'd felt the good honest weight of a brush in his hand.

VIII

HE'D LOVED ONLY ONE WOMAN. AFTER HER DEATH, HE'D KNOWN desire and lust, as wholesome and natural as hunger. And the women he'd bedded, warm as bread and good as apples, had laughed at his urgency, at his tousled mane of hair and his paint-spattered hands. Their bodies had met in tenderness, they'd tasted pleasure in each other's mouth, but they had not loved. And when he'd left them, at dawn or in the middle of the clear Tuscan night, these women had known his memory of them would be as fleeting as the scent of their perfume on his skin. They had not expected his devotion and he had not given it. But from the start, it had been different with Miuccia.

When she'd sat before him in the early morning light of the *bottega*, and he'd traced the limpid lines of her body, first with his eyes, then with the charcoal, she'd seen the cool, analytical expression on his face and had wanted to smash it with her closed fist. He'd not responded to her beauty the way the younger boys had. All of them, without exception, had fallen victim to the spell she cast on them. Some said it was the extraordinary luminosity of her flesh that entranced them, as though it had been made delicate and transparent by the kiss of disease. Others claimed to be moved by the serenity emanating from her, the imperviousness that had settled round her like a glow. She'd slept among lepers and had risen from their midst unscathed. Yet others were seduced by the depth of her gaze, or the sensuous curve at her waist, her abundant roan hair, her fine lips, her small, intelligent hands. To them, she was a goddess, sacred and untouchable. To Masaccio, she was the lovely distraction in the single-mindedness of his days.

She began to burn for him with an unholy passion the first time he impatiently cast parchment and charcoal aside and strode up to where she lay to arrange the veils draped across her body. She was a virgin of fourteen years, had remained pure despite the casual debauchery of Florentine society, had not been awakened to the mystery and delight of her own desire. When she'd seen him approach, this great, rumpled boy, she'd turned her face away from his cold eyes and his indifferent hands. She'd known she would see aloofness in his face and had been afraid of the ugly thing that would quicken in her breast at the sight of it. Wouldn't he be surprised, she'd thought, if my hand reached out like a cat's quick paw and clawed out his eyes? He could look upon me with his hard, calculating, dismissive gaze no more.

But the surprise that day was to be hers. As Masaccio slid the cloth across her body, muttering under his breath, the fleshy flat pad of his thumb grazed Miuccia's right nipple. She felt his touch move through her, stroking at her breast and nestling in her belly, an aching, voluptuous yielding there, that filled her eyes with wonder. Having adjusted the veils to his liking, Masaccio then took the girl's face between his hands and gently set the angle of her head. He could feel the fever on her skin, could feel her body hum with breathless astonishment. And he understood that he'd awakened in her a new and curious craving. Smiling to himself, he'd gone back to his place, picked up the charcoal and drawn Miuccia as the Samaritan Woman—with her well, her pitcher and her desperate thirst.

Because of the workshop's humble dimensions, she and Masolino's apprentices were thrown together in a sometimes awkward intimacy. While the younger boys crushed pigment and boiled the sizes, she made bread and cut up vegetables for soup. While they hauled water from the stream, she hung out the wash to dry. She would sit in the sunshine in the morning, brushing out her hair while they dug sleep out of their eyes and scratched at their groins. And when she bathed in the late evening, they would rise from their cots, their thin, naked bodies streaked with moonlight, and press their faces to the drawn curtain to catch a whiff of her warm, wet scent or a quick glimpse of her silhouette. She treated these youngsters with disdain, Masolino with respect, and Masaccio with the nervous impudence of idolatry.

To him, she was as beautiful—and as incidental—as the rain. He'd hardly notice her traipsing along beside him on the streets of Florence as he ran errands or dropped in on friends. She'd be right there beside him when he stopped in at the apothecary's shop to buy pigments or new brushes and sponges, she'd bury her nose in the folds of his cloak as they passed the butchers and the fishmongers along the canal, and open wide, shy eyes as they neared the wine-market. There, between the tavern and the hot baths, was the brothel—one of many the city now promoted in a vain attempt to curb the ravages of homosexuality. It had occurred to her, once or twice, that Masaccio might be of that persuasion. But when she'd seen how he could mislay people and things, lend money and never think to ask for it again, walk into walls, forget to eat, not know the time, the date or the year, she had concluded that his was not a case of skewed sexuality but of profound and advanced distraction. He was, simply, a *persona astratissima* and therefore, as she reasoned, not beyond hope.

It was at the morning of departure and at the evening of homecoming that Masaccio noticed her most. He would surround her then with affectionate, avuncular gentleness, kiss her brow and hold her hands, bid her take good care of herself and of the old master in the wicked foreign cities they were travelling to, or rejoice at their safe return.

When she and Masolino left Florence to go to Hungary, Masaccio's warm words of farewell accompanied her through the first three days of the voyage. As their sojourn in the distant capital stretched on, she thought of him every day, exaggerated his kindnesses and gentle attentions, talked herself into believing he was desperately in love with her. As a result, she worked herself up into a state of hysteria and nearly went mad with homesickness.

When Masaccio left Florence to paint the great altarpiece for the Church of the Carmine in Pisa, he enjoined her to ignore the lustful young men who would hound her footsteps and bay at her door during his absence, and wait patiently for his return. He promised they would walk out together, then, through the streets of Florence, and everyone would know she was his. A lovesick Miuccia had kept the homefires burning throughout the long, cold months of their separation, had turned his words over and over in her heart, had counted the days till she saw him again, had made herself desolately sick with longing. At his return, stricken once again by her extraordinary beauty, he had smiled warmly and embraced her, then had immediately forgotten her, Pisa, Florence and the whole world, as he'd lost himself in work.

Even when Masaccio had moved out of the workshop and taken a house on the Via dei Servi with his mother and brother, he and Miuccia continued to run errands together and to see to Masolino's welfare. As she grew older, he would chide her about her lovers and pretend to want to chase them away. She played along, threatening to abandon him and run off with some fresh-faced Florentine weaver or, when the time came for her to leave for Rome with Masolino, with one of the many sculptors hard at work now in the cathedrals of the city. He'd laughed then, his loud, engaging laugh, and declared that when next he went to Rome, he'd take her for wife himself under the noses of these paramours and at the very altars they had built. At this, Miuccia's head had filled with the clamour of her heartbeat, she'd felt the sky tilt and the earth shudder beneath her feet, and she had dared to speak. "We leave tomorrow at dawn, Masaccio. Today, I shall bake a wedding loaf and if you do not come to me tonight and eat of the bread and say before Masolino and all the *garzoni* present here that I am your betrothed, in Rome I shall do as I please and love whom I wish."

She'd waited with silenced breath as he'd thrown back his head and laughed once more before enclosing her in an embrace. Then, kissing her on the crown of her roan-red head, he'd promised he'd come at dusk to break with her the bread of their betrothal.

✣

It was a warm midsummer night, the Tuscan twilight seemed reluctant to deepen to dark, and Miuccia's heart was glad. Masaccio would have had many hours of daylight to finish the painting he'd begun, he would come to her satisfied with his day's work, drowsy with tiredness and soft with hunger. She would feed him and pour him cool red wine, she would listen as he talked of the completed *giornate*, she would watch him scratch distractedly at the orange and the Prussian blue on his fingernails. Then, when he'd pushed away the cheese and fruit, she'd bring to him the bread she'd baked. He would smile, recalling his early morning promise, and tear with his hands at the golden loaf. They would eat of it together, then, pulling her down onto his knees, he would bury his face in her breast and beg her not to go to Rome. All aloofness gone, he would plead with her to stay with him in Florence and be his wife.

So sure was she of the outcome of the day's events that, to Masolino's dismay, she had refused to pack her bags. And when he and the boys had gone to the baths, she had told them to expect a surprise at their return. As the hours moved on, and night hovered at the eastern edge of the city, she began to tremble with anticipation. It was now too dark to paint, the assistants would be lighting torches to clean up the day's mess, Masaccio would be even now making his way to her through the darkening streets. He would burst through the door, his hair wild, his eyes full of fire, and he would scoop her up into his arms and crush her to his heart. The one heady moment of unmitigated joy she would cling to through a lifetime of distracted lovemaking and absent-minded embraces.

✣

Light in the Brancacci chapel was still good. The last bit of sunset lingered on the pale walls and made St. Peter's gown glow. Even as he painted the ardent yellow of the robe, Masaccio's mind was full of doubt. Had he gone too far? Was he not exaggerating the aggressiveness of the confrontation? As each brush stroke fanned the flames of St. Peter's anger, Masaccio felt his confidence grow.

The story of the tribute money was a dangerously incendiary one, it was right that the actors in it collide in a brilliant flash of warring colours. He had not hesitated to paint the tax-collector's clothing a fiery vermilion. The man's round back, his open mouth, his wide, importunate hand stuck out palm up for money, nearly prodding Christ in the chest—every detail of his physiognomy was hot and angry. Saint Peter's reaction to the man's pugnacious attitude could be clearly read in the apostle's face. Masaccio had knotted his features and twisted his mouth with ferocious emotion. He had given him a misshapen left hand, blunt and graceless as a paw. And now, he was painting his robe an agitated yellow, exactly right, Masaccio thought, for a man as reckless and quick-tempered as St. Peter. Hadn't he slashed off the ear of the high priest's assistant in the Garden of Gethsemane? And hadn't Voragine claimed that Peter would have torn Judas to pieces with his teeth had he known what the man was up to? Doubtful no more, Masaccio applied the final shadows to St. Peter's robe as night sealed off the chapel windows.

By torchlight, he at last put down the brush and stood back to consider his work. He was pleased with its balance. The tax-collector's red tunic against the Saviour's deep blue robe. St. Peter's craggy countenance beside John the Evangelist's beautiful golden head. Judas's dark face among the bright ones, the sinister shadow in so much light. Now that the piece was finished—Del Giusto would see to the final touches in the morning—Masaccio felt weariness seep into his bones. But as torchlight played upon the chapel walls revealing blank expanses of coarse plaster—he ran his hand across the surface, pleased to feel its tooth beneath his fingers—all traces of fatigue vanished. He was anxious to take measurements and to begin making the preparatory drawings.

One of the best moments of the day was when, with charcoal and red ochre in hand, he laid out the scene's plan and set up the decorative scheme. All possibilities lay open to him then, ideas burst like fireworks, sprouted like tendrils on a vine, and it was often at the very instant of transferring the composition he'd sketched on parchment to the huge canvas of the wall that the finest inspiration came. The other privileged moment of the day was at the end, after the careful modulations of tone, after the browns and umbers of his landscapes, after the ruddy, tanned complexions of his figures, when he would direct light and cast shadow and make space real. In the Madonna and Child of Sant'Ambrogia, when he had bent hand and mind to painting the pensive inclination of Mary's head, he had noticed how placing a patch of light near the corner of her pursed lips expressed the thoughtfulness of her expression. He had not foreseen it. It had come to him as memory alights, unsummoned and unsought, the touch of a bird's wing, an unexpected breeze upon his cheek. Masaccio had learned long ago to be attentive to such grace. In his mind, in some mysterious way, these moments of sudden insight were inextricably bound up, entangled, infused with the smell and taste of Francesca.

It was very late when he finally rolled up the sheets of drawings and decided to head for home. The assistants had left him bent over the parchments in a circle of torches. He thrust each one in a bucket of water, let the hissing vapour envelop him like a veil against the encroaching dark. He crossed the church, felt the living presence there breathing its deep and peaceful watchfulness among the silent stones and painted effigies, then moved off through the nighttime streets of Florence. His mind set on the morrow's work, he had no eyes for the milky spill of the moon, no ears for the night thrush's song, no thought, either—not a single, hopeful, redeeming thought—for the lovely Miuccia.

✣

In the morning, when he arrived breathless at Masolino's door, he found the place empty except for a golden loaf in the centre of the table, a circle of bread, grown stale and hard from the night's long vigil.

Somewhere above the Atlantic
Thursday 2 May
I told the boys I'd take a cab—it was an early flight and I didn't want to wake them—so we said our goodbyes last night. But when I picked up the phone this morning to call Duffy's, I saw Nick standing in the hall, in his jockey shorts and a rumpled t-shirt, looking all of ten years old. I put down the receiver, gave him a hug and told him to go back to bed. But there was Alex at the door, already taking my bags out to the car.

We drove through the quiet springtime streets, while the sun came up orange in the east and, in the cars beside us, men sipped coffee and women checked their makeup in their rear-view mirrors. Nick launched into an improv on the faces we glimpsed through the windshields at the stoplights. That lady there, the one right next to us, was the vice-president of Marketing, had a husband and three daughters in a tony house in Lindenwoods, was wearing the red teddy her husband had bought her for her forty-fifth birthday and was considering this morning, on her way to work, the wisdom of entering upon an affair with the senior attorney in Legal. Whereas he, the guy in the red Camaro, had run into his ex-wife in the dentist's office yesterday and had been blown away by her good looks. As he revs the engine, he plots the logistics of a second chance meeting. The young blonde slipping the clutch in and out in that rusty old Toyota is replaying her conversation with the new copy-guy at Great-West Life. He has fine long fingers and a ponytail and she hopes he might be dangerous. And as for this guy, here, well, he's running away from home this morning, leaving two orphaned children for a woman he barely knows and a boring country full of tame rivers and clear-cut hills. And that boyo there....

I nearly missed it. I looked first at Alex but he shook his head and grinned. Then I turned around to look into Nick's eyes and, to my great relief, they were smiling too, and shining with mischief.

The boys didn't want to get out of the car—bad morning breath, they said, and sleep in the corners of their eyes. So I reached for Alex's hand and held on tight. But he shook me off, grabbed me by the neck and stared hard into my face. "Have a great time, Dad," he said. "And don't worry about us." I just nodded, too choked up to speak. Nick and I stepped out of the car at the same time. I wrapped his narrow body in my arms and crushed it hard against my own. He touched my cheek with a closed fist, said, "I love you, Dad," then jumped in beside his brother.

I watched them drive off together, Alex holding his arm straight up out of one window, and Nick hanging out of the other, doing the royal wave. I watched them till the car disappeared in a turn, knowing with sickening certainty that if anything happens to me while I'm gone, or to one of my boys, it will not have been worth it.

~

Magda was in the checkout line, looking stunning at five forty-five in the morning. I put a hand to my face as if to erase the seams the restless night had left there, felt the pouchiness of my cheeks, the rough old-man bristle of my chin, and was overcome with a sudden urge to go back home. But she was holding out my plane ticket and smiling, so I dropped my bags at my feet and stepped into place at the end of the queue.

While we waited to board, we had a coffee and talked a little shop. We were both still stinging from our students' poor exam results. Getting worse every year, she said. The scope of cultural references is growing narrower, the grasp of mechanics becoming progressively more tenuous. Art replaced by portraits of the rich and famous, literature subsumed by advertising and propaganda. I heard her say the words "philistines," and "pseudo-culture," I heard myself mention Mike Nichols and *The Designated Mourner*, but then my brain must have gone on automatic because all I can remember now of our conversation is the imprint of her lipstick on the cardboard of her Starbucks cup, and the golden flecks in the green of her eyes.

We sat together on the plane to Toronto—our hands sometimes touching and our glances colliding, such unnerving intimacy—and talked far too intensely, to my liking, for such an early hour of the morning. One of those exchanges that seem soft and flirtatious on the outside but, deep-down, are driven hard by the desire to impress. I imagine we were both a little nervous about the prospect of spending six weeks together and were trying to convince each other, and ourselves, we hadn't made a serious mistake. Though I was feeling a little high-strung, it was not an unpleasant sensation—a mixture of excitement, anticipation and sexual tension—and had nothing at all to do with regret. But then she began to talk about Toronto and the people who would be joining us there, and the first wave of nausea hit.

(It was when I was up there, flying with hysterical speed to the dense crush of a huge assassin of a city, that I felt myself dissolve. Nothing showed on my face—at least I hope not, Christie—but inside, everything was melting and sloshing around, my heart a big, hot, blubbery thing climbing up into my throat. The last thing I wanted to be doing this morning in May was flying into the smog and stink of people-infested jungles—Toronto, for God's sake, Paris and then Rome!—when spring was bursting into leaf along the lakes, and the rivers ran cold against the skin of my canoe. And it was there, when I sat in the scratchy blue plane seat beside a woman whose laughter was unfamiliar, that I realized the enormity of my mistake. I saw with frightening clarity that it was all wrong, that I had given up a spring I would never see again for exhausted dawns and tawdry afternoons, for—you said it best, old Wordsworth, my friend—*the close and overcrowded haunts, Of cities where the human heart is sick.*

And in Toronto, my worst fears were confirmed. After a bit of browsing in a bookstore on Bloor and a quick lunch at the Avenue Lounge, Magda and I walked to Massey College, where she'd made arrangements to meet with her friends. With high colour in her cheeks, she introduced me first to Për—a tall, blond Swede who is, I believe, a paleontologist, and then to Fiona, a woman with oddly aggressive spectacles, who teaches history of art at York. All three of them immediately began to talk about the colleagues who would be joining us in Florence from universities all over the world.

That's when the tingling alarm that had spread through me like an attack of nausea all at once became the dry heaves of regret. Where I had imagined myself sitting, alone, in a room filled with golden Tuscan light, or strolling, alone, down the cobblestones of a mediaeval *vicolo*, or sipping an espresso, alone, in the cool of the *ponentino*, I now saw myself bunched in with a group of tourists,

Nikon and Fodor's in hand, pointing and bleating—in hushed, reverential tones, to be sure—about the Benozzo Gozzoli, and the Luca Signorelli and the Rosso Fiorentino, and lining up at americanized buffeterias with trays and handfuls of Euros and pocket calculators to figure out the exchange, and being hustled onto buses and carted off in a blue diesel haze to the leaning tower of Pisa.

I can't tell you, Christie, how sorry I felt. Imagining I could write a better book there, in the suave Italian light, in the edifying company of scholars, I had talked myself into going to Tuscany to live and travel with a busload of university profs, as randy and as boisterous, no doubt, as freshmen on spring break. And it was too late to turn back. May and June would unfold along the Berens and I wouldn't be there to see it. I would, instead, be rubbing elbows with thick humanity in a world given over to dust and decay.

Like Saul Bellow, I found myself wondering, *Why was Coleridge's albatross following that goddam ship anyway? It should have been satisfied with stormy solitude. Why didn't it stick to seafood? Those sailors with their lousy English biscuits were the death of it. Also, longing for human company can be a fatal mistake.*

Right now, the three of them are sitting together somewhere ahead of me in this improbably huge silver bird. I am alone, thank God, and don't have to engage in repartee, or erudite allusion. I can write to you, or dream, or close my eyes and sleep, or drink too much Scotch, or read a few pages of Calvino, Coetzee or Seamus Heaney.

And the only company I long for, human or otherwise, is yours.)

Somewhere over Switzerland

Friday 3 May

Arrived at Roissy, feeling tired and crumpled. All I wanted to do was call home, then burrow into a bed in a dark, anonymous room. But it was morning in Paris, the sun was shining brightly, Magda and her friends had plans.

We had a three o'clock flight to Rome. Time enough, Fiona reckoned, to meet colleagues over brunch in the Latin Quarter. So on the first of our organized tours, we piled into a cab and raced through bright, slick streets beneath a sky bristling with significant shadow. The bistro, behind the Pantheon on Montagne Ste-Geneviève, was a warm candle-lit place with creamy white linen tablecloths and irises in slender glass vases. Fiona introduced us to two very pleasant-looking women and a gentleman with a goatee and, without further ceremony, we sat down to great blue bowls of steaming café au lait. And immediately, all around me, conversation flared like a well-fed fire—the French quick and fluent and sharp—while I sat back, my fingers wrapped around the warm bowl, and shamelessly eavesdropped. The usual academic formalities—enquiries as to the health and happiness of colleagues on both continents, words of congratulations on the publication of this book or that article, recent announcements regarding research grants and fellowships—were exchanged with smiles and brightening glances and I smiled too, and nodded my head, pretending to be *au courant*. But as I turned my gaze from one side to another, watching the emphatic nods and savouring the Gallic moues, I sensed with some alarm a sudden shift in the tenor of the conversation. All at once, I noticed that a new, worrisome thing was beginning to buckle up in the clear French brows around me. And then I heard it, the name Jean-Marie Le Pen, falling from someone's lips like an abomination. It sat there in front of us, smacked down on the snowy cloth like a slimy dead fish with a milky dead eye. And for a long time, among the fruit, the coffee and the crêpes Bretonnes, we talked of nothing else—the LePen phenomenon, the inexplicable success of the far-right National Front, the shocking ascendency of its racist leader. On Sunday, May 5th—two days from now—he will meet Jacques Chirac in a runoff for the presidency. There is no doubt as to the outcome of the election but Fiona's colleagues, and half of France, are appalled, wounded and humiliated that a hatemonger like LePen was able to make it this far. And so the conversation pivoted on this one central question—to what base instincts in modern French society did such a man appeal? The answers, suggested by my apolitical, cosmopolitan and artsy luncheon companions, were wide-ranging and eclectic, to say the least.

(But, as usual, I felt myself be drawn away from the discussion by the seductive pull of memories. Of the smoky dark cafés of Montparnasse, of fragrant espressos and ashtrays overflowing with *mégots*, of endless plotting with bearded Marxists in black berets, of exquisite jazz and of you. You wore your hair long in those days—how old were we then, that long-ago September in Paris?—and in its blondes, its ambers and its golds were all the shimmering lights of summer. You spoke in a low voice, your hands were quiet things, folded one inside the other, but your eyes were volatile and quick, their expression changing from minute to minute like a cloud-swept stretch of sky. I can remember watching those eyes and dying a little when they flashed for someone else.

Do you remember, Christie, how we cared, then, about the world? How we felt the urge to heal it beating in our chests like a second heart? Despair didn't tempt us, and hope had not yet been blunted on the dull edge of irony. Goodness hovered on the horizon like a trembling sun on the brink of the world. And it was you, and I, and they, those quasi-communists and poets, those sax players and lovers, those dime-store intellectuals and artists, who would be the midwives of the new dawn.

But we wait, still, for the shadows to lift and the dark has fostered new, more insidious evils. Even love, Christie, can be helpless in the face of fear.)

By the time I turned my attention to my companions again, they'd moved on to other matters. From what I gathered, a chapel in a mountain village in Tuscany had recently burned down. A vault has apparently been uncovered—a kind of crypt carved out of the rock beneath the church floor. And art historians the world over wait with bated breath to hear what treasures may turn up.

I tried to imagine it. A burned-out shell, blackened walls, ogival-shaped spaces paned with sky now, instead of stained glass. The broken stones and charred beams lie to one side beneath a thick coat of wet ash. The smell is an ancient one, evoking the long, bare bones of cold hearths, damp caverns, the woolly wetness of animal skins, the bloody scent of sacrifice. Towards the rear of the chapel, the floor has been scraped clean and in a depression in the mud, like the sinkhole of a toothless mouth, the outline of a trap door is visible. All around, men and women stand, quietly conversing, their calm countenances belieing the tension in the air. They are waiting for someone—to whom would be given the honour, I wondered, the local art historian, the village mayor, the parish priest?—to open the crypt and reveal its contents to the world. In a matter of minutes, after a quick survey of the mouldy-smelling boards piled *pêle-mêle* on the earthen floor, the eagle-eyed curators and scholars gathered there will know exactly what the discovery is worth.

Magda has told me about the altarpiece Masaccio painted for the Carmelite church in Pisa. Since the eighteenth century, when the polyptych was removed from the Scarsi chapel, dismantled and the separate pieces dispersed, the art world has kept alive the hope of one day finding two missing side panels. Magda told me it was very unlikely they would ever be found. The paintings had probably been cut into pieces, tossed out, or the boards used for something else—a work-table, perhaps, or as the canvas for another painting.

This, too, I tried to imagine. I tried to picture the workman—a carpenter, perhaps, in an impoverished village in the countryside—who has been called in by the vicar to see about hanging the two paintings that have recently been bequeathed to them. The panels are propped up against a pew and the carpenter casts a knowing eye over them, mentally taking their measurements, seeing how they might fit among the other humble paintings, frescoes and statuary adorning the walls of his ancient church. It strikes him that they are well executed. The figures represented on them are lively and colourful, the angels hover nicely, the emblems of each of the saints have been painstakingly reproduced—John holds a long cross, Julian, the sword with which he accidentally killed his parents, Nicholas carries three gold balls and Peter, the keys to the church. He would have stood back, this eighteenth-century carpenter, and taken a moment to admire the painter's artistry before finally deciding the panels were a little too large for his purposes. At approximately three and a half cubits high and one and a half cubits wide—sixty inches by twenty-eight—they would not fit in the blank spaces on either side of the confessional. So, being possessed of a pragmatic turn of mind, this good workman would have seen the advantage of having four smaller pieces that could be slipped in here and there, on either side of the two church doors, for example, to fill an empty space.

He lays one panel across his sawhorse, fetches his handsaw from his toolbox and, holding the painting steady with one large hand splayed across the face of a saint, he runs the teeth of his blade against the edge, takes a first bite out of the nice, flat, seasoned piece of wood. As I watched him work, steadily, competently, I saw the flakes of gold leaf lift in a fine dust and adhere to the blade, I saw the steps on which the saints stand cleave in two, I saw one falling fold of Peter's robe shred into slivers and shards of bright yellow-orange, and I felt my heart falter.

My mind full of thoughts of gutted chapels, of bigotry and sacrilege, I let out a soft, involuntary moan. Magda turned towards me, gave me a quick, quizzical glance. One look at the dismay in my face convinced her it was time for us to leave. A last gulp of coffee, *bises* all around, and we were off to Orly and the heartless, hopeless crowds of Rome.

Rome

Same day, much, much later

My heart clenched as we approached the centre of the city. Because of our late arrival time, we decided to wait until morning to rent a car and head up the A1 to Valdarno. I, needless to say, would have preferred a hotel on the northern outskirts, but Magda and her friends would not be swayed—they wanted to sip wine in the Independenzia, they said, and bask in the Baroque splendour of an Old Roman piazza. I was very tempted to let them go on without me but, at the last minute, decided to be civil. So, with a grim look upon my face, I went about the trying business of hailing cabs and hauling bags, I suffered the humiliation of baby talk with taxi-driving mafiosi, I wondered yet again if, at the venerable age of fifty-two, I hadn't bitten off a little too much.

(Magda is quite a bit younger than I. She is gorgeous and intelligent and full of youthful appetite. Unlike us, Christie, she thinks nothing of having twenty people in for a sit-down dinner on one or two hours' notice, or driving across town at three a.m. to meet a friend who's changing planes. She can drink red wine till the wee hours and get up the next morning to deliver a brilliant lecture at an international conference. She can shop the whole afternoon, dine out, catch a play and go for after-theatre drinks *all in the same day*. And I now know she can fly sleepless across the Atlantic, browse through duty-free boutiques on extended stopovers, fly again through one or more time zones, settle in a hotel room and find herself in the grips of an absolutely irresistible craving for Campari and the comforting loud intimacy only crowds can offer. As embarrassing as it is for me to admit it, I think I might find it difficult, some days, to keep up.

And so I won't even try. When all this business with departure and arrival and the general unrootedness of life in transit is over, I'll shut myself up in my room in the villa and bend all my energies into forging something solid out of the vague shapes that float and beckon like specks upon my retina, like *the ragged wings of birds against the changing tide of sky.* And I will look up now and then and let my gaze linger on the Tuscan hills, on the cypress trees and the vineyards and wait for you, my own golden angel, to appear.)

It was a lovely soft evening in May. Only the hard-core grappa drinkers were sitting inside the bar. Everyone else was on the terrace, enjoying the Roman twilight. Magda chose a table off to one side and ordered Cinzano for us all. It's hardly my drink, but somehow the bitter astringency of the stuff struck me as being exactly right. For the night, for the trip, for my life. I lifted the glass to my lips, felt the ice bite against my skin, heard it clink against my teeth, then swallowed with a grimace. I was thinking about the road we would be travelling in the morning—it appears I will be doing most of the driving; Për and Fiona are staying in Rome a few days to meet with friends—and already worrying about Italian cars and Italian drivers. Much more at ease at the wheel of a Jeep on overgrown tracks through the bush than on European autostrada, I was hoping to find the reassuring red line of a secondary road from Rome to Valdarno on my trusty Michelin map.

But Magda was clearly delighted to be here again. Despite the noise and the pungency of the piazza, and the careening, klaxoning cars, she was looking around with wide eyes, exchanging quick smiles with strangers, taking it all in. I heard her sigh contentedly. *Roma*, she said, *non basta una vita*. A lifetime is not enough. I sighed, too, suppressing the urge to argue. Instead, I blocked out the strident voices and the unpleasant smell of diesel fumes, and forced myself to take an interest in the conversation.

Për was talking about the latest archaeological finds in the Middle Awash. It was a fascinating subject, really, the missing link, Lucy, and the new *kadabba*, but I soon found myself distracted—and amused—by the subtle charm of his subtext. While ostensibly talking to all of us, he was in fact focusing his attention exclusively on Magda.

And no wonder, I thought.

She was wearing a narrow, sleeveless sheath cut from bronze silk. She sat close to the table, the cloth of her dress tight against her breasts, her pale arms open and stretched towards us in some kind of ingenuous gesture of appeal. Për's eyes kept running up and down the length of those white arms and lingering on the shallow dimple of the inside of her elbow. I could imagine that in full view of all the people seated at the terrace—Magda looked stunning, even in the semi-darkness, and all around us, heads kept turning—he would feel tempted to bend his head to the tender little hollow and press his lips to her flesh. I could imagine him wishing us away, Fiona and I, so he could concentrate all his attention on her every small gesture. He would watch her lick the Cinzano from her lips, run her fingers through her hair and, when she'd rise to leave, he would nearly knock over the table in his rush to follow. As they'd walk out of the bar, his old man's heart visibly pounding against the cloth of his new blue shirt, people at the tables they passed would all turn and stare. Though he is familiar with this, the world's frisson of disapproval at the spectre of aging flesh in a young woman's bed, it still manages to unnerve him. But tonight, as he walks with quivering step towards the rapture of sweet collusion, he turns a resolutely blind eye to the knowing glimmer of Italian glances and the cynical set of Italian mouths.

~

Have reread this last bit and can't help but laugh. "He," indeed. And as far as I can tell, the only old man around here is me.

Villa Saena Julia
Saturday 4 May
À rebours. It occurred to me, as we followed the Tiber River north towards Florence, that we were following the same route Masaccio had taken so many centuries before, some kilometres to the east and in the opposite direction. And I wondered if, like me, he had set out with dread in his heart only to discover after a few hours' travel that the road has unsuspected delights.

One quick look at the map told me that, till Orvieto, it made better sense to follow the highway and so, with clammy hands upon the steering wheel, I took the interchange that swung us quickly into the main stream of the A1. To my surprise, I soon found myself in the grips of a very heady, adolescent thrill—the little Fiat we rented responds very nicely, thank you, to the quite excessive demands I put upon it and speed, I had forgotten, has a lovely, bracing, cathartic effect.

Adding to the pleasure, of course, was Magda's presence at my side. My arm brushed against hers as I shifted into fifth gear and I could catch, whenever she moved, the lacy edge of the scent lifting off her hair. She was quietly rejoicing at finding herself in this part of the world once again. Her attention fixed on the landscape unwrapping itself before our eyes, she leaned forward in the car seat, attempting to absorb Italy though every pore of her flesh.

Her excitement is contagious. I have put aside every misgiving I might have had about this trip and am feeling as daring and adventuresome as Columbus himself.

Everything is so marvellously foreign. The trees shimmering silver instead of green in the morning sunlight and pointing to the sky with adamant fingers, the rigorous symmetry of the climbing vineyards, the dust and gnarl of the ancient olive groves, the odd shape of the exotic cars humming along beside us, the strange sound of the words I try to read on every road sign that we pass. And as I sound out the names of towns and villages, Magda nearly always has an anecdote to tell. That's the birthplace of X, she'll say, Y is buried in the church there, Z painted the altarpiece of the chapel in the monastery on the hillside.

Her knowledge of all things Italian never ceases to astound me.

Today, as we drove towards Orvieto, eighty kilometres north of Rome, she wondered if I'd be interested in checking out a relic.

"Oh, I love relics," I said. "Is it a tooth, a piece of the Virgin's camisole, a sliver of the True Cross? Or is it a vestige of very human love, like Donne's *bracelet of bright haire about the bone?*"

"It's something rather more shocking,"she said. "In Orvieto, people come to venerate a bloodstained host. Tradition has it that a doubting priest challenged God to make the host bleed at the fraction rite to prove it is indeed the body of Christ. Well, the host did bleed and, to dispel the doubts of all the Thomases of the world, is now on display in Orvieto."

Did we want to stop in Orvieto? The cathedral would be imposing, the monstrance impressive, but the Brancacci chapel waits, Magda has seen her share of relics and I, well, I no longer doubt.

~

We had lunch lakeside in Castiglione di Lago. While Madga introduced me to the wonders of Tuscan *cucina—cacciucco, finocchione, prosciutto de cinghiale*—I told her about Shelley. About his very young wives, his poems, his death by drowning in the Bay of Lerici, two hundred kilometres northwest of where we sat.

"His friends burned his body on a funeral pyre and made offerings of wine, oil and incense. For his gravestone, Leigh Hunt supplied a final summing-up: *Cor cordium.*"

"Heart of hearts. That's so beautiful," Magda said. "I think I would be glad to face eternity with those words carved on my tombstone. Wouldn't you, Daniel?"

I nodded my head, unable to speak because of the tears gathering at the back of my throat. As I tipped my glass of *brunello*, I wondered—why Shelley, why here, and, most mysterious of all, why tears? Sure, La Spezia was not far off, and sure, a meditation on death can bring the warmth of emotion to the eyes. But what associations brought the dead poet to mind, and what memory, or feeling of nostalgia, was flooding me with sadness? I was staring hard at the blank, blue surface of the lake when suddenly I heard myself say, "He was twenty-nine years old."

Magda set down her fork, pushed her sunglasses up into her

hair and tipped her head to look at me. "Really?" she said. "About the age Masaccio was when he died."

And then of course I knew. It was the idea of young death that was catching in my throat. In the morning hours of a life, the sudden swoop of darkness, the strangled breath, and the world a place of heartbreaking beauty. (From whose arms have they been torn, from what love? To what work did they owe their lives, to what passion?) I shifted my gaze from the stillness of the lake to Magda's face, to the throb of life in her throat, to the leap of green light in her eyes. I raised my glass of wine, touched it to hers and said, "To time, and to us, who make much of it."

Magda's rich laughter rang out over the water. She is on familiar terms with my obsessions, sees right though my façade of feigned nonchalance and into the dark and sweaty chambers of my anxious little heart. She gave me a look of mocking sympathy before turning her attention to the biscotti the waiter had placed before her. Then, slowly, while I watched, she dipped her *zucotto* into her coffee, took it into her mouth and, with exaggerated voluptuousness and a rapturous rolling of her eyes, savoured every lazy languorous mouthful. She was provoking me, of course, forcing me to slow down and let time move on without me. And after a few minutes of observing her, of letting myself become absorbed in her delight, I couldn't help but admit she'd won. As the warmth of the Italian sun settled on my face, and the blossom scent of the wind filled my empty head, I felt it well up in me like a small sea, the certainty that time is as well spent watching a beautiful woman eat as writing a page, or sketching a face.

~

The villa is superb. Just off a secondary road running between Montevarchi and Siena, it is a rambling old fortress made of amber stone, set among olive groves, fruit trees and ancient oaks. My room—very bare, almost monastic—looks out over the rolling green of the Chianti hills. Magda tells me there will be at least a dozen art history people living here during the next two months. But the villa is so large and ramshackle, and the grounds so vast, I think I'll be able to avoid group dynamics without much difficulty at all. I will be free to go off on my own to explore the countryside, on foot or on one of the bicycles I noticed lined up in the loggia. Tomorrow, at first light, I plan on taking one or two of the dirt roads leading away from the estate to watch the landscape as it shakes off the night. The way Masaccio might have seen it the morning he left Florence to travel to Masolino, Miuccia and Rome.

In the last couple of days, I haven't spent much time thinking about the direction the book might take, or what transformations it might undergo, now that I have fallen under the direct influence of this very distinctive Tuscan light. Tonight, as I paused on a terrace after dinner, watching twilight settle over the hills, it occurred to me it was in the last rays of this very sun that Miuccia would have sat, her face turned to the door of the *bottega*, waiting with beating heart for Masaccio to come bursting in, smell the yeasty warmth of freshly baked bread and remember his promise to her. As I lingered in the gathering dark, I tired to imagine the slow turning of her thoughts. How they might have moved from conventional images of romantic love—linked arms, touching hands, touching lips—and the warmer, redder, muskier images of sexual intimacy—her young girl's blood running hot at the idea of his clever hands on her fine body, of his face on her breast, of his hips pressed hard against hers—and the comforting images of gentle, connubial bliss—nestling together in a winter bed, sharing a bath, eating a pie out of the same dish—to something a little darker, a little less warm. As the night deepened, and Masolino and the boys returned from the baths, and still Masaccio did not appear, she would have begun to worry about him in the unlit streets of Florence. There were many poor squatting in the bushes along the Arno who would have looked upon even the penniless painter's cloak with covetous eyes, there were jealous artisans, too, who watched the comings and the goings of their more favoured brothers and plotted in the darkness. There were also, and Miuccia hated to think of them, all the temptations of street life that could call to a man and entice him, luring him off the path to home. The savvy women of the brothels, the young boys and their soft flesh, the casks of wine and the smoky camaraderie of the taverns, the cards, the die, the seductive charms of Lady Luck.

And he was so forgetful, her Masaccio. Distracted by a bit of warmth, a smile, a proffered glass of Trebbiano, he would let the thought of hearth and home and her slip his mind like a piece of old news.

At one point during her vigil, Miuccia might have left off wringing her hands and decided in a rush to slip on her cloak and sneak out into the midnight streets of Florence to find him herself. Masolino, who no doubt watched and waited in the shadows, would have had to struggle—his small hands barely strong enough to contain her flailing arms—to keep her from going out at such a late hour. Her fear and her determination would have pushed her to the edge of hysteria and she would have fought like a cornered cat. But in the end, hearing Masolino's calming words and heeding her own despairing heart, she would have lowered her arms and admitted defeat.

It was quite dark by the time I decided I should find my way to my room. The sky was streaked with purple clouds that had been drawn in the wake of the setting sun like dusky blankets pulled by a sleepy hand. While I stood with my head thrown back and my eyes on the earliest stars, I thought I could feel it, the bitterness that must have gathered on Miuccia's tongue the moment she realized he would not be coming home to her, not now and not later. It tasted of tears, most certainly, and of the acrid drink of life, it tasted of age, and of ash, of the thick, grey dregs of empty days and of lonely nights.

As I followed a dark corridor towards the stairway leading to my floor, I caught a glimpse of Magda and a few friends in one of the villa's common rooms. A fire was burning in the great hearth and the light danced in the glasses they held in their hands. The hum of their voices covered the noise of my footfalls on the flagstones of the hallway and I was able to sneak by unnoticed.

And so I sit here alone in my room and think, still, about Miuccia. And it occurs to me—to me who feels I have been dealt the cruellest of love's blows—that I am wrong. Of all the trials of romantic attachment—I see this clearly now—unrequited love is by far the most cruel.

(In this dim, unfamiliar room, light-years away from home and from you, I am reminded of a sharp panic that rose up in me one evening as we sat together in a darkened hall. It was in the late eighties, we were in a theatre somewhere watching a performance of David French's *Salt-Water Moon*. You remember the play, don't you, Christie, one man, one woman, and their whole future balanced on a yes or a no? In the tense silence gripping the audience, I could feel my body thrum to the giant beating of my heart. I watched, frozen, as two people, like lost stars in the night, pulled and pushed away from each other, moved in and out of the light, and nothing but the void to catch them. And I was filled with sudden terror at the precariousness of love. I saw, with a gasp, how easy it is to miss, how it never comes at all to some, how it takes nothing less than the collusion of all the earth, and the heavens, too, to make it come to pass. In the spinning darkness of space, in the hushed shadows of an artificial night, I reached for your hand and held it, like I would never let it go.)

IX

HAVING TOSSED THE HEELS OF BREAD AND THE MELON SHELLS among the empty wine crocks in her basket, Miuccia reached up to kiss Masolino on the cheek before turning in a wide fling of her long skirts and heading out the chapel door. She could still feel the warm flush on her throat where Masaccio's eyes had lingered, and she damned the fickleness of her flesh, rising for him, all hot and dewy and dimpled with desire. Seeing him standing there, with his long, sad face and his helpless hands, she had wanted to run to him, bury her face in his shoulder, feel herself small and safe in the warm fold of his arms. Though her limbs had trembled and her heart had knocked like a wild thing inside her, she had grabbed hold of her emotion and turned it inside out. No one would have guessed from her harsh laughter and taunting words that deep inside love lay, curled soft and yielding as a leaf in spring.

But her heart was wet and swollen. As soon as she had crossed the chapel threshold, everything proud and stubborn within her had dissolved to tears. She set down her basket, and, her face streaming hotly behind her hands, she lurched blindly down the aisle towards the golden Christ. Throwing herself to her knees, she sobbed like a lost child, her face pressed hard against the wood of the pew.

The storm was violent and brief. She breathed deeply, she wiped her eyes with a savage hand and recomposed her face. Raising her eyes to Christ's peaceful countenance, she tried to reason with herself. It was thus, and nothing she could do would change it. He was distracted, feckless and incorrigible. And though she wanted nothing else for her life but his dark eyes and his beautiful hands, she would have to learn to let him go. She would marry no other, but would wait patiently upon him, storing up in memory the soft look, the caress, the gentle word that, in passing, he would give for her to keep. Drawing in a broken breath, Miuccia turned her face to the sun on the cathedral wall, and prayed to be made whole. She felt as though her life were spread like ashes on a cold and empty hearth.

Through the benevolence of Cardinal Branda da Castiglione, Masolino and Miuccia had at their disposal a suite of rooms in a nearby *palazzo*. It was understood that Masaccio would take up residence with them there for the duration of his commission in Rome. Recalling the stark austerity of the room they had set aside for him, Miuccia gave some thought to making it more pleasant. Besides changing the bedding—or, at the very least, giving it a good airing—and sweeping the floors and carpets, she could pick flowers, the tawny autumn wildflowers Masaccio loved best, and place them in pots around the room. It would be easy to please him, she thought. He expected so little and she knew him so well, his habits and his tastes as familiar to her as her own. And she would serve him with gladness in her soul. Like the vestal virgins Masolino had pointed out to her in the Forum, she would make of her life one long devotion to him, her own particular god, she would watch with hushed heart over the sacred fire burning in his breast. She would be his slave, his grace and his muse and if, in a moment's abstraction, he turned to her in his need, she would be his lover, too.

Considering then the many, many nights that lay ahead, when after the evening meal Masolino and Masaccio would endlessly linger at the table talking fresco and tempera, Miuccia felt a warm flood of tenderness well up inside her. It would be like the old days, when the three of them would sit amongst the crumbs and the dregs, and Masolino would drag his short, intense index finger through a wine spill to demonstrate a stroke and Masaccio would quote Cennini and talk about sight. About seeing, and not seeing, about repeatedly overlooking the evidence of the eyes. As the night wore on, and wine made their tongues grow thick, and the weight of the day pressed into their flesh, Miuccia would listen and watch as the gods before her metamorphosed into men. Their words would grow fat and self-important, their unperishing visions would fall to dust, and Miuccia, her heavy head nestled in her folded arms, would let herself slip into sleep.

When she awoke in bright mid-morning sunlight, she would find herself tucked into her bed, dressed in her nightgown, her aprons and robes spread neatly on the chair beside her. And she would smile at the thought that it was a weary, wine-besotted Masaccio who had tended to her in the night, who had picked her up from her chair at the table and carried her to her bed in his big arms. Masaccio who had undressed her like a child, drawing the nightdress over her naked arms, careful not to wake her, before kissing her on the forehead and leaving her to her dreams. Now that the three of them were together again, these long midnight conversations would round out their days once more, but this time, Miuccia would not let them end in sleep. She would take advantage of the darkness and Masaccio's muddled gentleness, and make room for him beside her on the bed. If, as a result of these tender, wine-drenched encounters, she became big with child, Masaccio would have no choice but to see her through different eyes. She would no longer be Masolino's Miuccia, she would be wife and mother, his very own flesh-and-blood Madonna.

Miuccia bowed her head in prayer once more, submitting to the guidance of divine light. *E'n la sua volontaté è nostra pace.* In Your will, Lord, is our peace. After a few moments of silent invocation, she raised her head, opened her eyes and was greatly startled to find someone standing close beside her. A woman, a little older than herself, simply but finely dressed, was staring intently at her with an unhappy look upon her face. Miuccia stood up, at once embarrassed and displeased to have been interrupted at prayer, and asked of the stranger what it was she required. Her voice, though whispered, was a peremptory hiss and the woman recoiled as though she'd been struck.

"Please excuse my boldness, *Signorina*. I saw you come out of the chapel," she gestured towards the rear of the church, "a moment ago, and I was hoping you could tell me how work there is progressing."

Miuccia was tempted to tell her to leave off disturbing others and to take the trouble to go see for herself. But looking the lady over once again, taking quick stock of the quality of her cloak and slippers, Miuccia decided she had better be courteous. The stranger could very well be a member of the Cardinal's family. She answered instead, "From what I have seen, *Signora*, the chapel frescoes are most beautiful. And now that a very fine painter from Florence has arrived, work will proceed at an even quicker pace. This man—"

"I know him," the stranger said. "He is my husband."

Miuccia had to bite back the urge to laugh. Patroness or not, she had to set her straight. "Surely not, *Signora*. Some other painter perhaps."

"No, *Signorina*. I speak of Masaccio, the Florentine painter. I wait for him now, and grow weary with waiting. But I shall be patient till his work here is done and we can make our way home together. Should you see him as you leave, be so kind as to remind him that his wife waits without."

She hesitated a moment. And then she said, "Please forgive my importunity, *Signorina*. For fear of disturbing him at his work, I disturbed you at prayer instead. A much greater offence, I am sure."

With a stunned, incredulous look, Miuccia watched the stranger move away from her and settle into a distant pew. Blinking away the tears that sprang with a bitter pricking to her eyes, she let herself sink back down onto her knees, felt her body shrink and dwindle beneath her billowing gown, felt her heart grow hard as bone. She looked up at the placid Christ on his pretty cross, tasted the salt of the spittle gathering on her lips and wiped it from her mouth with a weak and awkward gesture. For one brief moment, she felt her mind slip. It slid off into some dark place, caroming off the edge like a stone skips across water before sinking beneath the wave.

It was anger that brought it back. A clean, cutting anger, as sharp and as cold as a winter wind. She was angry with the woman, angry with Masaccio, angry with the indifferent god who even now gazed down upon her with his blank and bloodless eyes. Tell me, Lord, was it for this You saved me? Her tongue was silent but the words rang out in her brain, louder and louder with each question she threw in his dead, impassive face. For this betrayal? Was it for this humiliation that You rescued me from deformed limbs and mutilated flesh? Better my body, Lord, than my poor heart.

Turning away from Him, Miuccia rose from the pew and strode out of the church. As she passed the door to the chapel of Saint Catherine, she heard Masaccio's voice, distant and muffled, as though in a dream, or from some far-off world. With a rueful laugh, Miuccia remembered the bed-chamber she was going now to prepare for him and his wife. Instead of gathering for them the gold and russet flowers of fall, she wished she could fill the room with the purple petals of the deadly belladonna.

X

As soon as Miuccia had left the chapel, Masaccio became painfully aware of his stomach. Breakfast at the Rienzi's villa now little more than a memory, he regretted not having partaken of the workers' midday meal. His innards were beginning to make sounds, cavernous growls that both amazed and infuriated him. His body—so generous an instrument, so implacable a master. As often as he'd marvelled at its suppleness, its stamina, its brilliant adroitness, so, too, had he raged at its incessant demands. Like a spoiled child, or sometimes, Masaccio thought, like a fickle god, it exacted continuous, plentiful tribute in exchange for a few hours' peace. And he deeply resented its ascendancy over him. He wished he could work without bread and wine, could think and draw and paint without ever seeking relief in sleep, or in a woman's arms.

Well, he thought (a little smugly), at least that particular requirement has been taken care of for the present. Thanks to Eloisa. Eloisa, who lies in wait for me without. Tired, hungry and alone.

By the time he'd moved around the workers and up and over their pails and planks, he had decided on a plan. He would take her to the inn they'd passed on their way to the cathedral that morning and sit her down to wine and fruit. And he would let her speak. Let her talk all day if she wished about her beloved brothers and father, about her absconded husband, yes, even about Rome. ("The name came from Ruma—breast—because of the shape of the Palatine Hill," he remembered from the morning's lecture. He supposed she would pick up exactly where she'd left off.) And he would listen with a kind and attentive ear. He owed her that much. It occured to him that he also owed the sausagemaker at home. Then, he began to wonder if he'd paid the debt of six fiorini he owed to Andrea del Giusto. Slowing down beneath the arch of the door, he tilted his head back to think, cast his eyes heavenward, and was immediately distracted by a play of light on the wall. The one where he was to paint the Annunciation. Gabriel and Mary. The angel and the virgin. He had painted angels before, in a fresco in Sant'Ambrogio, in Ser Giuliano di Colino degli Scarsi's chapel in the Carmine of Pisa, and had not given them much thought. But this one, *this* one, would have to be given special consideration. For he was Gabriel, the messenger of God, come to tell the humble maiden that through her, eternal energy would be poured into the field of time. Of the four evangelists, only Saint Luke had written a Gospel describing this visitation and, as befitted the mystery of the occasion, only the sketchiest of details had been recorded. As usual, Masaccio's imagination would have to flesh out the rest.

He found a roll of parchment leaning in a corner and a bit of charcoal between two olive boards, so, in the roaring rising up from his guts, he sat cross-legged on the floor, the paper spread before him, and prepared to outline the scene. The first thing he wanted to set down, the thing his hand had ached to draw from the moment the image of the angel had sprung fully formed from his brain, was the wings. The great, virile, swan wings that had cleaved the air with a rush of wind and had filled Mary's heart with fear. But now that he was about to put charcoal to paper, Masaccio was suddenly filled with doubt. Would Gabriel really have dared to appear before a simple peasant girl in the guise of an angel? Wouldn't it have been more plausible for him to come to her as a man, a handsome stranger dressed in a luminous white robe? But think, Masaccio, think of the terror she would have felt at his sudden presence in her house. And was it in fact in her house that he'd appeared to Mary? Or was it in the fields among the sheep, or in the gardens, between the rows of lush green leaves swaying in the desert winds? Masaccio's hand moved across the paper in fits and starts, at once spurred on and arrested by contradictory images. Then he heard a sound above him.

"So this is the man the Cardinal has sent to us to teach us how to draw. See how his hand hesitates to set down the first mark. I have seen more resolve in the scribblings of a child." San Salvi gazed down upon him from the height of a low scaffold. He was painting gilded haloes *a secco* while, beside him, his assistant worked at the foliage of trees.

Masaccio looked up and smiled. "Tell me, my friend. Did Gabriel appear to Mary indoors or out?"

"Indoors, without a doubt. She was a good Hebrew girl. She spent her mornings weaving and her afternoons making unleavened bread. One day, she looked up from the work of her hands and there stood Gabriel, the tops of his great wings folded beneath the lintel of her door."

"Hmmm," said Masaccio.

The image seemed right. A private moment, a vision appearing in the intimacy of prayer. And yet, his instincts leaned towards a pastoral setting. He wondered why. Did he want to portray the reversal of the expulsion? Was he projecting on Nazareth the luscious landscapes of Gianlucido's walls? Was Mary in the garden simply another version of Francesca in the vineyards?

"Of course you disagree." San Salvi, dramatically bent in half, stared into Masaccio's face. "The Annunciation as seen through the eyes of a painter from the wilderness. Who would, naturally, miss all the significance of the angel's visitation within the woman's chambers. Don't you see, my charming little rustic, the symbolism of such an apparition? It's an invasion, a form of *penetration*." His rear end still up in the air, he batted his eyelids a few times. "Am I beginning to make myself clear?"

The charcoal forgotten in his hand, Masaccio stared into space. San Salvi's mention of symbolism had set him off on a new track. In this fresco, he would paint the Virgin and the angel (indoors or out), he would paint light and awe and humility, he would paint a world imbued with the sense that *nothing is impossible to God*, he would capture, in paint, a moment of ineffable grace. But what would he add to all these elements to evoke in the mind's eye that higher reality, that greater grace—the mystery of salvation? Would there be, in Mary's garden, three trees on a low horizon? Should there be, hanging from a trellis, or spilling out of a pottery bowl, the grapes of Christ's passion? (The suggestion made Masaccio's forehead pucker into a frown. In the Virgin and Child of the altar-piece in Pisa, his baby Jesus solemnly eats from a bunch of grapes. He did not wish to use the image again.) Would there be a lamb somewhere in the painting, in Mary's arms, perhaps, or caught in a tangle of thorns? Or would he draw upon the symbolism of centuries past and represent the gift of immortality by a rose?

He felt his head begin to throb with the press of ideas and his hand ache with a deep and urgent craving. Like an animal too long held captive, it lunged forward on the parchment, driven by an instinct all its own. Masaccio watched as a kneeling Mary took shape beneath the charcoal, her face upturned to greet the light. Then he drew her standing, her gown falling to the ground in heavy, mortal folds, her hands palm up by her side, already saying yes. He drew her face, the one and the many, the smudges of the charcoal alternately suggesting fear, and wonder, and deep and abiding peace. Luke had not put the word fear in *her* mouth, Masaccio recalled, but in the angel's. Could he read into her heart, this divine white bird? Could he know she'd been waiting for him from the very instant of her conception?

"Oho, I see the reports we've received on your account are full of despicable lies." San Salvi, descended from his scaffold, leaned one shoulder into the wall and gazed down on Masaccio's drawings. The expression on his face was half-hidden by the greasy locks loosely tied at his nape, but the look in his eyes was unmistakable. He was being eaten alive by jealousy, a barely contained desire to deride and discredit. "They told us, dear Masaccio, that you paid no attention to detail. That your hands have no fingers and your faces no eyes."

"It's true, San Salvi. Tommaso does not trifle with the insignificant." Masolino's measured tones undercut San Salvi's tiresome falsetto.

Hearing his voice, Masaccio raised his eager eyes to his. "Tell me, Maso, what does Aquinas tell us about angels?"

He had spoken in a loud voice. His question had reached the ears of all the workers and each of them, like well-trained catechists, called out an answer.

"They are God's servants," one assistant said. "They live in heaven and act as messengers between God and human beings."

"The word *angel* means *messenger* in Greek," someone else called out.

"They are bright, powerful spirits that appear in dreams and visions and protect people."

"There are nine orders of angels," said Giuliano. "The seraphim are the highest ranking, followed by the cherubim, the thrones, the dominations, the virtues, the powers, the principalities, the archangels and finally the angels." He tried to go on, but his erudition had so impressed the men that they filled the chapel with whistles, applause and hoots of laughter. When the noise abated, San Salvi nodded in his direction and said, "I had no idea you were so well versed in these matters, Giulio. Celestial hierarchy, no less! So that is what your brain is stuffed with. Small wonder you can't think and paint at the same time!"

Masolino had pulled up a bag of plaster beside Masaccio and seated himself upon it with a sigh. Masaccio looked into his eyes and understood, now, what had aged the master so. All these months, he had had to struggle to keep this San Salvi, this *prima donna*, under control. The energy he should have put into his painting had been eaten up by this ravenous, egotistical monster.

Lowering his voice, he gently nudged his old friend. "And so, Masolino. What about the angels?"

"Aquinas taught that angels were necessary to fill the gap between God and human beings. He said that countless numbers of angels existed and that they were immortal. He claimed that angels knew everything except matters that depended on human choice and things known only to God."

"Gabriel knew, then, that Mary would recognize him as an angel whether or not he had wings?"

"He knew."

"And *did* he have wings?"

Masolino hesitated a moment. Then, in his inimitable, unerring way, he cut through the dilemma with one quick stroke. "What Mary knew and what the people who will gaze upon your fresco know are two very different things."

Masaccio had his answer. Bending eye and hand to the task, he quickly sketched before the kneeling Mary a figure dressed in ethereal robes, with glorious great wings upon his shoulders.

It did not occur to Masaccio when, at the end of the day, he and Masolino and all the painters repaired to the inn for supper, that it was the very place to which he had intended to take Eloisa. The aroma of roasted meat and peppers floated up to greet them at the door, a table was laid and red wine poured and Masaccio let himself be fooled into believing he was in Florence once more, at the hostelry a few doors down from his studio in the Piazza San Apollinare. The men here were louder, though. One of them, in particular. He was also a nag and tenacious as a terrier. The *arricico* had been prepared for the frescoes Masaccio was to begin painting the next day and San Salvi was determined to discover how "big, ugly Tom" proposed to transfer his drawings to the wall without a *cartone* and *spolveri*. Everyone in Rome used patterns and dusted pounce marks now. Only the most backward of fresco painters worked directly on the wall. When Masaccio patiently explained to him that he would do as he'd always done, that is, snap vertical plumb lines into the plaster to establish the axis of the standing figures, and incise lines to mark the straight edges of the architecture, San Salvi raised his hand to his forehead and cried out in mock dismay, "My Good Lord, the Cardinal has sent us a primitive! Heavens, man, even old Giotto tried to keep up with the times."

Masolino raised a weary hand to silence him. "San Salvi," he said, "you speak foolishness. Giotto, were he here, would weep before the verity of Masaccio's compositions. You will watch him work, *goffo*, and you will learn. Now, pass me the bread and hold your peace."

San Salvi turned glowering eyes on Masaccio and did as he was told. But the wine turned to vinegar in his mouth, and the meat to ashes on his tongue. And in his heart, something rough and brutish began to take root. A dark plant with darkly bruised blossoms.

Thursday 9 May

It took a little time, but I've finally settled into a routine. For the first three days, I woke up early every morning with the intention of sitting down at my desk and writing a page or two before the house stirred. But I would look out the window and see the landscape winking at me through the mists rising off the wet green of the hills and it was more than I could bear. So, turning off the laptop, I'd slip on a jacket against the freshness of the dawn, grab a piece of fruit on my way out, climb onto one of the villa's creaky old bikes and head out on the country roads that cut through the vineyards and the ilex trees. And I would fill my senses with the Tuscan morning—its birdsong and its angelus bells, the chalky smell of its night-damp earth, the tang of its smoky breeze and the fall of its thick blond light. Sometimes there would be workers in the vines, trimming the canes or replanting cuttings, and one or the other would catch a glimpse of me as she straightened her shoulders, and give me a wave and a smile. And though the fields and coppices I cycled by seemed to stretch on to the very foot of the Chianti hills, though they lay silent and still all around me, I could feel the beat of feet on cobblestone, the heat of human fever, like a seething in my bones. And I would stop, set my boots down in the red dirt of the road, lean on my bike and wait for it—the glow of satisfaction that would spread through me at the thought of everything that lay beyond the fields before my eyes. And I knew I would have it all—the mediaeval walled cities, the frescoes and the cathedrals, the paintings and the ruins—all of that and the golden mornings, too.

By the time I made my way back to the villa, the professors would be tucking into their breakfast of *pecorino* cheese and ripe fruit and discussing the bas-reliefs and the cameos they would see on the day's excursion. I went along with them, those first three days, because I knew the best hours for writing were gone, because I knew the book would have to wait till my giddiness wore off.

It was, in fact, nothing less than drunkenness that made my head spin those first few days. The very air I breathed seemed thinner, the light more potent, the sky, an intoxicating shade of blue. So, with the meekness of the secretly inebriated, I stood in line with the others, climbed onto the bus and shared a seat with a woman whose grey pageboy stuck out beneath her Tilley hat, or sat beside an earnest young instructor with a bulging camera bag on his lap, or with an old man in a summer linen suit and panama, a walking stick leaning against his knee. And the pleasant Italian chauffeur drove us on Monday to Siena, past the moonscape summits of its landscape, through its gates, to the polychrome marble of its cathedral. On Tuesday, he took us to San Giovanni Valdarno and a visit to Masaccio's boyhood home. And yesterday, he drove us to Arezzo, the birthplace of Petrarch and Vasari. All around me, those hours on the bus, people talked in a multiplicity of accents, and I would listen distractedly and occasionally pick up a fact or two. I learned, for example, it was the ancient Etruscans who introduced cypress trees to the Tuscan landscape. That, as early as the thirteenth century, the streets of Tuscan cities were paved. And that Tuscan is the purest of the Italian dialects—the language of Boccacio and Dante. I also saw churches, campaniles, piazzas and marketplaces, I saw gold and silver and lapis lazuli, I gazed out over the fields and olive groves and imagined I could see smoke rising in phantom shapes from this old volcanic terrain. And still, I could not shake off the drunkenness.

Then, when we returned to the villa and sat down to *crostini* and *vignarola*, I would stumble into the middle of quite heated scholarly debates and find I could contribute nothing because of this reeling, rocking mind.

But yesterday, when I awoke, I opened clearer eyes. A fog had lifted, a convalescence had ended and, like a weaver at his loom, I took up in my hands the nearly spent threads of Masaccio's story. I saw him putting charcoal to parchment, I overheard his quiet words to Masolino, the sharpness of his exchange with San Salvi, and knew all at once, but inexplicably, that it was over. It was time to turn away, leaving him to the angels and the virgin and the serpent hissing in his ear.

And so I went walking. Blissfully alone in the yellow afternoon. Everyone else had gone on excursion and I had the grounds of the villa, or so I thought, all to myself. I was very surprised, therefore, upon my return, to discover Magda seated at one of the tables of the terrace, sipping Campari. The symposium begins tomorrow—and runs till next Wednesday—so she'd spent the afternoon gathering her thoughts. We talked a long time about this place. The villa, the scholars, the food, the vistas, the images on the chapel walls. She was delighted to hear I'd started to work again, relieved to know I had no regrets. I thanked her once more for including me on this wonderful adventure. She smiled, her mouth a thin line of dismay, before apologizing for the rough manners of some of her colleagues. "I'd forgotten what ego-bashers a few of these guys are," she said. "What insufferable pompous asses."

I told her not to worry. Their derision, I said, had served me well. I'd put their mocking tones into San Salvi's mouth. And then, *sans crier gare*, I found myself telling her why I was finished with Masaccio. "Now that I'm here," I said, "in the shadow of the Pratomagno mountains, now that I've walked through the house he lived in as a boy, and can look out on the slopes that greened over for him every spring, I confess I am appalled at my presumption. Who am I to tamper with this man's life, Magda? What gives me the right to play fast and loose with the facts?"

Magda's alabaster forehead folded up into tiny pleats. She leaned in closer to me and said in a low voice, "What do you mean, you're done with Masaccio? Have you written the last chapter? Is the book finished?"

"No, no. Not even close. But oddly enough, when I was at home, I found it easier to imagine him. Back there, far away from this place, indulging in conjecture seemed a perfectly innocent exercise. I sketched him out, drew an outline of the details we know about his life then filled in the blanks and connected the dots. But here," I spread my hands wide to indicate the land, the sky and the Tuscan sun, "it seems almost sacrilegeous."

Magda didn't say anything at first. Simply turned her gaze to the vineyard and considered—what? I wondered. Its bare wires, its new green, the secret latency of its ancient wood? Then I heard myself say, "*Mais on vit, et les autres rêvent votre vie.*"

Magda quickly turned back to me and said, "That's exactly right, Daniel. You are rounding out his life with a dream."

"But Madga," I said, "I have no idea how his story finishes. And who am I to meddle with the truth?"

She gave me a stern look and said, "You have a number of plots to choose from."

With an impatient toss of her head and counting them off on

her fingers, she began to enumerate the possibilities. "He might very well have been poisoned—the Italians, you know, were notorious poisoners. The Pope might have had him murdered because of the anti-Papal subtext of the Brancacci frescoes. Masolino, or some other minor painter, might have slipped something into his wine out of jealousy. He might have been killed off by an angry creditor. He might even have faked his death to escape his creditors. Or, most probable of all, he simply died of plague or fever contracted during the dangerous Roman summer." I recognized the list of speculations from Douglas Preston's *New Yorker* article, and admitted I'd read and considered them all. Magda continued, "There are no recorded facts about his death, Daniel. All posterity has is a copy of his tax return, written in Masaccio's hand, on which his name has been crossed out. In the margin, written in some other hand, are the words, *Dicesi è morto a Roma*. Said to have died in Rome. So you see, you are free, then, to invent to your heart's delight."

It was my turn to gaze out over the fields.

I must have been lost in thought for some time because when I next looked up at Magda, she had finished her drink, put on her shades and adjusted her hat upon her head. She was also standing by her chair, her notes and books tucked underneath one arm. I couldn't see her eyes anymore and I couldn't read her mood, but there was warmth in her voice as she bent her face to mine.

"Did you know, Daniel, there is no Inuit word for *art*? Making art, they say, is turning something from the real to the unreal." Then she put her lips to my cheek, touched her fingers to my hand and slowly moved away.

I sat a long time at that table on the terrace, thinking about Masaccio and thinking about truth. And managed to arrive at only one conclusion. For now, for the time I will spend here beneath Tuscan skies, I will turn my attention to characters born only of my imagination. Cecilia, Eloisa, San Salvi. And I will leave Masaccio on the threshold of the chapel, with an aching hand and a teeming brain, with a vision only he can see.

Friday 10 May

This morning I rode the bus to Florence with the others. But when they piled out at the Uffizi where the first lectures were being held,

I waited a while, and let them move off without me. I should, of course, have attended Magda's presentation. But I was in Florence at last, and could not resist going—alone—to gaze upon the frescoes of the Brancacci chapel.

I spent the day staring at walls, considering colours, juxtapositions, bones and bare bodies, the drape of clothing, contrast and light. I saw Peter walking on water, taking money from the mouth of a fish, preaching at Jerusalem, baptizing the neophytes, distributing alms, raising a dead woman, healing the maimed with his shadow and resurrecting a prince. I saw porphyry panels, turbaned heads and palm fronds painted against an azure sky. I saw clasped hands, pointing fingers, curly hair and naked toes. And above all, I saw time.

As I walked around the chapel, my gaze moving from one detail to another, my heart beating with some unreasonable hope, I suddenly became aware of a strange unease stirring deep within me. And I remembered all at once that I was in a tomb. I remembered that this *capella*, standing in the right transept of the conventual church of Santa Maria del Carmine, had been built as a burial place for Piero di Piuvichese Brancacci, a wealthy silk merchant and his family. He'd had money to spend, apparently, and a reputation to uphold, so he'd asked the great painters of the day to decorate his final resting place with images from the life of St. Peter, his patron saint. And what had he hoped to accomplish by doing so, this shrewd Florentine businessman? What lesson had he wished to give?

As I considered the tomb and its cryptic meaning, I felt my mind slowly filling with confusion. I found I could no longer concentrate on St. Peter's miracles, or on their significance in the context of the story of Adam and Eve. All I could think about was dust, flesh and paint. The dead, the dying and the immortal. And how they merged, these three things, how they meshed, and became one.

And so there it was again, the laughing face of time. As I stumbled out of the chapel and into the midday sun, the words of the "Doomsday Song" rose up in me to the tempo of some macabre jingle: *Jumbled in one common box Of their dark stupidity Orchid, swan, and Caesar lie; Time that tires of everyone Has corroded all the locks Thrown away the key for fun.*

I found a table in a nearby trattoria and ordered something by pointing at the menu. The woman seated nearby noticed I didn't speak the language and asked if she could help. I thanked her, said it really didn't matter, the Italians were incapable of preparing a bad dish, but she sidled over to my table all the same and set her glass of wine between us. I sighed inwardly at first, then decided the distraction might do me good. There was something big weighing on my mind and I didn't have the courage, just then, to take its full measure.

She was from Manhattan, staying with friends on the Tuscan coast. She'd come to Florence today to shop. Had I seen the leather goods in the kiosk by the Duomo? Or visited the boutiques along the Via Tornabuoni? Then she reeled off a list of designer names I'd never even heard of. But she was attractive—had a freshly scrubbed look to her that made me think of sunshine and beaches, fluttery unpainted lids and striking violet eyes. *Pervenche*, I think the word is. I let her call the waiter and change my order, I listened to her suggestions as to which restaurants to avoid and, at her dictation, took down her address and phone number at the villa on the coast. She wanted to know where I was staying. I had only the vaguest directions to give her but I knew if she made up her mind to find me, she undoubtedly would. She is that kind of woman.

While we waited for the antipasto, I listened, half-amused, to her animated chatter about goldsmith and jewellery shops, about concerts and black-tie parties, about the wine bars—the *enoteci*, she called them—and the tavernas. Not a word, I noticed, about Santa Maria del Fiore, Santa Maria Novella or San Giovanni. But then I heard her inviting me, this very evening, to a party she's throwing at her villa near the seaside resort town of Castiglioncello. Her car was parked around the corner—she could drive me to the coast this afternoon and tomorrow, or on Sunday, one of her guests could surely give me a lift back to Florence. While she talked about the people I would meet there—a British ex-pat or two, wealthy Berliners on vacation, a young French comte and a few Belgian diamond magnates—I tried to imagine what it would be like. The seaside, first of all. The Ligurian coast, south of Livorno. Driving in an open car with the smell of salt water filling my head. The palm trees, the pines, the blue water cresting white with breaking waves. The sailboats dotting the bay. The long empty crescent of beach, the rocks, the kelp, the climbing tide.

All I had to do was say yes. I could leave this table and this foreign square, follow this stranger to her waiting car and let her drive me away to some other life. On the tiled terrace, or in the sunny high rooms of the villa, I could take on, for a while, some new persona, invent broader parameters for the close, cramped hours of my days. And it seemed to me, as I considered the sea from my restaurant chair, it was precisely the kind of escape, the kind of *fugue* my soul was yearning for. On some wind swept stretch of sand, in the frivolous blue air of a Mediterranean beach town, I could maybe forget about time for a while, and its dusty, smothering clutch. I could walk down to the water's edge, roll up the cuffs of my flannel trousers and wade into the sea. It would wrap its chilling fingers around my pale, bony ankles and fix my attention, for once, on that instant and on nothing else. And I could lift my gaze to the horizon and see sky and water touch, see the sun stop in its long, smooth arcing to the sea and burn an indelible spot on the retina of my eye.

Then, in the breezy rooms of the villa—I thought from the safety of my restaurant chair—I could pick up the *lingua franca* of the seaport town, learn to laugh the laughter of its well-heeled crowd, to be glib and amusing, to avoid the questions, to evade the questions, to lie and lie again. I could become lost in my inventions, lost in the fragrance of women's arms, of women's hair, and, while the evening turned to dark, I could drink too much Montepulciano and stumble on my words, and wake in the morning in some strange bed with the taste of strange flesh upon my lips.

By the time Sandy motioned to the waiter for the bill, I'd already decided it would be wiser for me to forsake the beach-brown women of Castiglioncello and throw in my lot, once again, with the grey-boned scholars who, even now, were taking notes at the Uffizi. And then I heard her talking about thermal waters and Saturnia, and inviting me, once again, to come along. Shaking off the daydream, I looked into her Elizabeth Taylor eyes, smiled and asked her about art. "When you come to Florence," I said, "don't you spend some time with Titian, Filippino Lippi or Andrea del Sarto?"

"What do you mean?" the lovely new-world Sandy said. "You

mean all those flaky old paintings on walls? Those crucified apostles with their phony haloes and their pointy beards? Listen to me, pal. Life's too short to spend it looking at crumbling plaster and faded paint."

She reached into her bag for her cigarettes and missed the star-

tled—no, shocked would be a better word—expression on my face. By the time she had lit up and lifted her heavy-lidded gaze to my eyes, I had taken a deep breath, calmed down and realized, all in one stroke, that she had unwittingly revealed to me the source of my unease this morning in the chapel. As I'd walked around Signor Brancacci's burial place, it had come to me in a whisper that the paintings I was contemplating were something less than permanent. They partook of the same substance as old Piero's bones and of my perishable flesh. They did not speak to me of eternity, they did not promise everlasting life.

(And I found myself longing for home, Christie, for the cool black water of a running river, for the smell of spring in a black-spruce stand, for the china-blue face of a prairie sky, and for you.)

Saturday 11 May

Writing went well this morning. Was on familiar terrain with the pleasant, wholesome Cecilia, still young enough to believe in immortality. (Oh, aren't I the worldly one. Until yesterday, Christie, I believed, too. Believed, like Bellow's Henderson, *that chaos doesn't run the whole show. That this is not a sick and hasty ride, helpless, through a dream into oblivion. No sir! It can be arrested by a thing or two. By art, for instance. The speed is checked, the time is redivided.* But now, after listening to that oh-so-recent Sandy, after seeing the tired paint and the restorer's brush on the walls of the Brancacci, I know that art arrests nothing. And anyway, why should it be permanent, when nothing else in the world is?

As you have taught me to see, nothing lasts, nothing is imperishable, save the timeless love in which you dwell, and in which you wait for me. As for the rest, there is nothing but this instant of my life.)

Spent the afternoon sitting in the variegated shade—the *sfumato* chiaroscuro—of the villa's pergola, thinking about woman. About how, in these last few days, I have seen her represented in statuary, in tempera on wood or canvas, in gilt bronze and in fresco. I was trying to put this young Cecilia of mine in clearer focus, trying to see in what role I could cast her, when my thoughts were interrupted, towards the end of the day, by familiar loud voices. A group of professors, having returned from a day trip to San Gimignano, were discussing Berenson, yet again. The poor man's name comes up frequently among these scholars and opinion about him is quite dramatically polarized. Considered a swindler and an art racketeer by some, he is literally worshipped as "il grande professor Berenson" by others. The younger professors had also taken on the the older ones (sigh!) once again, laughing at their formalist talk, dismissing it as dilettantism. I was not in the mood to have the serenity of my sun-dappled arbour shattered by these braying voices and so I quickly challenged them, these men and women of art, to choose among the myriad images they carry always within their minds the most striking representation they have ever seen of *l'éternel féminin*. Because they are, like me, so amazingly easy to distract, I soon found myself in the midst of a very lively discussion on the female figure in art throughout the ages. In the first rush of competition—we are such children and in such terrible need of approval, we doctors and fellows and professors emeriti—the usual names were dropped with unthinking abandon—Mona Lisa, Venus, Salomé—but soon, very interesting ideas began to emerge.

Woman as mother goddess, someone said.

Hathor, someone else answered. An Egyptian mother goddess. Usually appears in the relief sculpture and wall paintings of the neolithic civilizations of the Middle East as a cow-headed woman. Sometimes portrayed feeding milk to an infant king, or wearing a headpiece displaying a disk of the sun, or as a cow whose belly—I love this image—forms the sky.

Woman as sacred mother.

Yes, yes. The Madonna. Enthroned. In glory. The pastoral. The domestic.

Or Kali. Consort of the Hindu god Shiva in her manifestation of the power of time. But she is a destructive mother goddess, frequently depicted as a black, laughing, naked hag with blood-stained teeth, a protruding tongue and a garland of human skulls.

Cecilia, I decided, was too young to be a mother goddess figure, destructive or otherwise. Eloisa, on the other hand....

Woman as heroine, someone else said. Woman as victim, or as temptress.

This is more like it. Cecilia as young seductress, or, at least, as *fille de joie*.

Then, of course, someone else said, there are all those wonderful *putas*. And Willem de Kooning's savage portraits of women, and Goya's mysterious *majas*.

They began to refer to portraiture—Velázquez, Frans Hals and Ingres—of people and paintings I am unfamiliar with, and my attention started to drift. To what woman represents to me. (To what you represented to me. And I caught myself smiling.

The women I had known, the women I'd dreamed of, were all swept away on that beach, that summer, by one small gesture of your hand. I was smitten, seduced, completely won over by the young blonde in a blue bikini who could outswim me and outsail me and match me beer for beer. Who knew the name of every tree that swayed in the boreal forest. Who knew the difference between a buteo and an accipiter, and who could call them on the wing. I knew Orion, but she knew Betelgeuse. I knew Sirius, but she knew its white dwarf star. And when we lay beneath the constellations on long, cool summer grass, her laughter in the darkness, the touch of her fingers on my skin, made me feel I was the most alive thing in the whole world. And she was one woman and all women, lover, friend and little girl, sharp and lingering as the taste of sweat on love-wet skin, deep and mysterious as the pull of moon on secret blood.

~

At night, in the silence of the sleeping house, I listen to the beating of my hopeful heart and wonder if, in the angel, a trace of woman remains.)

~

Cecilia, I have decided, will be a study after Carravagio: wanton as a young nymph, she will be half strumpet, half waif, with red, chapped hands and torn skirts, with light in her smile and a surprising darkness, too, in the depths of her eyes.

Sunday 12 May

Woke up to rain and quietly rejoiced. Put in a good morning, then, at *mezzogiorno*, as I settled into a sheltered corner of the terrace to have my lunch, I was called to the phone. For a second, I felt a squeeze of annoyance at the thought Sandy might have tracked me down. But at the first hello, I recognized Nick's voice and was immediately swept off my feet by a wave of homesickness. *Nostalgia del cupolone*, as the Florentines have it, but my own particular nostalgia was not for the dome, but for my son, my sons, so far away and alone. The conversation was brief. He was calling to ask if Maggy could move in with us for the summer. She was fighting with her mother and the creepy boyfriend again, and she had no money for rent. A small, a very small problem and I breathed a sigh of relief. Of course, I said, as long as it's all right with Alex. And I resisted the urge to ask where she would sleep.

When I returned to the terrace, I saw George from Chicago settled into the chair across from mine. The sun had come out and he was sitting among the dripping vines with his arms crossed and his eyes closed, warming his back and purring like a big old tomcat. I like George. He's short and round and toothy, has bright pink cheeks and a most engaging smile. He speaks quietly. Listens eloquently. Makes you believe you are the most brilliant conversationalist he's ever met, and life, your life, the most surprisingly delightful he's ever had the pleasure to know. He is gracious and tactful, but at the same time so warmly, so wonderfully familiar. It seems to me quite likely that George is the sweetest man I've ever met. I quickly invited him to share the pizza bianca—topped with smooth and fragrant Tuscan olive oil—and a carafe of red wine.

We've already covered many topics, George and I, in the short time we've been acquainted. Professionally, he specializes in imperfection. In the art of the quattrocento, he is on intimate terms with truncated arms and elongated necks, the unnaturally steep fall of shoulders and the awkward hingeing of limbs. He has inventoried all the liberties Renaissance masters have taken with nature and to what effect. And he has explained to me how deliberately incorrect anatomy can add to the beauty and harmony of a design.

"Consider the *Birth of Venus*," he said during an early conversation. "Botticelli has given us a slightly deformed but ineffably graceful goddess. And it is precisely her imperfections that enhance the impression of an infinitely tender and delicate being, wafted to our shores as a gift from Heaven."

"She is flawed," I said, "like all of us, and all of art." And he smiled as I went on. "Doesn't every work of art," I asked, "have at its heart a secret fault, a poignant imperfection?"

"Beauty," he said, "with the mark of Adam upon its face."

I understood, after this first conversation, that the man is a poet.

Another time, we talked about age. We are at approximately the same place in our lives, he and I, caught between regret and hope, and full of a vague, fond sadness. But that day, we chose to laugh about it. We shared stories about having reached the stage at which memory—in us and in our friends—can no longer be depended upon. It has become a tricky thing, fickle, fleeting and unelastic, and whatever it manages to retain, we have noticed, is largely a matter of chance. And so we find ourselves telling friends the same news over and over again, their surprise each time as genuine as our delight in telling it, or buying books we believe we've never read before only to find two other editions in our library at home, or launching in on an amusing anecdote in the middle of a lecture and suddenly being filled with twitchy misgiving—was it to this class or another I've already told this story? Or we feel sudden grief well up in us at the thought of so much about the past that's been mislaid. Through the changing prism of time, in the tenuous hold of our memories, details blur and faces fade and the truth is forever lost.

We'd smiled at each other a bit ruefully, George and I, because we know only too well our forgetfulness is no longer the consequence of professional distraction, but of simple senile dysfunction.

I understood, after this second conversation, that the man is a wayfarer, like me, surprised to find himself in a dark wood in what he thought was the middle of the afternoon.

Today, we talked about sex. I told him about the phone call

from Nick and confessed it was preying on my mind. He understood why. We fell silent for a moment, both of us considering the sometimes unhappy consequences of young, impetuous love. But then, I felt George's gaze upon my face—warm, amused and tender—and I knew what he was thinking. "Ah," he said. "The first time. Tell me, Daniel, do you remember the very first time?" And he began to tell me the story of Miss Elisabeth Lennox, his piano teacher, and very first lover. She was thirty-six, he was seventeen. He had been stopping at her house once a week on his way home from school since the second grade. She had a very fine studio on Chicago's Near North Side, with oak wainscoting, wall sconces, stained glass piano windows and a fireplace. And up in her room, a four-poster bed with a white eyelet spread.

"She'd been old Miss Lennox to me for so long, I really didn't notice the change until it was too late. When I turned fifteen or sixteen, maybe, I found that images of her were beginning to linger in my mind's eye, long after I'd left her. The freckles on the skin of her arm, for example, the very white half-moon of her cuticles, the tendrils of hair at the nape of her neck. When she stood behind me with her hands on my shoulders to tap out the measure, I caught myself concentrating on her scent instead of on the music, thinking about the space between her belly and my back, and imagining that, if I turned towards her, from my position on the bench, my face would nestle in her breasts. As she sat at her desk writing out my lesson, I would stare at her narrow ankle in the sheath of her nylon stocking, and try to imagine her bare legs, her bare feet, the inexpressibly tender cleavages of her small toes.

"Then, when I left the studio, I would wait till I'd rounded the corner of her street before reaching into my bag for the books she'd taken into her hands and flattened with her open palm, and I would press them to my face. And I would breathe it in, the vestige of Houbignant or Chanel lingering there among the inky smells of sheet music. And at night, in the secret of my room, she would come to me, Elizabeth, Liz, Beth, Betty, and, edging into my dreams with her fingertips and the point of her tongue and the loose, deliberate weight of her hair, she would soon take up all the place, her white body spread before me like a *mappemonde*, and I, a new Vespucci.

"I did not learn much music in those later years. My practice sessions were fraught with distraction, and the arcane language of notes and rests on a staff seemed to call me to a richer, deeper mystery. Then one day, when I had come ill-prepared yet again for a lesson, I became aware, suddenly, of an icy silence beside me. The tension in the room, the heavy pressure of unspoken reproach, had all at once metamorphosed into a cold, dark void. Furious with me, Elizabeth had withdrawn to some place I could no longer reach. I was stumbling through the ten miserable pages of Chopin's 'Impromptu' when, without turning my eyes to Elizabeth's face, I knew all at once she wanted me to stop. So I did. I lifted my hands from the keyboard and folded them in my lap. And waited. She rose from her chair, closed the pages of the music book and grabbed me hard by the chin. Lifting my face to hers, she said in a voice I'd never heard before that I should be ashamed of myself for wasting her time. That she deserved better, and, my God, what about Chopin? She held me tight between thumb and forefinger, her face pushed up against mine, and looked straight into me with the blackest eyes I'd ever seen. Very soon, my own eyes began to fill up with tears, big, salty and steaming, and pouring like a river down my cheeks. And then, before I could close my eyes, she was kissing me, her lips wet with my tears, her salty mouth searching for mine. And I felt my heart splash in my chest as she pulled me to my feet and led me upstairs to her four-poster bed with the white eyelet spread."

George didn't look at me as he finished his story. His gaze fixed on the distant blue hills, he was lost in memory, I knew, awash with longing and desire. For youth, for innocence, for the heady drink of first love. When he finally remembered me again, he added, "I still play, you know. And the first bars of the 'Fantaisie-Impromptu' never fail to take me back to that room under the eaves, to the memory of my hands on her body, glowing like a star in the dull winter light of a February afternoon."

So I said, "You'll have to play it for me sometime." We smiled at each other then, and lifted a glass. We drank to Elizabeth, to the deep, secret joys of sex, to the cunning of body and the ripe fruit of flesh.

~

Late this evening, after spending the afternoon tramping up and down the hilly roads of the countryside, I went prowling through the villa, looking for Magda. The image of a face had accompanied me on my long walk through new sunflower fields and, at first, I hadn't recognized it. It came to me in fragments—the texture of a lip, the fine grain of a cheek, a tangle of blonde lashes, a smile, a frown, a sudden arch look in the eye. It came to me, too, in subtle wafts of scent and, finally, in the memory of a mouth moving towards my face. I knew then it was Magda who had followed me through the landscape, having slipped into me, without my knowing, like warm, sweet wine slips into the blood.

When I found her in the main floor common room, she was sitting before a fire, a glass of sambuca in her hand, deep in conversation with Për.

PART TWO

_Checkout Receipt

_ Charleswood Library
_ 24 Aug 2017 03:20

****

_ A possible life /
_CALL #: FICTION CHAPUT
_ 33097060899033 Due Date 14 Sep 2017

_TOTAL: 1
****

Manage Your Account Online or By Phone
Renewals * Notices * Online Payments
Call TeleMessaging at 204-986-4657 or
1-866-826-4454 (Canada/US toll free)
Go online winnipeg.ca/library
****

Overdue Fines:
dult Items 40 cents/day per item
hildren's Items 20 cents/day per item
xpress, Bk Club kits $2.05/day per item

CECILIA

XI

NIGHTFALL SEEMED LESS TERRIBLE NOW THAT SHE'D FOUND A travelling companion. Cecilia would have been hard pressed to explain how this boy, who spoke a northern dialect and was young and small and blind, could have saved her from any of the dangers of the dark, but somehow, in his presence, she felt reassured. He'd been separated from his fellow pilgrims in the *Mercato Vecchio* in Florence, and had since been forced to rely on the goodness of strangers to help him find his way to Siena. It had taken the better part of a week for him and his friends to travel the two hundred and twenty miles from Padua to Florence, and three more days for him to reach Siena alone. But now that God had placed Cecilia on his route, he knew he would make good time to Rome.

It was his voice raised in song that had first alerted her to his presence on the road ahead. The earth was still wrapped in shadows, dawn was a pink smear in the eastern sky and Siena crouched like a cat at her heels, watching its prey fly away. When she'd discovered the kind painter from Florence had not waited for her before leaving for Rome that morning, she'd hesitated only a minute before deciding to take to the road by herself, in hopes of catching up with him somewhere between Siena and the Holy See. As she'd hurried through the quiet streets to the city gates, her movements hampered by the layers of skirts and stockings and bloomers she wore beneath her cloak, she'd turned again and again, casting worried glances behind her, convinced she was being followed. Her heart pounded like footfalls in her ears and the wind whistling through her hair was full of the sound of her name. She could not believe her freedom would be so easily had. In exchange for a life of toilsome drudgery, this open road, this heady exhilaration, the promise of adventure and romance in faraway Rome. When Ettore's voice had reached her, Latin words lifting to the sky in plainsong, she had turned no more towards Siena, but had gathered her many skirts in her hands and had rushed towards him as the rising sun lit up his face. When she'd come up beside him, he'd not left off chanting, nor turned his unseeing eyes upon her, but had smiled around the words of the "Pange lingua gloriosi."

Cecilia had seen at once that he was a much-travelled pilgrim. On his long grey gown, beside the red cross stitched to his scapular, he wore many palms, scallop shells and vernicles. The wealthier pilgrims from the north who had travelled through Siena on their way to Rome had often stayed at her father's inn. Over the years, Cecilia had learned the significance of the emblems sewn on their caps and tunics. This boy, this Ettore from Padua, as yet too young to boast a true pilgrim's beard, proclaimed by the many badges on his tunic that, despite his downy chin and cheeks, a true pilgrim's heart beat in his breast. Cecilia noted with relief that at least his feet were not bare, and his lips and nose were still intact. She had often been repulsed by the sight of mutilated faces and bloodied feet at the inn door and had wondered how pleasing it was to the Creator to see his works defiled.

As the last notes of the Gregorian chant drifted off over vines and olive groves touched now by the morning sun, Ettore turned wide, sightless eyes upon her and asked her her name. He explained in his strange, broken Tuscan that he was from Padua, that he was a rich man's son, going on pilgrimage to obtain from the saints the favour of sight. "They are being stubborn, these men and women of God. They find it amusing to watch me stumble blindly from shrine to cemetery to altar to church, and are not yet willing to give up their entertainment. But I take pleasure in travel, and believe as many of my fellow holy nomads do that 'the further ye go, the more ye shall see and know.' Since I trust they will grant me the blessing in the end, these obstinate saints in heaven, I am quite willing to *indulge* them all yet once again."

The pun was not lost on Cecilia. She laughed a little, in spite of the squeezing at her heart. Though the *marcheurs de Dieu* were numerous, and the indulgences promised to them as numberless as the stars in heaven, she knew miracles were a rare occurrence among the sick, the halt and the blind who visited the shrines. They took curative waters, they circumambulated holy objects in ritual procession, they mounted sacred staircases on hands and knees, they venerated relics—articles as false as phials of the Virgin's milk, parts of her girdle and veil, a lock of her hair, slivers of the one, true Cross, even portions of the manna fed to the Israelites—then returned to their homes uncured but resigned, perhaps, to their fate. On these pilgrimages, they walked with the faithful, prayed with the devout, ate, slept, gambled and sang with the lame and the hale, and learned through it all one true and everlasting thing: that they were not alone. Christ came not to abolish suffering, but to fill it with his presence. Therein lay the miracle.

The young man said, "You have run away from your father's house and you are afraid he will catch you before day is done and drag you back to the fires of his kitchen."

Cecilia looked with surprise on the boy's calm face. "How is it ... how did you know?"

"I hear the thicknesses of your gowns as they sway against your legs on this uneven road. I hear your heaving breath as you strain beneath the weight of too many clothes. I hear in your scrip the uneasy clinking of the *fiorini* you stole from your father's table. I smell fear on your skin, the sour sweat of a small, threatened thing. The thick cloying smell of roasted meat clings to your hair, and the smoke and the ash of the kitchen hearth ground into the hem of your skirt mingle now with the dust of the road. Why to Rome, my pretty?"

"How do you know I am pretty?"

Ettore paused, and, taking Cecilia by the arm, he forced her to stop beside him. Lifting his hand to her face, he traced her features with his fingertips, his empty, dark eyes uncannily fixed on hers. When he was done, he resumed walking, his vacant gaze now lifted to the startling blue of the sky.

"Unlike me, you, my sweet Cecilia, can see. The mirror has confirmed what you learned, long ago, in other people's eyes. The gift of beauty, of divinely superfluous beauty, sets up a longing in the soul. One you seek now to satisfy."

At his words, Cecilia felt her heart burn within her. Who was this young man that he could know a stranger's deepest, most secret desires? How had he guessed that her restlessness was born of the conviction that her *bellezza*, her *pulchritudine*, had set her apart from the rest, had conferred upon her privilege and distinction? Since he already knew so much, she decided to tell him of the famous Florentine painter who had asked her to travel to Rome to sit for him as a model of the Virgin in the great frescoes of the Cathedral of San Clemente. She spoke these words with feigned humility, head bowed to the ground, and waited for Ettore's response. When he did not answer right away, she thought perhaps he did not fully grasp the momentousness of the request and so quickly added, in an enthusiastic attempt to enlighten him, "Don't you understand what this means? Me, my face, will be immortalized upon the walls of one of the great churches of Rome. A gifted painter looked upon me in the rooms of my father's inn and saw in the lowly servant girl who laboured there the likeness of the Holy Maiden of Nazareth. I have been chosen, Ettore, my beauty has marked me out. Like Mary, I have been called upon to serve."

Ettore did not smile. His mouth disappeared in a thin, disapproving line and his eyes, the burnt-out candle ends of his eyes, glowed then glistened with tears. "He has deceived you. You go to Rome not to serve God, or faith or beauty or even yourself. But only this man. He has called you to his side and you will serve him on your back, Cecilia. He has summoned you to Rome to be his *puta*."

He seemed to expect her to be scandalized. She humoured him by stammering a few horrified exclamations. But there was, in truth, nothing shocking in this revelation. Cecilia had not been so naïve as to imagine that aesthetic considerations alone had motivated the painter's request. It would be a normal part of the bargain, she supposed, for her to be called upon to satisfy his other, more carnal, appetites when painting was done. But there would be pleasure, she believed, in being taken by a man who, all the day, had gazed upon her and admired her, who with eyes that saw had seen her. Better that than being pawed in the dark by blind and brutish lust that corrupted even graceful flesh with the coarseness of its touch. But she did not share these thoughts with Ettore. Instead, she cried out, "Surely not," and "You must be mistaken," and convinced him of her innocence. Giving her arm a reassuring pat, he promised to leave her in the care of a convent of Franciscan nuns he knew in the Holy City. "With them, my love, your virtue will be safe."

Cecilia murmured her thanks and silently vowed to lose this godly boy before the gates of Rome.

✣

It was a long and difficult road and, with each mile that she walked, Cecilia's memories of the comforts of her father's house grew fonder and more misty-eyed. It was hot in those late August days and, by nightfall, the tender, swollen flesh of her feet would be bursting out of the seams of her wretched shoes. The late summer flies buried themselves in her hair and took away chunks of her scalp, the wasps stung her lips as she bit into fruit, the beds in the inns were hard and bug-ridden, and the cheese she was served was often rancid and green.

The other travellers she and Ettore met along the road sometimes eased the strain of the endless walk—their anecdotes were amusing, or the songs they sang were clever and lewd—but more often than not, these pilgrims simply added to the miseries of the road.

Between Viterbo and Rome, each of the men had tried—at least twice—to get into Cecilia's skirts while the women travellers, for their part, had concentrated their considerable skills on relieving her of her purse. As long as she stayed near Ettore, she was safe. The moment she strayed from his side, she felt their avid fingers reaching out like sticky webs to catch her. For some obscure, superstitious reason, the pilgrims seemed to fear Ettore. Cecilia had felt it the moment they'd been reunited in Viterbo. When she and the blind boy had come upon a group of them in the courtyard of the town's inn, she'd seen them sprawled in the grass in drunken squalor, and had heard them, two by two, grunting in the bushes. As soon as he'd appeared, the wine-sacks had been quickly put away and the women had come staggering out of the woods, straightening their skirts and pulling twigs and leaves from their hair. Cecilia at first supposed it had something to do with his infirmity. Ettore was a blind boy, a child of God, and harming him would call down damnation on the head of the guilty. Or perhaps they feared him, his blindness calling to mind the wages of sin. But she soon discovered that the power he held over them was of a different order entirely. Having observed the largesse with which he distributed his father's *soldi*, paying for all the pilgrims' food and wine with unstinting hand, she'd understood that these supposed men and women of God were driven only by cupidity. At the same time, she was filled with wonder at the grace that had protected the boy from the unscrupulous hands of confidence men and murderers through so many long voyages. What else, besides God's loving grace, could have kept his young life safe?

During the evening, he asked Cecilia to stay at his side. They ate together and talked, and, over red wine mixed with a little water, he told her the marvellous tales of his many travels. He showed her the guidebooks he carried in his scrip describing the pilgrim circuits of Rome. In the more ancient one, *De locis sanctis martyrum quaė sunt focis civitatis Rome*, Ettore explained, the pilgrim was led out of fourteen gates in the Aurelian wall to visit all the cemeteries between the Porta Cornelia and the Porta Flaminia. In a more recent book, Adam of Usk set out an easier itinerary for the pilgrims to Rome. In order to lighten the heavy toil of visiting them all, he confined the circuits of full indulgence to seven churches, and, within the church of St. Peter, to seven of the altars. Ettore confessed he had touched every sacred place in the city of Rome. He'd had these books read to him so many times, he knew them now by heart. Just as he had memorized in his skin and in his bones the smell and feel of every shrine from Canterbury to Jerusalem. He told her how the pilgrim's heart filled with dread as he approached the gates of each new city: would plague or some other fearful epidemic be raging within the town walls, waiting in ambush on unsuspecting flesh? Would the food in these far-off lands be wholesome and fresh, or would both fish and fowl make the foreigner ill? He told her of hunting lice and vermin on board the pilgrim ships, of sharing large beds with strange and dirty men in the hostels established by confraternities and brotherhoods to ease the pilgrims' way. And then, pulling from his scrip a curious array of vials and inlaid boxes and pouches made of skin, he set before her eyes his treasury of relics. These, he assured her, were true. No, Cecilia, not all of it was lies. He knew without a doubt, for instance, that the piece of cloth lying at the bottom of the tooled leather case he took in his hands and offered like a chalice was cut from the Virgin's camisole. The one she wore when she gave birth to the Christ child, the one true relic around which the great cathedral at Chartres was built. And he knew, as well, that what they said about the depiction of Christ in the chapel of San Lorenzo in Rome was unmistakably true. The face of Jesus on the chapel wall had been painted there by a non-human hand. Ettore said that standing before it, his blind face lifted to its saintly radiance, he'd felt there the presence of the spirit. He'd heard Christ breathe, had felt on his cheeks the heat of His living flesh, the warmth of His living gaze. This one, thought Cecilia, requires a leap of faith I, with my heavy feet of clay, can never hope to make. But she murmured words of wonderment, soothing, pleasant sounds to erase the anxious furrow in Ettore's crumpled brow. He began to feel among the objects placed before him, intent upon finding one particular thing. And while he ran his fingers along the edges of the boxes and held sacks and bottles in the palm of his hand, he declared to her in a proud, almost arrogant way, it was not a simple matter to gull the blind.

"The seeing are a bizarre lot. When asked to believe, they demand to see. And having seen, it does not occur to them that sight does not begin and end with the body's eyes. It is only the blind eyes of the heart that can really know. So when the keepers of the relics tell them the stone placed before them on the altar of the Oratory on the road to Ostia was used in the martyrdom of St. Stephen, they see a stone there and believe. When they are told the rock in the porch of St. Lawrence's church was the one supposed to have drowned St. Abundus, they see a rock there and believe. They see chains in Rome and believe they were St. Peter's; they see a gridiron and believe it was St. Lawrence's. If they were to close their gullible eyes for the merest of seconds and open their hearts to the invisible, they would know at once that which is true from that which is not."

He found at last among his treasures the corked phial he'd been looking for and pressed it into Cecilia's hands. "I give to you now neither relic nor momento of life long fulfilled. What you hold in your hands, Cecilia, is the promise of death. When you are held in thrall by some evil power and your life and your virtue are threatened, a drop of this poison in a goblet of wine will deliver you from the enemy's hands. It is the deadly venom of the Egyptian asp, a gift to me from a pilgrim of the East. We met among the sellers of jewels at the doors of Santa Croce in Gerusalemme, and, like the gold and silver on those merchants' stands, this poison is worthless to me. Man and his works hold no terror for me. God is my stronghold and my shield."

Cecilia lifted the dark bottle to her eyes, then smelled the cork and grimaced. She was touched by the boy's thoughtfulness (though a little surprised at his glibness about dispensing death). Tucking it into one of the pockets of her skirt, she reasoned it might come in handy as currency. A phial of snake's venom in exchange for bread and wine, for instance, or to pay for a room at the inn.

XII

BEFORE THE *TE DEUM* OF THANKSGIVING HAD LIFTED FROM THE pilgrims' lips at the first sight of Rome, Cecilia had slipped away by herself. Hidden among the maize in a peasant's cart, she was taken straight into the heart of the city. Asking directions of everyone she met, she made her way to San Clemente and, drawn there by some unerring instinct, found the unfinished frescoes of the chapel of St. Catherine. A few workmen were moving scaffolding along one wall; others stood before completed frescoes, a paint brush in one hand. Standing in the doorway, she looked from one man to the other, trying desperately to call to mind the features of the Florentine painter she had glimpsed in the bath. It occurred to her he might not even be there. It was late in the day and most of the workmen, she presumed, had gone home for the evening meal. The thought made her stomach leap with hunger. She imagined the men sitting down at tables laden with sausage and bread and she hoped she could count on the unknown painter to provide her with food and lodging that very night.

Day was dimming. There was no time to lose. With clammy

skin and stone-cold blood, she walked resolutely up to the workman closest to her. He stood on a low scaffold, adding touches to a painting of Jesus and St. Christopher.

"Excuse me, *Signore*. I am looking for a friend."

The man heard the small noise she made but did not hear her words. He took a few steps to the edge of the platform and gazed down upon her, one eyebrow lifted quizzically. She raised her head and spoke up. "He's a painter from Florence, only recently arrived."

Cecilia cringed at the echoing sound her voice made in the hollow vault of the chapel. She had spoken far too loudly. From the corner of her eye, she could see a sudden stilling of hands and a slow turning of heads.

"You must mean Masaccio, *Signorina*. I am afraid you are too late. He and the maestro have left for the day. If you return tomorrow...."

Masaccio, Cecilia said to herself. No, it cannot be. I have not come all this way to throw myself upon the mercy of a man called Masaccio, an ugly, slovenly lout. But if not.... A slow despair began to surge through her. It had a whiny, miserable voice, thick and sticky with tears. I must see him. Perhaps I will know him when I see him. And her frightened thoughts becoming panicky words, she suddenly cried out, "But I must see him tonight."

The man shrugged his shoulders and called out to the others. "Does anyone know where Masaccio sleeps?"

Cecilia spun quickly around to look up at the other men. As she did so, her hood fell from her hair and exposed her lovely face. One painter, standing at a rough table spread with parchment, had not taken his eyes from her since he'd heard her speak. His gaze fixed upon the fine features of her face, he now moved towards her, letting his eyes slip the length of her body, his tongue a hungry, animated thing at the corner of his lips. Cecilia watched him come near, she saw his sallow skin and pockmarked cheeks, saw the ugly rat-tail of hair hanging across his shoulders. Ettore, she said to herself, even the weak eyes of the body can see this man is evil. The stench of it rises off him with the smell of his sweat. But she stood her ground. Perhaps he could lead her to the kind Florentine painter.

"Go back to your work, Alonzo. Leave the *signorina* to me."

Alonzo snorted with laughter. Before turning to the wall once again, he looked down at Cecilia and said, "*Signorina*, this is San Salvi. Unacclaimed genius and unsung marvel of the great city of Rome. But one day soon, the whole world and you, my lady, will quiver at the very mention of his name."

"Your tongue, Alonzo. It needs trimming with a knife."

"Not by you, you ambitious whoreson."

With these words, Alonzo took up his paint brush with a laugh and bent to his work once again.

✣

He was disappointed to learn she was not Masaccio's wife. Not his lover, not even his friend. Just some young fool who'd taken it into her head that her face would look nice on a chapel wall. He had looked forward to the challenge of seducing her, of stealing her affection from the great Masaccio, then sending her home to him, humiliated and defiled. On the way home from the cathedral, he had imagined how he would win her over. Without overtly disparaging Masaccio's work, he would show her his own drawings and speak of the frescoes he had painted in the churches of Rome and Naples. He would, in a very modest way, allude to his fine reputation, and confess he was much solicited by the nobility and the papal court. He would install her in his rooms and bid her wait while he fetched her friend. He would then return, his arms full of food and drink, to tell her Masaccio was momentarily detained, that he would come to them as soon as he possibly could. Then, when she was sleepy and sated and vulnerable, he would speak of her beauty and praise her sweet grace. He would beg her to let him draw her, he would work hard and cunningly to overcome her reluctance, and when at last she'd agree, he would pose her reclining on a low bed, and slowly, so slowly, he would remove all her clothes. And when he took her, as take her he surely would, he'd exult in the knowledge that the great master Masaccio sported newly sprouted horns.

Cecilia had fallen into a pleasant, inebriated stupor. She did not once ask for Masaccio, seemed content to prattle on about her father's frightful temper, about adultery among pilgrims in the leafy bowers by holy wells, about roasting ducks and skinning hares. She confided to San Salvi her dream of becoming a painter's model, swore she would do anything to be immortalized in fresco and finally admitted she could not, for the life of her, remember Masaccio's name. It's something ugly, she said. Not a pretty name at all. And as the evening wore on and the wine rose like fever through her veins, San Salvi's face began to change in the room's dim light. Its cadaverous angles took on a sculptural quality, giving him a high, intelligent forehead, prominent cheekbones and an imposing Roman nose. A piece of marble sprung, perhaps, from Donatello's hand. His thick lips, hung upon his skeleton like fruit from a bough, seemed to her intoxicated eyes the very picture of sensuality. Here was a man, she thought, who bit deeply into life and sucked with smacking mouth at the marrow of the bone. He moved well across the room. His back was straight and his buttocks firm, and his hands, cleverly tucked into his wide sleeves, were like small surprising animals, imbued with a life of their own. In short, he no longer seemed repulsive to her. Not evil at all. So when she saw San Salvi take out parchment and charcoal, she let out a cry of delight. Hurrying to arrange candles on tables around the bed, she lifted her arms and unpinned her hair, then proceeded to undress. San Salvi watched in amazement as she removed each layer of clothes. When at last she lay naked before him, the skirts and bodices she had let fall to the floor at her feet billowed like a ship's sails around them. And at the heart of all those woollens and linen cloths was a tight, young, white body.

"No, I must not," San Salvi had planned to say when she would invite him to leave his drawing and come lie with her. "Such pleasures weaken the painter's hand, leaving it as trembling and uncertain as leaves in the wind." But when he saw her lying there, saw the seductive roundness of her belly, the downy curve between her hips that begged and begged to be stroked, he felt through all his flesh the aching pull of desire. He wanted to go to her at once, lay his emaciated body against her ravishing white flesh and harrow it in long, punishing strokes that, at last, would make them both cry out in wonder. He felt his throat clot up with heat, grew dizzy with the rushing rhythm of his heart, felt his knees weaken and his hands begin to shake. As though to mock him, his body began to tremble in the horrible dance of the old. With dismay, he watched as the charcoal jumped like a live thing between his fingers. Placing one edge of it against the parchment, he willed it to steady. Tracing first the clean line of Cecilia's leg, he managed to carve her hip out of darkness before tucking into the cleavage at her waist. But soon his fingers betrayed him. Lust, rising in him like thickening blood, splayed his hand like a paw. He tried to draw her breasts, but turned the sweet swellings into the long, bloated goatskins on an old hag's chest. He gave her a sinewy throat and a wide, plump face, he botched the eyes and smeared the mouth and made a seaweed tangle of her hair. Angry now, and in a frenzy of arousal, he threw the drawing to the floor. Striding across the room to Cecilia's side, he fell on her at once and, hoisting his tunic above his hips, he ground himself into her in a blind fit of lust. She rocked beneath him, her breath beat out of her in gasping cries but, even in his rage, he felt her distant, distracted, away. After a brief, puny shudder, he lay heavily upon her, his fury unspent. When at last he raised himself above her to look into her face, he saw she lay with her head lifted and turned away from him, her eyes fixed on the fallen parchment. With one extended arm, she was trying to snag the corner of the drawing lying just beyond the reach of her wiggling fingers.

San Salvi groaned. Then, rolling off her body, he lay on his back and covered his face with his hands. He felt her scamper away from his side, heard the parchment rustle in her hands, heard her wade with bare feet through the heaps of clothing on the floor. He knew she was taking the drawing closer to the light. A hush fell suddenly upon the room. The paper was quiet in Cecilia's hands, her quick, young breath had died in her throat. Then, as San Salvi waited with clenched teeth, a wail rose up from some ungodly place and broke like shattering glass into a thousand sobbing pieces. Cecilia stood in candlelight, blue shadows dancing all over her white body, her eyes fixed upon the image of herself. With her face screwed up in disgust, she studied her fouled reflection, then tilted her head back, opened her mouth and howled.

Beside himself with anger, San Salvi sprang from the bed and tore the drawing from her hands. In three quick, furious movements, he ripped the parchment to shreds and threw them in her face. Then, raising one bony hand, he began to hit her. And with each swing of his arm, he screamed out vile names, his mouth foaming with the words of his raging. Shielding her face from him, Cecilia bent to retrieve some of her clothing and, cowering beneath his blows, she stumbled blindly to the door. He kept at her, wielding one hand like a whip, the other raking at the gown she held to her breast. One of his fingers caught at a fold and tore the garment with a ripping sound. It burst like a gutted sack, spreading coins and beads and pins and combs all about the floor. San Salvi paused, glanced down at the scattered trinkets, caught sight of the phial—Ettore's dark gift—gleaming in the shadows. Reaching out to grab hold of Cecilia's arm, he scooped up the bottle in one hand and, drawing her twisted face to his, spoke to her between gritted teeth. "Here, you slut, before I throw you in the gutter. Tell me what evil potion it is you keep in this bottle."

Wrenching her arm free from his grasp, Cecilia stepped away from him and backed through the door. Then, shaking her wild witch's hair at him, she croaked out from a heaving breast, "I would kill you, San Salvi. With my bare hands, I would rip your head from its scrawny neck. Poison is too sweet a death for such a dog as you."

The torn gown pressed to her body, she turned from his door and fled through the dark streets. Clenching the bottle tightly in his hand, San Salvi stood and watched her run. Then he slipped the phial into his pocket, went into the house, gathered up Cecilia's scattered clothes and threw them into the street.

✣

She took refuge in a garden, concealing her nakedness in a grove of cypress trees. Other than a slash in the cloth where the pocket had been torn away, the gown was still intact. Trembling in the coolness of the late evening, Cecilia hurried to slip the dress over her head. Feeling the rough wool against her bruised skin, she was grateful, nevertheless, for its winter weight. It would hold her in good stead.

But she already knew she would miss her shoes. The grasses at her feet were heavy with a chilling wet, and in this city of fragment and shard, sharp edges waited everywhere upon the unsuspecting sole. Swept away, suddenly, by a wave of despair, she let herself crumple to the ground amid the heavy dew. The contusions on her face and body began to ache, and at the thought that her beauty had been marred, perhaps forever, she was overcome by a fit of weeping. Pulling first at her hair, then at the grasses around her, she began to gather them up in clumps and press them to her face. They were cool against her skin, and sweet-smelling, and she wished she could swathe her body in them, wrap herself in their soothing, healing scent. She wished she could lie beneath them until her flesh mingled with the earth and her bones lay, unstartling things, like stones upon the ground. She longed to feel the grass pushing through her skin, growing out of her mouth and the sockets of her eyes, taking root in the garden that she had become.

Tuesday 14 May
Rode the bus into Florence with the others again this morning, but parted company with them at the doors of the Accademia. There are only two more days of lectures but I can already feel restlessness setting in. The symposium lured them here but now that they've tasted the smooth sensuality of Tuscany, they huddle in the dark halls and watch the Power Point presentations and feel an ache rise up in them at the thought they could be walking along the *sampietrini* of narrow mediaeval streets, or sipping Valdinievole in a taverna on the Piazza della Signoria. I'd promised myself I'd attend at least one of the lectures—one of Magda's preferably—but found I could not bring myself to give up even one of my free hours to speculative theory. (I'm sure my absence was not a cause for much concern.)

Remembering Sandy's recommendation, I went in search of the leather boutique close by the Duomo. I had the vague idea bags might make nice gifts for the boys, buttery soft skin brief- or attaché-cases, packsacks or shoulder bags, a souvenir they could use for a lifetime. I had no trouble finding the place but it wasn't open at that hour of the day, so I spent some time walking around the cathedral, admiring Brunelleschi's dome. I tried to imagine the mood in Florence the morning of August 7, 1420, when building materials started to pile up in the piazza. Recalling the pages I'd read in Vincent Cronin the day before, I knew that "one hundred and twenty *braccia* of stone, cut brick-shape, two hundred planks of olive-wood, one hundred fir trunks for making platforms and eight planks of pine-wood" had been carted into the middle of the square. "The Works department had taken a lease of Trassinaia quarry on the hill of Vincigliata, ordering ten gallons of lime and sixty blocks of *macigno*—hard golden brown stone to be supplied daily, except when it rained. As the blocks began to arrive, two hundred and twenty-three chisels were sharpened to work them." Townspeople must have stood around and watched, shaking their heads in dismay as workmen hammered scaffolding together and built the four hundred steps to the cathedral's uppermost walls. They knew that, some seventy years earlier, the dome of Hagia Sophia in Constantinople—bearing a cupola roughly the same dimension of the one Brunelleschi now proposed to build—had partly collapsed. I imagined them staring up at the sky, these skeptical men and women, squinting against the late summer sun, convinced that "Brunelleschi was going to build a city up there, and that Maestro Arnolfo's church would be crushed beneath it."

Cronin tells us there were eight master builders involved in the project who were paid by the day at the usual rate of one lira twenty soldi. The tradesmen's attendance was marked on two large slabs of plaster that hung conspicuously on the construction site and Giovanni di Ser Benedetto provided a sand-glass by which the hours of work could be reckoned. No builder could descend from the cupola during the working day, no wine could be sent up unless it was previously mixed with water and no one could work on the dome during Lenten sermons because of the noise of the mallets and chisels—not even the great Brunelleschi himself. According to reports, he worked the hardest of all. He went himself to the lime ovens, he invented a new kind of barge to bring Carrara marble for the ribs of the cupola up the Arno from Pisa, he designed the *ulivella*, the grappling iron worked by oxen that allowed large stones to be lifted by a crane without ropes. And—a detail I have special affection for—he carried turnips in the pockets of his gown, ostensibly to gnaw on when his stomach began to growl, but also to carve into three-dimensional models as illustrations for the carpenters. Then, after sixteen years of toil, "on the last day of August, 1436, the final stone was laid in place and the great dome closed." When Brunelleschi died, ten years later, a wax model was taken of his face—of his fleshy pug nose and his receding chin.

As I walked around the cathedral in the clear Tuscan morning, my eyes full of the dancing illusions produced by the play of green, rose and white marble, it occurred to me that poor Masaccio never had the chance to see his good friend's project completed. Brunelleschi, born twenty-four years before Masaccio, died almost twenty years after him. I could feel myself growing maudlin as I considered yet again the brevity of life and the old hag's indifferent shears, when suddenly I saw the fact for what it was: an interesting footnote in the annals of art history, nothing more. I feel convinced, now, Masaccio would not have cared about dying so young or about leaving so much work unfinished. I feel sure that as he left the world, he hadn't a thought for cathedrals or domes or frescoes or even the unequal span of years. I believe that at the moment of death, he must have felt grateful, certainly, for the work that had occupied his mind and his hands, for the sunlight that had warmed his flesh and graced his days, for the beauty that had stopped the very breath in his throat, for the bread he'd broken and the wine he'd shared. But what must have filled his heart to the brim, as he stood at the threshold, was the memory of, and the nostalgia for, awkward, fumbling, glorious human love. At the end, when everything else fades into insignificance (as you and I have learned, Christie), we see with remarkable lucidity that our lives are defined and shaped by nothing else but love.

The boutique was still closed, so I bought a *Herald Tribune* and a caffe latte and settled into a terrace on the sunny side of the street. Cast a distracted eye on the news—the twentieth highjacker still praying for the destruction of the United States, the Cardinals still forgetting about the children, kids still packing guns to school, Bush still mishandling the Middle East. I was more interested in a couple of elderly tourists—brothers, I wondered, or childhood friends?—sitting at a table next to mine, quietly planning their day over breakfast. Spry old guys, the kind I hope to be as I round the corner to eighty. I gathered they had recently come to Florence from Assisi, where they'd stayed in a Franciscan monastery—one gentleman referred to the mural on his cell wall, painted, he said, by Giotto. The remark started me thinking about the Giottos I still haven't seen. I've already spent a little time with the Ognissanti Madonna at the Uffizi, and the lives of the saints in Santa Croce, but I'd like to go to Padua to see the fresco cycle of the lives of the Virgin and the Christ in the Cappella degli Scrovegni, where Giotto painted the first blue skies to appear in Western art. I'd also like to go to Assisi, to decide for myself whether the frescoes of the Upper Church are of Giotto's hand or not. Giotto di Bondone in Colle di Vespignano—ah! those plump, profligate Italian names—venerated for his attention to *dear and dogged man*. As I sat in the shadow of the campanile he'd designed, at a stone's throw from the place where his body rests, I was reminded of the words of the epitaph carved on his tombstone: "Lo, I am he by whom dead painting was restored to life, to whose right hand all was possible, by whom art became one with nature." High praise, indeed. And Masaccio, said Berenson, was Giotto born again.

The gentlemen beside me had finished their breakfast and moved on, leaving a few Euros beneath a saucer and a couple of pamphlets among the plates. I picked one up as I walked by and saw it was a Franciscan tract with the monastery's address printed on the back. I folded it up and put it in my pocket. Then I sauntered over to the boutique, smiled at the shopkeeper and immediately fell into a memory.

(It was the smell, of course, that beckoned you to my side. We were young again, your long hair lay like a mantle of sunlight on your shoulders, and you kept turning your face to me as your hands caressed the leather, your eyes shining with undisguised avidity, with pleasure, with shame, already, at the great bourgeois sin we stood on the brink of committing. I don't recall what the bag was worth, remember only its suppleness in my hands, the heady scent of its tawny buckskin. We were talking in low tones about the folly of blowing a week's worth of meals on a single souvenir when the young Italian salesman approached us to see if he could help. He was beautiful, I remember, his dark eyes catching the spare light lingering in the shadows of the shop. He had a mouth like yours and long, fine hands, and his English was thick with husky Latin inflection. And, like a devil out of Dante, he spoke into your hair, and brushed your breast with the back of his wrist as he pretended to straighten a strap, and let his fingers lie in the crook of your arm with a deep and intimate insistence. I said nothing. Just watched your eyes and waited. Hoping you would shake him off like you shook out the sleepy storm of your hair in the morning, with a yawn and a shrug of your shoulders. But, still stinging perhaps from a thoughtless word of mine and a little hungry for revenge, or tempted, for a moment, by a bit of sexual mischief, you did not turn away from him or give him the withering look I kept hoping would appear in your eyes. No. While I stood there and watched, my mouth dry, my hands knotted into fists, you and the lovely Italian boy engaged in the deliberate, passionate dance that was then, and is always, just world enough for two. In the few seconds I stood by and endured it—I still remember this, Christie, with a painful catch at my heart—I was filled with an eternity of longing. As I watched you flirt with this dark young stranger in the heavy odour of animal skin, in the dusky light of an exotic sun, I was touched and kindled and torn by—how to express it, now, so many years later?—the infinite varieties of desire. For another life, another face, another me. For other places, riddled with unfamiliar fragrances and strange, unsettling stars. For giftedness. For song. For raving madness on the knife-edge of love. For love. And for yielding, again and again and again. But as I watched the movement of his fingers on your bare arm, I saw myself through the glassy eyes of a feverish brain, an overgrown boy with large hands and unruly hair, too earnest, too fearful, and certainly too fond of dead poets and their foolish way with words. No match at all for a gorgeous stranger with burnished skin and eyes bright with moonlight and fire.

There was nothing for it but to turn away, find the bus back to the hostel, and spend one last lonely night in Florence before heading down the highway to Rome.

My memory of the gardens of the palazzo we stayed in on the outskirts of the city is probably much clearer than yours. When I arrived in the late afternoon, the sun was slanting through the cypress trees, making the ground bristle with shadow. There were the usual clumps of travellers sitting around the tables on the terrace, drinking wine and sharing stories, but I had no taste for conversation. I had some serious decisions to make and a seriously wounded heart to mend. So I went walking beneath the trees, head down and brow buckled like the moody Romantic I imagined myself to be, and sat awhile among the statues and the reflecting pools. If the memory is so clear to me, Christie, it's because I had come to a crossroads, unlike any I had known before or, for that matter, since. I sat there in that strangely muted garden, with its quiet olive greens and its silent silver water, and picked up my life and held it, and turned it over and over in my hands. It seemed a very foreign thing to me, made up of nothing I could recognize, with its sudden aloneness, its unrootedness, its terrible, terrifying freedom. I remember feeling my heart beat, feeling it fill me with a pounding fear as I understood, I think for the very first time, that my life was my own and only mine to live.

I stayed in the garden a long time, till the light leached out of the sun and darkness spread like a stain across the sky. By the time I headed towards the loud voices and the lights of the palazzo, I had made up some improbable plan, involving a Greek isle, a fishing boat, an unfinished book of poetry and the American blonde who kept turning up—alone—at every stop we made. I don't remember how I made it out of the garden and into bed—whether or not I ate, or spoke, or washed, or cried myself to sleep. I remember only the fat yellow face of the moon staring down at me through those high palace windows and the noisy breathing of the boys in the dormitory room. I slept, I know, in spite of the grief that kept welling up in me like tears, because when you sneaked past the night-watch, crept up to my cot and bent your face to mine, I thought I was dreaming. But it was really you. There you stood, your hair falling like a golden rain into my eyes, your warm hand pressed against my heart. Then, without making a sound, you slipped your smooth body next to mine, tucked your head into my shoulder and, with one shuddering breath, quieted all my fears.

That was the night, remember, Christie, you said yes, forever.)

~

There was a lot of beautiful leather in the boutique and a few bags I know the boys would love but, somehow, I couldn't make up my mind. I wandered out into the piazza and into the neighbouring streets, and let the sun bear down hard on my bones and sink into the marrow. The markets in the town squares were shiny with the fat skins of fresh fruit and petal-bright with flowers and the air was thick with summer scent. I forced myself to think of Eloisa and her encounter with the lonely hostler boy, or of her brothers' murderous wrath, but, try as I might, there was absolutely nothing going on in my brain. I was nothing but skin. Sensation brushed against me in waves of smells and sights and sounds that washed over me, then receded without leaving a mark. I had no mind left, certainly no memory, and only a handful of disconnected words. And my heart felt as buoyant as a bubble in my chest. When I stopped to wonder at the source of this gleeful idiocy, it took me only a second to recognize spring fever, that fleeting, euphoric state visited upon overwintered Canadians caught between snow and daffodils. So I walked on, smiling stupidly into the sun, letting my vacant head fill with sunshine and song.

That's when I saw her. I recognized her dress, the one she was wearing this morning when we boarded the bus. A periwinkle blue, with tiny white flowers. She had tied her hair in a thick coil at the nape and, through the store window, I could see the curve of her neck as she bent over a book. I wondered what she was reading so intently, wondered which perfume she wore—I know them all, by now—and which jewel at her throat. Still empty-headed and fond, I imagined myself walking into the store, coming up quietly behind her, and pressing my mouth to her small ear. She would be surprised, quickly lift her eyes from the page and smile warmly when she saw it was me. I was already grinning, had taken a step or two towards the door, when Për suddenly appeared between two banks of bookshelves. He moved in close beside her, then stood with his hands tucked into his pockets, his handsome face bent over her book. I backed quickly away, feeling pale all at once, and inexpressibly foolish.

~

I can't say how I spent the afternoon in town, what I had for lunch, or where I bought this bottle, but I've been sitting here since supper, filling glass after glass with fingerfuls of this wonderful peaty Scotch. I spent the evening profitably, catching up on my mail. Had a message from Alex, who wanted some suggestions for a fishing trip he's planning to make with a few friends on the May long weekend. Nick wrote to tell me Maggy broke her arm rollerblading and had to quit her job and is it okay if she can't pay rent for a while. Fine, I answered. No problem. And how's the set building going? And have you learned your lines? And how are you travelling to and from work? (The day he called to ask if Maggy could stay at the house, neither of us mentioned the obvious: that he would be moving out of the rented shack by the river—and away from those wild actor friends of his, thank God—into the quiet, safe comfort of his bedroom. A space he's only too happy to share, I am sure, with his broken little bird. And I ask you, Christie, which is worse? Imagining him with those maniacal drama school types through the four full moons of summer, or playing house with a savvy, hard-headed woman who can teach him a few things about love? You would tell me, I know, I am getting soft in my old age. And I would remind you, with a gentle nudge of reproof, you once knew but perhaps have forgotten that I am utterly defenceless in the face of love.)

Brendan also wrote and forwarded some bad dentist jokes. Sheila gave me a very comprehensive report on the boys and on Maggy, whom she seems to like, and told me she was having them over for dinner this coming weekend. Gavin and his new love are off to Montreal next week to catch a performance of the Bill T. Jones / Arnie Zane Dance Company. He sounds very high, and, therefore, very much at risk. I will be home for the crash, which is a very good thing. Also had a message from Clara, with a list of Web sites that specialize in matchmaking, and four e-mails from students asking for letters of reference. Sent them off, then spent the balance of the evening sipping at my Scotch and staring at the lights on the hillside. And trying desperately to come to terms with this astonishing fact: in spite of this afternoon's blithe assumption I have fallen under the spell of springtime in Tuscany, the truth is I have been swept off my feet by an achingly beautiful woman who, in all likelihood, has fallen in love with someone else.

Wednesday 15 May

And so I realize, with something of a shock, that for many days now I have been acutely aware of her presence. Even as I bent to the task of writing Cecilia'a story—her childish hope, her fear, her humiliation—I was distracted by the sound of another woman's voice and summoned by another woman's scent. Every morning, at the same hour, I shift in my chair, angling my face away from the page and towards the window, watching and waiting for her to appear. And then, when I finally catch a glimpse of her silhouette, marked in shadow against the early light, and see her fine white arms, her damp roan hair, I can't help it, I want to go to her and take her in my arms and breathe in the smell of the morning on her skin, the subtle musk of the night, and feel her body fold into mine. I've caught myself imagining her at dawn, slowly waking from her dreams of saffron and cerulean blue, and I've seen her, in my mind's eye, rise from the warm nest of her bed and move to the window, her white shift unfolding from around her hips and tumbling to the floor. She is naked beneath the sheer cotton and, as she lifts her arms to part the drapes, I can see in the loose cut of the sleeve the soft, warm curve of her breast and wish with all my heart I could be there to press my mouth against it. But she doesn't have a thought for me. Standing at the window, gazing with the level green light of her eyes on the misty shimmer of the hills, she remembers, she smiles, she is filled with delight. Then, as she readies herself for the day, I want to stand with her beneath the hot rush of water and take her in my hands and slip my soapy fingers across her body and into the thick dark tangle of her hair. I want to feel her body against mine, want to feel her go slack in my arms, weakened by heat, by pummelling water, by merciless desire. And I want to drink deeply of her, lose myself in the terror of her lips against mine, of her breath stealing mine. And when she is towelled off and moving naked through the room, polishing her skin, oiling her limbs till they shine, I want to stand by and watch her slip on small, summery underthings of silk and lace, and narrow summer sheaths, and summer sandals on her fine brown summer feet.

But all she gives me, these mornings when I wait for her to appear, is the vision of her silhouette against the sky and the sound of her voice lifted in friendly greeting for someone other than me.

Thursday 16 May

Try as I might, I cannot concentrate enough to write Eloisa's story. So I gave up this morning, dug out the old notebooks I brought with me and settled in for a warm, nostalgic read—my life with annotations. Journals, I suppose I should call them, or *Markings*, like Dag Hammarskjöld—these collections of jottings and quotations and memories that survive like traces of feldspar on a cave wall. (The first one I picked up was the last one you bought me—a pocket-sized book from G. Lalo, with unlined pages, marbled covers and red-linen corners and spine. It was a record of 1992–93, when Alex was twelve and Nick was ten. And, for a few stolen hours, I gave myself over to memories of swim meets and hockey practices, school plays and family birthdays, canoe trips and snorkelling expeditions, I leafed through old ticket stubs, airline tags and program notes, and read with a pang of rediscovered joy the quotations I'd carefully recopied from the books I'd loved best. A whole tapestry of life, a time so intimately present, Christie, it seems impossible to believe it's now irremediably lost. A page turned, a chapter closed, blue eyes forever dark.)

I was thumbing through quotations and fragments of poetry when I came upon words that sank in me with the cold blade of recognition. A character in a novel I'd been reading then said he could not concentrate on his work with a beautiful woman close at hand; he confesses that he is *unable to remove her body from the page*. When I reread those words, I realized that I am like that fictional writer, fighting to contain distraction, to repress the longing that's broken free somewhere inside me and is running loose, like an illness, or a fever, and I so sick now with desire. A profound conversion is taking place within Eloisa, some kind of spiritual upheaval that deserves my full and careful attention, and yet I feel myself being pulled away, again and again, by images over which I have no control. As I watch myself write about a mutilated face pressed against a fine linen gown, or about murder in a garden, I am aware of fumes rising up around me, thick, scented, smoky vapours that seep into my brain and cloud my eyes and fill the empty chambers of my heart. I try to ignore them and focus instead on the corpse sinking in the muddy waters of the Tevere, or on Eloisa's face as she feels the hand of God upon her, but they come between the words and me, these ascending fumes, this subterranean heat, creeping like a secret tide, rising and rising, until I drown.

Monastery Monte Alverno, Assisi
Friday 17 May
And so I have run away. Courage, in French, means "running" but I know I have not been brave. I have simply chosen to remove myself, for a time, from the misery of temptation. I have a novel to finish, I have a friend whose love I must learn to not want.

I arrived at the monastery late last night. When I reached for the door, I had a thought for Aunt Helene. The anecdote, not apocryphal by any means, simmers steadily in the family's collective memory, a gentle, awesome, well-kept flame. Off on a weekend retreat, having reluctantly agreed to accompany her sister Eveline through two days of prayer and meditation, Helene had taken her bag and made her way to the Oblate Sisters' Convent House. It was on the wide steps at the convent entrance that the summons had come. The minute Helene had placed her hand on the doorknob, she'd known, without the edge of a doubt, she'd never leave that house again. She'd been called, she told us, the voice in her heart clearly speaking her name.

I have never been cynical about religious vocation. I believe sincerely, with the callow faith of my youth, some men are born to the priesthood as others to poetry. And know, had I been a fisher on the Sea of Galilee, that man's eyes in mine would have been enough to make me leave my nets on the shore and follow him. So I've come to this place with my soul on my sleeve, ready, like Blake, to be surprised by God looking at me through the window.

During the night, in rhythm with sidereal time, I rose with the monks to listen to them sing the hours. I've eaten of their bread, partaken of their silence, tasted of their solitude. I spend much time walking alone among the trees of their olive grove, or shut myself up in the clear white stillness of my room. It is not Giotto who has adorned the walls of this narrow cell, but some more ancient, less earthly painter, still in love with an ideal world. I am able to write here and to read a little, and find I can sit a long time in quiet contemplation of the fresco of the Madonna that covers the wall at the foot of my cot.

It occurs to me I could easily have been a monk. Living out my days in splendid, cloistered isolation, in heightened communication with a transcendent world, in love with *dearest him that lives alas! away*. I suppose the word that best conveys the essence of my relationship with the metaphysical is *humility*. I know human smallness, am intimately acquainted with human unfaithfulness, and so am touched to the very soul by the goodness of a god who believed we were worth dying for.

~

It does not seem too strange a turning, here in this place of miracles, for Eloisa's sudden reimagining of her life. Human history is full of such awakenings, and Assisi is famous for at least two. It seems fitting, here in this place of prodigies, to imagine a woman who, like saints Francis and Clare, walks away without a backward glance from the dark cloy and clog of wealth and into illumination. Who sees, with the insight of inspired vision, the true purpose of abundance and the true power of time. When Eloisa stands before the glass in her chamber with her messy hair and muddied gown, she reaches out an unadorned hand to a strangely altered reflection. Some new flame is burning bright within her, some immortal clear white light, and she knows, all at once, she is standing in the midst of the divine.

~

Chesterton on St. Francis: "He listens to those to whom God himself will not listen."

And again, "He wandered about the valleys of the world looking for the hill that has the outline of a skull."

And yet again: "One night the people of Assisi thought the trees and the holy house were on fire and rushed up to extinguish the conflagration. But they found all quiet within, where St Francis broke bread with St Clare and talked of the love of God. It would be hard to find a more imaginative image for some sort of utterly pure and disembodied passion than that red halo round the unconscious figures on the hill; a flame feeding on nothing and setting the very air on fire."

Passion: from the Latin *pati*, "to suffer."

Love that hurts, love both sacred and profane.

Monastery Monte Alverno, Assisi

Saturday 18 May

Assisi rises out of the plain of Umbria like an altar carved out of rock, a walled fortress, impenetrable to everything but the breath of the spirit. And it is palpable here, amidst these shrines and holy temples, as real as the smell of woodsmoke and of roses. Pilgrims and tourists throng the streets and the back alleys, toiling up and down staircases and through the vaulted lanes, filling the small piazzas and milling around the fountains, buying relics and postcards and crucifixes and effigies of the saint surrounded by wolves, lambs, fish and birds. Today, slipping in amongst them—these earnest tourists in walking shorts—I visited the basilicas, saw Cimabue's fresco of St. Francis, Simone Martini's smiling horses and the twenty-eight episodes of the *Poverello*'s prodigious mystical adventure. Then, moving with the pilgrims through the shady, flower-scented streets, I entered beneath the wings of the rose and white basilica of Santa Chiara and saw the crucifix that spoke to Francis, and the tunics they'd worn, he and Clare, so very long ago. Then, towards evening, I followed the crowd to the fortress of Rocca Maggiore and watched as a golden mist rose up from the darkling valley of Spoleto.

Tonight, as I made my way to the monastery, I expected my mind to be crowded with images of polygonal transepts and crypts and geometrical landscapes, morsels of the visual banquet that had been spread today before my eyes. Instead, to my surprise, I was accompanied through those quiet mediaeval streets by flashes of strangers' faces. People I had never seen before, glimpsed in passing, as they walked together or sat and looked into each other's eyes, their hands linked, their shoulders touching, their heads bent in private conversation. In short, what I had observed most of the day was not the fresco painter's art, or Saint Francis's youthful sparkle, or the dark flanks of Mount Subasio, but lovers. And on their faces, strange to me but somehow familiar, too, I had superimposed my own and Magda's. And ached that it could be so.

The realization filled me with shame.

I had come to St. Francis's home hoping to learn, by him and through him, to divest myself of an impossible love. I'd hoped the spirit that hovers in this place would infuse in me the strength to resist and the wisdom to relent. I'd prayed to be possessed, once again, of that other, purer, more unearthly love.

Before entering the monastery for the night, I lingered awhile among the olive trees and, after some reflection, finally admitted the truth: my love for Magda is wrong. I stood there beneath the greening trees and a fingernail of moon and, with lips set into a hard line, put a name to each of my sins.

Lust, first of all. What else to call this compelling and obsessive preoccupation with Magda's body? It has reduced me to a craven, snivelling puddle of desire, has made my very skin throb with unutterable tenderness. I confess to being aware, some days, of nothing else but the small blue vein that beats at her temple, or the tender swell of her bottom lip. And though I know her young flesh would recoil at the thought of my old man's hands upon her, their splotches and their gnarls and the ropes of their veins, I can't help myself from wanting her.

Secondly, arrogance. Pretentiousness. Conceit. The over-weening sense of self that deceived me into believing I could be a match for a woman like Magda. What made me think my fiction could measure up to her hard-earned facts, or my tired body and slowing mind could arouse anything but contempt in her young woman's heart? As I stood blindly beneath the monks' silvery trees, my eyes burning with anger and anguish, I was forced to admit, in the face of all the evidence, it is not love that has made a fool of me, but ordinary, vulgar vanity.

Thirdly, neglect. The confession of this sin made me cringe with particularly painful remorse. (It's because of you, Christie, because of the exemplary mother that you were. You would not be pleased that I've left the boys alone for the six weeks of this Italian sojourn. True, they are not children anymore. They will spend the summer gainfully employed in work they both enjoy. They are quite capable of preparing their own meals and keeping the house relatively tidy. And if, on more than one occasion, they have some friends in to share a few boxes of beer, well, it will not be the end of the world. But you, I know, would see it differently. You would insist upon the importance of being there for them, as they picked up the empties and the lipstick-stained glasses. In case they wanted to talk, after all the others had left, about one girl, maybe, the one in the tight white jeans and bare midriff, the one with the indigo tattoo across her narrow loins. In case the long, long night had left them with a serious dose of the blues. You would say that, even now, it's important for us to be vigilant. Instead, I've gone off with a woman almost young enough to be their sister, on an extended holiday in the groves of Bacchus, a decrepit old satyr panting after a nymph.)

Fourthly, unfaithfulness. I am *already* deeply and everlastingly in love. How exactly do I propose to turn away from Christie and cleave unto this other woman and, in effect, cheat them both out of a whole and undivided heart? (Replacing you is unthinkable. I feel everything inside me rise up in revolt at the idea of forsaking you. And yet, I would go from you to this other, and you would smile, I know, and lower your eyes and look away, because you have not forgotten that I am only human.) Still I know I am being false, because my heart is not mine to give.

Finally, covetousness. A direct transgression of one of the Ten. It is obvious to me, and to everyone else, she and Për are in love. They spend all their free time in each other's company, are clearly kindred minds, smile warmly, their cheeks flushed, when they come together unexpectedly. I have watched them in a crowd or in quiet conversation and have felt each time that green-skinned thing raise its ugly head inside me. What perverse will is there in me that wants for a woman I purport to love a slightly skewed version of the true and natural thing? And when, in my lifetime, have I ever wished to steal from a man that which is rightly his?

~

The list was longer than I'd imagined, each sin blacker than the last. I left the garden with a heavy heart and shut myself up in my silent room. And now, as I wait for the midnight call to prayer, I ask St. Francis again, and St. Clare, to release me from the bonds of this mistaken love.

Sunday 19 May

The night brought solace. I let myself be carried by the chanting of the monks, I surrendered to the spirit that inhabits these walls. When I left for the tour this morning, it seemed to me my soul was in a still and centred place. Even though the tourists were busy and loud, I found I could sit in the hermitage and in the convent of San Damiano and feel in touch again with the serenity that had stolen over me in the hushed hours of the night.

It was in San Damiano that God spoke to St. Francis and asked him to rebuild His church.

I've heard it said that very young children can still hear God's voice. As they grow older, and as the noise of the world drowns out

His voice, I wonder if they forget how it sounds, of what tones it is made, of what deep reserves of gentleness. Or is it forever set in their bones and in their flesh, the memory of this voice beyond and across time? So that when a man like St. Francis is spoken to in the quiet of the woods, does his heart immediately recognize the voice as the one he's heard within him since before the world was made?

At the Eremo delle Carceri, I saw the grotto where St. Francis prayed and, while the other tourists gathered before it, jostling for a better view, I wandered awhile among the green oaks. And understood there, in the quiet of the forest, that if God were ever to speak to me, it would not be in the ruins of a church, or before a tabernacle somewhere, or even in the darkness of my room, but certainly in a space like that one, a cathedral of trees, a temple of rivers, a shrine of ancient rock. In fact, I could not be sure, this morning at the hermitage, He had not done so once or twice before.

~

I returned to the monastery in time to pack my few things, leave a donation with Brother Alfonso and take one final look around my little cell. I was feeling quite solid in my resolve, sincerely believed my prayer had been answered: I was learning to not want Magda's love.

Before leaving the room, I bent down to see if I'd inadvertently kicked a sock or a pen under the bed and saw a book lying on the floor in a thin coat of dust. It was not one of mine; had obviously been left behind by the previous occupant of the room. I reached for it and saw it was an Italian edition of Augustine's *Confessions*. I opened it to the flyleaf, read the name T.L. Barcley signed in purple ink. And beneath it, in quotation marks, a line from Augustine that spoke straight to my heart and, in one fell blow, undid all my resolve. "Love," it said, "and do as you will."

ELOISA

XIII

THE SEXTON FOUND ELOISA WHEN HE WAS MAKING HIS LAST ROUND of the day. She had fallen asleep, her head cocked at an awkward angle in the corner of the pew. His first instinct was to let her be. She had obviously taken refuge in the church for a very good reason and he was reluctant to wake her to whatever trouble had followed her there. And then, she was a woman. Always a delicate matter. As much as he hated to put her out into the street at so late an hour, he could hardly be expected to invite her to stay the night in one of the friars' cells. And wouldn't she, upon waking and seeing a man of God standing before her, ask for confession or—at the very least—good counsel for her problems? Against all desire, he would then find himself caught up in matters that had always left him feeling inadequate, completely at sea. Questions of the heart and of the womb that invariably involved many tears and a great wringing of hands. He would have to listen and nod, compose for her benefit a wise and saintly countenance, while inside, his guts would churn with the fear of drowning.

While he deliberated, his eyes fixed on a sputtering votive

candle at the foot of the statue of the Virgin, Eloisa began to stir. A painful crick in the neck had pulled her from sleep. The good friar had to resist the temptation to run. He stood to one side while she sat up and looked around. When he saw she was not afraid, he approached her with outstretched hand, a gesture in this case more pleading than placating. "It is very late, *Signora*. The streets are dark and you are far from home."

Eloisa shook herself like a cat shedding water, and looked up at him. "Tell me, Father, have all the painters left?"

Before he spoke, she knew what the answer would be. It was far too dark to paint, and even if the men had lingered to discuss the morrow's work, at this hour they would all be in their beds. She asked for the friar's blessing. Then, genuflecting before the golden Christ, simmering now, shimmering in the shadows, she rose and bid the man good night. As she passed before the arched doorway of the Chapel of St. Catherine, she did not pause to look inside. All her thoughts were for Masaccio—and for the woman by whose soft side he (no doubt) slept.

The night was cold and the light cloak she wore did nothing to keep the chill off her back. She felt it slip in beneath her gown and place its icy fingers upon her skin. She felt the darkness, too. It walked beside her and in front, it pressed its heavy hand against her face. But as she hurried down the Via San Giovanni, her small figure hunched up against the cathedral wall, neither cold nor fear were big enough to fill the emptiness that gaped within. Losing Masaccio meant she was losing her second and final chance. She had not been able to hold on to Gianlucido. God had looked down upon her and taken pity on her loneliness: He had sent her Masaccio. If he slipped away in the night, as completely as the other had, no one would come again to replace him. She would be condemned to the spinster's cold and childless existence. Eloisa felt all her instincts surge up within her, a deep and urgent craving to be mother and wife, to be rooted in love all the days of her life.

Distracted by sadness, she did not hear the footsteps that suddenly rang out behind her, cried out only once when a sack was forced over her head. She felt herself hoisted into the air and thrown across someone's bony shoulder. When their bodies made contact, the wind was knocked out of her and she hung there, gasping for air, while the man dug his fingers into the soft flesh of her calf. She assumed she was going to die. This abductor, whoever he was, would rape her, then slit her throat before throwing her into the Tevere. To her surprise, she was filled with peace at the prospect. There would be an unpleasant bit to be got through at first, of course, but then there would be darkness (does a darkness exist, she wondered, more dark than the inside of this sack?) and, at last, the silence of stilled thoughts. The ache in her heart would vanish, her mind would grow quiet, she would roll as gently into death as into sleep.

Meanwhile, there was nothing gentle about this midnight pick-a-back ride. As the man twisted and turned down lane ways and around corners, he did not concern himself with protecting her head or her feet, and she felt blows rain down upon her from branches and buildings and rough brick walls. And when at last, after a great, huffing flight of stairs, he set her down upon her feet and she could hear voices a little ways off in the distance, as if from the inner room of a house, she felt at once disappointed and relieved. Surely nothing too horrible could take place within ear-shot of a crowd.

When she no longer felt her abductor's arms around her, she dared to lift the sack from her head. As a candle bloomed into light, she was astonished to see a table set with food and drink in the middle of a low, mansarded room. Two chairs were placed on either side of it and a young man was turned away from her, his hands busy putting the flame to a great number of candles.

Well, she thought, he went to a great deal of unnecessary trouble to bring me to this place. Had I known he was offering a feast, I would have come willingly. Now, who in the world would have prepared such a surprise for me? With hope leaping in her breast, she tried to find Masaccio's strong shoulders in the stranger's narrow back. When she could not, when she knew without the shadow of a doubt this man was any man but Masaccio, she lost all interest. Dropping the sack to the floor, she sighed an unhappy sigh and let herself fall to the edge of the stranger's bed. Her eyes fixed upon her linked hands, she wondered idly if perhaps he would let her rest awhile before doing to her whatever it was he'd planned to do. A short nap would be nice, she thought. I very much would like to sleep, she thought again as her eyelids dropped and her head keeled forward upon her breast. She fell into a deep and immediate sleep, and was almost instantly drawn out of it by the sound of Masaccio's voice. Beyond the wall, or maybe through the floor, he was explaining in sonorous tones some artistic principle that, judging by the silence with which it was received, held everyone enthralled. Eloisa was on her feet and at the door at once. But before she could make another move, she felt a hand grip her wrist and draw her forcibly into the room.

When she turned to face the man, she found herself gazing at the top of his head. He had his chin to his chest and his eyes turned towards the floor. With bowed head, he gently led her to a chair. Her wrist still firmly in his grasp, he sat across from her, then, lifting his head, he raised terrified eyes to her face. Eloisa saw a low forehead and thickly planted hair, she saw sand-coloured brows and dusky brown eyes, and, as he lifted his chin to the light, she saw a gaping hole where his nose had been, and the open wound of his mouth. No teeth, no lips, nothing but a stump for a tongue. Her heart climbed into her throat and she began to retch, a horrible wrenching sound that filled her with shame. For she knew this boy, had seen him lurking in the marketplace, hiding like a leper from the crowds. He was the innkeeper's son, one of many poor hostlers who had taken a horse's hoof in the face.

The apothecary who had tended to him after the accident had prescribed simples tied in a piece of linen and pressed to the wound. He'd declared he could do nothing for an injury of that nature and had expressed regret at not being able to treat the boy for gout. It was his cure for this particular ailment that had established his excellent reputation in the city of Rome. To the gawkers who'd stood around watching the boy writhe in pain, he'd explained that for gout, he would wait until summer to find celandine, a red stone that grows in the stomach of the swallow, which he would then tie in a small linen sack and sew in the patient's shirt under the left breast at the nipple. "It produces," he'd declared to the impressed crowd, "the same effect as the sapphire which has occult virtues, the specific one of preventing evil humours from going to the joints." While the boy had screamed in agony, he'd then proceeded to pick out the teeth and bone fragments imbedded in his flesh. As he cut off what remained of the tongue, the good apothecary had said he was quite sure the boy's brain was now as riddled with tooth bits as a cheese pudding with raisins. The people in attendance had laughed, then turned to their homes and their supper as the boy choked on his blood.

Eloisa covered her own mouth with her hand and looked at him with apologetic eyes. He closed his own and shook his head. She needn't feel ashamed. No one could look upon him without feeling sick. He motioned in silence to the plate before her. He wanted her to eat. Eloisa waited a moment for her heart to steady, then, locking her eyes on his, she reached for a cup of wine. Drinking greedily, she felt its vigour fill her mouth and calm her nerves. She could do this. She would do this. Glancing around the dingy attic, she imagined the countless lonely suppers the boy had taken by himself, night after night, hidden away and despised even by his own people. They had chased him away from their table, claiming no doubt that the very sight of him cut their appetites. Left to the four slanting walls of this mean room, to the stables and to the indifferent gaze of the horses, he was, through no fault of his own, excluded for all time from the warmth of human intercourse. Made mad with solitude, it was no surprise he was driven from time to time to kidnapping strangers on the street and forcing them to sit and face him, and break with him the lonely bread of his exile.

Eloisa felt her heart grow big as she began to grasp the depth of the boy's isolation. (Her own loneliness in comparison seemed a slight, insignificant thing.) Fortified by the wine, she raised her eyes to his face and did not shrink from its horror. As she examined the ragged edges of the wound and its dark, damaged flesh, her gaze returned again and again to the boy's gentle eyes. And soon, she saw only his eyes. Soon, the bottom half of his face was obscured by nothing worse than shadow, everything beyond the light of his eyes fallen into shadow. She found she could eat, each morsel of roasted meat tasting better than the last, she could listen to the laughter and the shouts and the sound of Masaccio's voice beyond the wall and feel her heart fill with happiness, she could smile on this young stranger, lift a hand to his face and touch it gently to his cheek.

Later, when all but one of the candles had been blown out

and the plates had been wiped clean, Eloisa had settled onto the boy's low bed, her back propped up against the wall. Then, with a wide, embracing gesture, she had invited him to come sit beside her. Making soft, animal sounds, the boy had snuggled at her side, wrapping his arms around her waist, letting his ruined face lie against her breast. Eloisa had held him there till he'd fallen asleep. She'd listened to Masaccio talking with his friends over their late supper, she'd heard the far-off sounds of their merrymaking, she'd felt upon the linen bodice of her gown the spreading warmth of the boy's breath. And for some inexplicable reason, she'd felt peace like a river carry her away.

XIV

VITTORIO HAD PACED UNTIL DAWN. HE KNEW IN HIS BONES THAT something was not right. Eloisa and her husband had been gone all day and all night and Vittorio knew better than anyone that, after sunset, the streets of Rome were unsafe for man or beast. When he'd seen his sister arrive alone shortly after sunrise, he'd run out of the house to meet her, demanding in an angry voice to know the whereabouts of her feckless husband. Eloisa had calmly responded that, first of all, he was not her husband, and secondly, she had no idea where he had spent the night. Vittorio had immediately gone into a rage. What did she mean, Gianlucido was not her husband? And how was it, that on the second night of their marriage, they had slept apart? By this time, Vittorio had followed her into the house, had watched her remove her cloak and wet slippers. When he'd seen her dishevelled hair and the dark stains upon the bodice of her dress, he'd grabbed her by the shoulders and shaken her hard once. "Tell me, Eloisa, what the animal has done to you. I swear, if Gian has dishonoured you yet again, I will rend him limb from limb with my bare hands."

Eloisa looked into her brother's dark eyes and smiled. "It's over, Vittorio, the marriage is over. And no one is to blame, and no one deserves to die. I will go on living here as before, with my father and my brothers, and I will grieve no more."

"Where is Gian now? Where does the cowardly bastard hide?"

But Eloisa did not answer. Going quietly to her room, she let the curtain fall between her brother and herself and went to stand in front of the square of polished metal hanging on the chamber wall. She gazed in silence upon the soiled linen of her gown. It pleased her, somehow, to see the fine cloth marked with wine stains and drool, it made her happy to see her bare feet sticking out at the soiled hem of her skirt. Reaching up to her throat, she unclasped her necklace, and removed the bangles of gold and silver from her wrists. She pulled all the rings from her fingers and, holding her hands up to her face, she wondered what it would feel like to wear a crown of dirt beneath each fingernail. It occurred to her then that she'd never dug in the earth with her hands, or kneaded dough, or laid a fire. This morning, she could still feel the roughness of the hostler's coarse hair against her palms, could feel the stickiness of his skin between her fingers. His smell, a mixture of boy and horse, of manure and hay, lifted off her flesh and she smiled. It was a messy, warm and wondrous smell. The smell of life itself.

Behind the dropped curtain, Vittorio's angry face blanched with fear. He need not be afraid of Eloisa. He knew that no power on earth could ever convince her of her brothers' guilt. But this Masaccio, with his bewildered look, his disarmingly innocent eyes, *he* was a force to be reckoned with. When their uncle Domenico had announced upon his arrival from the north that Gianlucido Villani was on his way home to Rome, that his niece's wedding night had not been cancelled but only delayed, Vittorio and his brothers had exchanged puzzled looks. Then, when Masaccio, looking so much like an older, more mature Gian, had presented himself at their door, the brothers had dared imagine, for a moment, that the events that night in the garden three years before had never taken place. Only Vittorio, with his macabre turn of mind, had looked upon Masaccio and seen a ghost. A vengeful phantom, come back to prey upon his mind and drive him mad with guilt.

It was obvious, now, that he'd been right to expect the worst.

Masaccio's forsaking of Eloisa sent the clear message that he was not willing to step into another man's shoes, that he thumbed his nose at both wife and fortune. This insult to Eloisa filled Vittorio with blind rage. In love with his sister from the moment he'd drawn first breath, it was inconceivable to him that anyone could set eyes upon her and not be immediately swept away. And Masaccio *had* been taken with her beauty, Vittorio knew it could not have been otherwise. It was impossible that a foreigner, of lowly birth and station, a simple, rustic artisan, for God's sake, could look with scorn upon the gift of Eloisa. But he had walked out on her and, to Vittorio's mind, there could only be one explanation for his desertion. He had guessed the truth and now feared for his life. Well, Vittorio would prove to him he'd been right to be afraid. He would act alone this time, would not even consult his brothers, trusting to *la dolce cantarella* to do the job quickly, without leaving a trace.

It was still very early, the painters would not yet have arrived at San Clemente. If he hurried, he could greet them at the church door. Going first to a hidden drawer in the *cassoni* of his chamber, he then went to the kitchen to prepare some food and a goatskin of his father's best wine. He wanted to go to Masaccio in peace, offering friendship and goodwill, wanted to scrupulously avoid arousing the man's suspicions. Wrapping himself in his great cloak, his parcels tucked beneath his arms, he slipped into the garden behind the sleeping house and paused a moment beneath the trees of the orchard. It was there, in the lemon grove, that Gian had met his death.

Vittorio had not cared for Eloisa's lover, had in fact been appalled that his sister had chosen such a fey, effeminate man for a husband. Had been appalled, if truth be known, that she had condescended to being touched by any man at all. To his eyes, men were all the same. Like him, rough, dark, hirsute creatures with long, simian arms and hands that sprouted coarse hair, warts and thick, tumescent veins. As a boy, even then a round, furry cub of a child, he had looked upon his sister's smooth skin with an amazement tinged with shame. Beside the small, perfect features of her face, his own large eyes, big, splayed teeth and droopy lips had seemed a cruel caricature and it had struck him as quite impossible they'd been born of the same flesh. He'd been afraid to touch her when they were children. Afraid his hands would leave some grotesque, indelible mark upon her skin, break the fine bones of her fingers, or crush the breath in her throat. And when he'd caught a glimpse of the smooth, finished roundness of the mound below her belly, he'd been filled with humiliation at the ugliness of his own body. Wrinkled, wattled and pendulous, the apparatus hung between his legs had seemed a horrible joke played by an uncouth god, a constant reminder that he was more goat than man.

He and his brothers had hidden much from their sister. Afraid, always, of offending her gentler sensibilities, they had taken their brawls out into the garden, had traded bruises and bloodied noses far from her chamber door. They had never bragged, in the evening at the supper table, of skinning cats alive or stoning dogs to death, had waited till she'd left the room to count the money they'd stolen from the beggars on the street corners, the thick coins tumbling through their fingers like rounds of dirty bread. She would have wept, they knew, if she'd seen them try to skip the *fiorini* across the face of the Tevere, tossing the paupers' coins into the water like so many worthless stones. Later, when they'd weary of that game, they would turn to the bushes on the riverbank and root through the branches and the soft earth, hunting for something to kill. Plunging their rough fingers into whatever nests they found, they would crush eggs and tiny furred heads, they would yank off legs and tails and break off fledgling wings, they would take in their hard hands, the warm bodies of brooding birds and still their racing hearts with the point of a pin. All this, too, would have made Eloisa cry.

Later, when Vittorio and his brothers had begun to spend their lust on the house's serving wenches, taking the young girls from behind, standing up, in the kitchen or the stables, they'd known that if Eloisa had come upon them fornicating like monkeys in her house, she would have thrown them out into the street. Their bodies would have disgusted her and their dark and shameful cravings, their cruel hands, would have woken loathing in her heart. So they'd hidden from her, washed the blood off their hands and the smell of sex off their skin, scrubbed the stink of slaughter from their clothes.

As Vittorio approached San Clemente, he felt a strange agitation come over him. He was on his way to meet his sister's lover, to kill him yet a second time. It seemed to him, as the church loomed nearer with each step, he might fall apart within its doors. Find himself incapable of going through with the murder, be driven by guilt to confess his sin and beg for forgiveness with broken and contrite heart.

When he and his brothers had discovered they'd accidentally killed Gian that night in the garden, he'd felt no real remorse. Annoyed, mostly, that the man had succumbed so easily, he'd resented the trouble he'd had to take to dispose of the body. It was only afterwards, when he'd seen his sister grow thin with languishing, when she'd grieved long and deeply for her lost lover, that he had known regret. He'd not imagined for a second that feeble, foppish Gian had been capable of inspiring such faithful love in a woman like his sister. He'd held her as she cried, as her narrow shoulders had been wracked with sobs, and he'd cursed his drunkenness and his taste for perverse pranks.

The morning after the wedding feast, the bleary-eyed guests had gathered at the newlyweds' chamber window and begun clapping their hands and calling out their names. The night before, they'd carried Gian and Eloisa off to bed, hoisting them on their shoulders and bearing them jubilantly throughout the garden and the rooms of the house in a candlelit procession. Guests had thrown petals into the air and carried poles hung with a carrot and a pair of onions, huge, oversized bunches they'd laughingly dangled in the newlyweds' faces. When the curtain had been dropped across the door of the marriage chamber, the party had moved back into the great hall and had continued with unabated fervour till dawn. Then, with the rising sun lighting up their drawn faces; the guests had made their weaving way out to the garden and clamoured to see the bloodied sheet before going home and retiring to their beds. But that morning, they'd called out in vain. No happy couple had appeared at the window, no bedsheet had been spread for the world to see. Eloisa, abandoned and afraid, had stayed huddled in a corner of the room, far from the light streaming through her window. In the end, it had been her brothers, appearing suddenly at the rear of the crowd, who had dispersed the guests with a shrug of their shoulders and a lascivious wink. All was well, they assured them. Go home now and sleep off the wine. Gian and Eloisa are well.

Turning into the Via San Giovanni, Vittorio thought of how difficult it had been two nights ago to convince the guests to leave the party early. When Masaccio and Eloisa had disappeared from their midst, Vittorio and his brothers had quieted the musicians and recorked the wine. The groom, they'd told their friends and family, is weary beyond imagining. There will be no procession tonight and no wedding breakfast on the morrow. The greatest good we can give them on this night is the gift of sleep. When the crowd had roared its disapproval, Vittorio had amended. Yes, of course, he'd said, love first, three years' worth of love, and then a deep and healing sleep. As he'd watched them turn and grudgingly go, he'd remembered it had been at that very hour of the evening that, three years before, he and his brothers had gone into the garden to taunt Gian.

At their sister's wedding, Vittorio, Rinaldo and Ignazio had drunk till they were sodden. As the wine had peeled off layer after layer of civilized veneer, they'd shown themselves to be, by turns, maudlin and coarse, cruel and romantic. They had entertained the aunts with sweet stories of their childhood, had regaled their young male cousins with tales of their sexual exploits, then tried to pinch the bottoms and the titties of their friends' prudish daughters. When their throats had become raw with singing, and their heads spun, their legs ached, and their faces stung from being slapped, they had stumbled out of the house, a laughing, lurching threesome, and fallen into the soft night of the garden. Tangled together like bear cubs, they'd rolled about in their brocades and silks, cooling their hot foreheads in the heavy dew before sprawling spread-eagled in the grass, their eyes full of throbbing stars.

It was Ignazio, the young swine, who had first suggested they spy on the newlyweds. It would be interesting to watch how Gian moved, he said. Instructive to see how a faggot fucks. Vittorio and Rinaldo had tossed and turned in the grass, trying to stifle their laughter, and, with soft, drunken hands, had slapped Ignazio about the head. When the younger brother had set off on all fours towards the light in the bedchamber window, Vittorio had reached out and grabbed his ankle while Rinaldo tackled him flat to the ground.

They'd lain there, heaving with hysterical laughter as Ignazio had struggled to get up, buttocks lifted high into the air, his face ground into the earth. When he'd managed to throw his brother's weight off his head, he'd gone toward the window once again. This time Rinaldo had made no effort to stop him. Sitting up, his watery eyes straining to focus, he'd watched Ignazio crawl through the darkness with slow, encumbered movements. But Vittorio had had another idea. Getting waveringly to his feet, he'd put out one muddy slipper, and, leaning hard into his brother's side, made him topple to the ground. Then, grabbing both of them by the scruff of the neck, he'd whispered loudly in their ears. "Spying is a children's game, you louts. We are men. I wish the same could be said for the sissy who even now hoists up our sister's skirts. Let us draw him away from her for a moment. Let us call him to us and make him prove he is a man." Releasing his giggling brothers, he'd stumbled up to the window and stood off to one side.

The wedding music was still tumbling around the house and out the windows in loud, rolling waves. But when Vittorio raised his hands and cupped them to his face, the soft whistle escaping from his lips cut through the noise like a sunbeam in a storm. It was the thrush's song he made, with the bowman's expert skill, and he knew its haunting melody would be as clear a summons to Gian as the sound of his own name. On a night like this, thick and mellow with summer's last heat, his heart would be brimming and his veins running hot with desire. Anything at all, an errant perfume, a musky taste upon his tongue, the thrush's sweet song, would split him open like ripe fruit.

While Vittorio whistled, his brothers waited in the shadow of the citron trees. By the time Gian had appeared at the window, his ear cocked to the sound of the bird's song, Vittorio, too, had melted into the darkness. He'd watched with beating heart as Gian had hesitated, then turned to speak a few words to Eloisa. As Vittorio's song rang out again, Gian lifted a leg over the sill and stepped out into the garden. He'd taken a few steps, his face raised to the sky, his eyes turning this way and that in search of the bird. That's when the brothers had fallen upon him, taken him by the arms, and drawn him off into the depths of the garden. There'd been much laughter at first, and a great slapping of backs, and, after the initial start of fear, Gian had relaxed and let himself be led by his new brothers-in-law.

In a clearing in the grove, the men had made a circle around him, and, with gentle pushes and shoves, had passed him from one set of arms to another, whispering lewd things into his ear. Rinaldo had caught him first and, pinning his arms behind his back, had pressed his big, black face into Gian's hair. "You are too anxious, my new brother, to taste my sister's kisses. She wants neither your hurry nor your haste. Tarry awhile with us here. While she waits, desire grows."

Then he'd tossed him into Ignazio's arms. "Forget your charcoal and your brushes tonight, Gianlucido. It's a real live woman who lies within, and a real live tool she hankers for. For if your cock be as limp as your wrist...."

But Vittorio had grabbed hold of Gian and wrapped a great arm around his throat. "Remember my sister is not one of your painter's whores, Gianlucido. Not a sack of flesh in which to spill your seed. She is a lady and you are dirt. Remember this always, Villani. You are not worth the dogshit she scrapes in disgust from the sole of her slipper." Then, with a hard shove, he had sent him spinning once again into Rinaldo's arms. Rinaldo had flung him back to Ignazio and Ignazio to Vittorio. On and on, from one brother's arms to another's, and with each turn, the push had become a little rougher, the hold on Gian's shoulders a little tighter. At one point in the nightmare circle, one of the brothers had dealt Gian a sharp blow to the nape, making his neck lash back at an unnatural angle, making his eyes roll white in his head. Caught up in their drunken frenzy, none of them had noticed how Gian's body had suddenly crumpled in their hands, or how his head had begun to loll about like a broken puppet's. It was only when he'd slipped through their fingers and fallen into a heap on the grass that they'd stopped and looked, their heavy lids blinking stupidly in the moonlight, and realized what they'd done.

Then had come the sordid business of disposing of the body. (Vittorio cringed like a guilty mongrel whenever he thought of it.) It was he, the eldest, who had flung Gian across his shoulder and carried him through the trees to the shed at the edge of the orchard. Rinaldo and Ignazio had followed behind, darting from shadow to shadow, mindlessly giggling at the absurdity of the game. Their brains still befogged with drink, their voices rising, then quickly hushing, they had argued disjointedly about the most expedient burial for the man who lay like a mound of rags at their feet. In the end, they had all agreed Vittorio's plan was the best. Carry the body away in a sack and, at the riverside, fill it up with stones, tie it securely, then heave it into the water. By the time the currents had torn the body away from its mooring in the clay of the riverbed and brought it bobbing to the surface, the water would have eaten at the flesh, rotting it beyond recognition, Gian's face a swollen blue mush and his painter's hands eroded to the bone.

The brothers had rooted around in the darkness of the garden shed till they'd found a large piece of rough sacking. It was not a bag, only a large rectangle of jute, the kind the workers placed beneath the olive trees at harvest. While Vittorio and Ignazio laid the corpse out on the cloth and began to roll him in it, Rinaldo cast about in the shadows, looking for a length of good, solid rope. In the end, they'd had to make do with a ball of twine. Winding it around and around Gian's body, they'd made a tidy package of him, a rolled rug, with a tuft of hair sticking out at one end and a pair of wedding slippers at the other. Vittorio had lifted Gian onto his shoulder once again and, with his brothers in tow, had set out for the river. They had crossed no one in the streets and alleyways between their villa and the Tevere, and no one had witnessed their awkward pantomime in the slippery mud of the bank. Having lain Gian among the reeds and the decaying fish, they had set about gathering rocks, their fine garments dragging in the duck shit and the muck. Vittorio knelt by the body, his knees sinking in the smelly soup of the riverbank, and worked stones between the layers of sacking, fitting them beneath the crisscrossed webbing of twine. At last, he had tied one rock to each of Gian's feet and one more to his neck. It was this heavy, awkward bundle of bone and stone that, in the end, they'd had to pick up and heave with a huge wrenching of their limbs into the fast water of the river. It had made a great splash that had risen up in a wave and caught the glimmer of the moon. Then the body had sunk into darkness.

Vittorio and his brothers had turned towards home, their

drunkenness washed cleanly from them, their hands smelling of nothing worse than fish.

It was only much later that it had occured to Vittorio they'd consigned their sister's lover to a watery grave without a prayer or the sign of the cross traced in mud upon his forehead.

At the door of San Clemente, Vittorio became conscious of the weight of the packages he held in his arms. Poisoned gifts were heavy, he decided, and best disposed of without delay. He raised his hand to the church door, and felt his heart falter within him. He could not bring death within these walls. And this fellow, Masaccio. He was not such a bad sort, after all. Perhaps he suspected nothing. Perhaps it was a mistake to make him die. He was about to turn on his heel when the door suddenly opened before him. It was Masaccio himself, wearing a weary look upon his face. Without another thought, Vittorio stepped up to him and reached out a murdering hand.

Wednesday 22 May

I have never killed anyone off before and I'm not sure I like it. Life is nothing but a crapshoot at the best of times, our coming and our taking off as incidental as the tossing of the dice. We carve out a place in time, we build houses, bring children into the world, plan and project, talk about tomorrow with a possessive, proprietorial smugness. But then, some blind, lumbering beast comes hurtling down the highway, or a vein explodes, a cancer spreads, and we are just one more on a long list of failed experiments. In my fiction, I never had a hand in this kind of arbitrary ending, resisted collusion with the absurd—my own small, personal revolt against the wanton gods—until now. So I am uneasy about this death, feel I've given over like some easy slut to violence, to casual slaughter, to meaninglessness.

At the same time, I am ashamed to admit I'm taking real delight in writing this novel. Unlike anything I have ever done before, it is at once historical romance, adventure story and mystery—genres I have hardly ever read, let alone written—and I find the constraints of the form paradoxically liberating. Like a good Scotch, it softens inhibitions without clouding discernment. For the past three days, since my return from Assisi, I have lost myself in Eloisa's metamorphosis and in the sordid details of Gianlucido's murder, and have barely cast a glance out the window at the hills, the sky, or a certain silhouette. The weather has suddenly turned cool, anyway, keeping most of us indoors and, even in the evening, I have not gone in search of company. Unwilling, perhaps, to come once again upon the cozy tableau of Magda and Për in a fireside tête-à-tête.

In keeping with my promise to refrain from imposing a fictional life on a most factual Masaccio, I still write only about characters of my own invention. The stories of Cecilia and Eloisa are now finished. The next chapters will therefore deal with San Salvi—Masaccio's rival, Masolino's affliction, the harrow and scourge of womankind. With this third character, all the elements of Masaccio's undoing will be in place. He will stand at the very edge of death, about to be killed off by the usual cabal: by himself, by the woman he knew, by the woman he did not know, by the man who envied him, and by the man who feared him. Dispatched by hate *and* by love, he will go, the poor, feckless, innocent artist, from this place of sorrow and darkness into realms of unending light.

Thursday 23 May

I cycled to the market in Montevarchi to replenish my supplies of grapes and cheese and bread and wine. They have sustained me, these ancient sacramental fruits of the work of human hands, through the teeming silence of my long sequestration. The clouds were low on the horizon when I set out before noon and I'd hoped to make it home again before the rains began. But as I was counting out the Euros for a few slices of prosciutto, I heard a crack, and saw the flash, and watched as great drops of rain splashed in the dust at my feet. Tucking my parcels inside my jacket, I cut through the marketplace, then ducked into a side street full of boutiques—stationers, milleners, antique and linen shops—and, at the very moment the skies opened up, found refuge in the recessed doorway of a bookstore. I was leaning against the shop window, struggling with the zipper on my jacket, my eyes turned toward the sky, when I caught a familiar perfume. Magda had come out of the shop and, standing right beside me, head down, was attempting to juggle her umbrella and the bulky package she held under one arm. I didn't say a word—couldn't, for the noisy pounding of my heart, and simply reached to take the package from her. She saw my hands, knew at once it was me, and waited a moment before raising her eyes to mine. And when she did, I could see they were wet with tears. She didn't say anything. Simply lay her head in the hollow of my shoulder and heaved a shuddering sigh.

"I thought you were gone," she said. "I was sure you'd left without saying goodbye."

I wanted to hold her against my heart and bury my face in her hair but the parcels were between us and all I could manage was an awkward one-armed hug. So I bent to kiss her on the cheek. She stood very still, eyes closed, while I breathed her in and then, in a slow, deliberate motion, she turned her mouth to mine.

It was a fumbled kiss, a botched embrace, a cruel parody of the one I'd rehearsed a thousand times. I kept thinking Për would suddenly appear, catching us in each other's arms (and I thought of you, Christie, of how she was the first woman I'd kissed since you've been gone), and there was nothing on my lips but terror. She sensed it, she pulled away and turned her attention to the umbrella. I wanted so badly to tap her gently on the shoulder and ask if we could maybe try again, if she would be so kind as to give me a second chance, but I could still taste the panic on my lips. Instead, I offered to buy her a coffee. I had to work hard to conceal my disappointment when she told me she was sorry, she had to meet Për in a restaurant in a neighbouring street—they'd planned to finish up the final draft of the concluding chapter over lunch.

"Final draft?" I asked, my voice carefully casual in spite of my leaping heart. "Who's writing a book?"

She looked at me with surprise. "Didn't you know?" she asked. "Didn't I tell you? Për and I have been trying to put the finishing touches to this thing for the last year or so. And now, it's finally done and we can at last go our separate ways."

A savage joy ran through me then and I had to fight to suppress the idiotic, adolescent exclamations that were bursting like fireworks in my brain: They're not lovers! They're just colleagues! Planning a book together! A book, you simpleton, not a life, not even a six-week holiday in Tuscany! Nothing but a lousy little book! But my smile must have given me away. Because she paused a moment before disappearing beneath her open umbrella, she gave me a soft look and said, "I never meant for you to get the wrong impression." And then she was gone.

~

I walked home in the pelting rain. I was halfway down the road to the villa when I remembered the bicycle I'd left in the stand by the marketplace. I had no hat, no scarf, no gloves, and within five minutes, I was soaked through to the skin. It was cold, too, and quite windy and my thoughts flew around in my head like so many screaming storm birds. I was full of vague, ominous feelings—that old familiar sadness—pierced now and then by a bright yellow shaft of hope.

George caught sight of me from an upstairs window and rushed out to meet me with an umbrella. It was too late for that, but I appreciated the gesture. I was shaking with the cold and he was the one warm thing in an otherwise chilled and desolate landscape. He bustled me off to my room and ran a hot bath while I struggled out of my wet clothes. Wrapped in a towel, but still shaking, I dug out my suitcase and found the plaid flannel pyjamas Nick had packed for me, that long ago day in April. He'd ignored my protests, insisted I'd be glad to have them, assured me that fireplaces and woollen blankets and, yes, even Scotch, don't cut it against springtime dampness. Hugging them gratefully to my chest, I made my way to the bathroom, dropped everything and slipped into the tub. As I sank my livid, trembling limbs into the steaming water, I heard George moving in the next room and then the door closing softly behind him.

I don't know how long I'd been soaking before he reappeared with a couple of glasses in his hand. He'd made us a grog, he said, with hot water, lemons and brandy. He placed one glass for me on the edge of the tub, and settled with a contented sigh into an armchair outside the bathroom door. "Just what the doctor ordered," he called out. "And as for me, well, what the hell." And then he launched into a monologue punctuated with frequent interruptions. "So, Daniel, what do you think?" "And how does that strike you, Dr. Clevenger?" "Any comments you care to make, Daniel?" waiting, before resuming his lecture, for a sound, any sound, from me. I suppose he was afraid that, seduced by the heat and the insidious lethargy of strong liquor, I'd fall asleep in the bath. As it turned out, after a rather thorough disquisition on the growing threat of global warming—"we are the makers of our own misfortune, Daniel; it has our fingerprints all over it"—it's George who fell fast asleep, mouth gaping open, head thrown back against the hard edge of the armchair, glass precariously balanced in a very slack hand. I covered him up with a blanket, then settled into bed with this notebook and a pen and a very strong urge to sleep.

Castiglioncello

Saturday 25 May

Impossible as it is to believe, I seem to have run away again.

I am sitting at a terrace, overlooking the sea. Palm trees rustle in the wind off the water, there is a sailboat moored a short distance from the beach and, from here, I can see Kenneth loading the dinghy with the day's provisions. The sky looks promising, Delft blue strafed with lines of stunningly white cirrostratus. The sea, from the terrace, appears calm but on closer inspection will reveal itself to be cunningly pleated with wave. The smell is exactly right. Salt and iodine with, in its underbelly, the pungent aroma of fish. Also tanning oil and sunscreen and somehow, somewhere, the citrus burst of lime. I am still reeling from a late, late night. The sun seems rather brighter than necessary, and the gulls wheeling around this stretch of sand screech with astonishing, hysterical stridency. Like storm birds. Screaming and thrashing with visions of things to come.

~

I woke in a cold sweat in the middle of the night. It took me a minute to find my bearings, coming, as I was, from a long way off, but then I immediately remembered George. Opening wide eyes against the darkness of the room, I looked for him among the shadows of the far wall and saw, at once, that he was gone. I hadn't heard him leave. He'd folded up the blanket and left the room without disturbing my sleep. Settling down into the warmth of my bed, I was thinking of George and his good, generous male heart, when I felt the chill of my dream come over me once again. Something deep inside of me broke, a strangled sob rose up in my throat and I buried my face in my hands.

We were walking a treacherous path in a dense forest—boreal, rain or the black spruce bogs of the north?—moving between lakes, or jungle lodges or rivers, and the sky at both ends of the trail was clear of cloud and blue. But it was wet in the forest we were hiking through, the rain was steady and cold, and the path we were walking ran like a river around our ankles. Our boots were soaked through and, with each step, we could feel the squish of our sodden woollen socks, the water drenching our feet by turns warm and then miserably cold. Beneath our soles, the clay had turned to soap. Eroded by the rains, the mud ran thick and yellow as though the earth was bleeding, as though its flesh had been cut, a vein laid open and the hemorrhage would never cease. My eyes riveted on

Christie's back—it was her, it could only be her—I watched as her boots slipped and churned through the mire, as her knees buckled under the weight of her pack, as she wrenched her body to avoid a fall. I could see her rain gear was of no more use to her—could feel the cold wetness of the skin of her neck spreading in shudders to her shoulders, the shiver of her scalp beneath the mat of dripping hair.

As I watched her take each measured step, I became aware of a turmoil of emotions within me. Solicitude and love, certainly, but also an almost panicky sense of urgency, the need to reach out to her and help her, take her by the arm and steady her through the most perilous passages, lift the load off her shoulders and take it on my own, pick her up in my arms and carry her to the open blue space beyond. At the same time, I knew I was helpless. My arms, my love, my strength could avail her no more. As if to prove it, she began to move away from me, her stained, hooded figure disappearing around turns in the trail, growing smaller and smaller as the distance between us increased till she finally stopped at the edge of the blue. There, she turned around on the trail to take one last look behind her. Desperate to catch up with her, I ran though the bush, the mud flying in spreading splashes around me, my pack caroming off trees and flinging me from side to side as my feet slid and my ankles twisted in the runny brown muck of the path. Though I ran fast, my breath coming hard, the tears carving warm streaks on my chilled skin, she stayed always beyond my reach. My body ached, my lungs were bursting, my heart crashed around in my chest. Then everything went still as I watched her raise her head against the rain and look at me. Though I stared and squinted and strained, though my eyes burned as bright as torches in the dark, I realized with a bone-chilling grief that I could not see her face.

I woke from the dream as from a fever. I searched the shadows of the room, wondered at my beating heart and waited for the sorrow.

~

When I walked out onto the terrace of the villa, it came to me with a shock that it was long past mid-morning. The sun was out, the mist had risen off the vines, the day promised to be warm and yellow. The old professors had dragged out the chairs from beneath the dripping arbour and sat beneath the crisp blue vault of the sky, or walked on the edge of the gardens, the round toes of their shoes pearled with heavy dew. I was wondering how I was going to spend the day—how, for that matter, I would survive the next hour with such a wobbly, wooden heart, when I saw Magda coming through the trees, her sandled feet jewelled with water drops, her hair loose around her shoulders. And I knew I couldn't face her.

I was about to turn and go back into the villa when I saw a car come up the drive. It was an aqua Alfa Romeo with the top down. The woman at the wheel wore big sunglasses and a bright blue kerchief wrapped tightly round her head. Though her hair was concealed and I couldn't see her eyes, I recognized her burnished, beach-brown face at once.

She'd come to find me. Had spent a few days in Siena and, that morning, as she was about to leave, she'd remembered the Canadian she'd met in a trattoria in Florence. So she'd taken a drive to see if she could ferret me out and drag me off with her for a weekend by the sea. From the corner of my eye, I could see Magda standing by a table beneath the arbour, watching me as I talked with this lovely stranger, and recoiling a little when I climbed into the car beside her. As Sandy pulled a U-turn in the drive, I smiled sheepishly at the gathering on the terrace and raised my hand in a vague salute. And I left as I was: with a heavy heart, with chinos and loafers and a cotton sweater slung over my shoulders.

As we headed toward Castellini, she turned to me and asked who the redhead was. And should we have brought her along. I shook my head, my eyes glazed over, a painful grin frozen on my face. We didn't speak again till we reached the coast.

~

The drive was better than I'd imagined. Sandy likes speed, and the wind on my face had a bracing, cathartic effect. As we followed the curving road down towards the sea, I sensed the change in the air, the mellow golden light of the Tuscan countryside becoming starker, more diffuse, almost granular with brine. We drove deeper and deeper into the salty white light, while, behind us, the hills folded one upon the other, swallowing up the road, the vineyards and the villa *Saena Julia*. I closed my eyes, bent my face to the whip of the wind and felt relief flood through me, like in the aftermath of a narrow escape.

Over lunch, she explained about my thumb. Fifteen days ago, at the restaurant in Florence, she'd noticed the peculiar angle of my thumb—the overextended metacarpal, the sharp jut of the bottom knuckle—and thought she'd recognized wealth. I looked, she said, *expensive,* and since she was pathologically attracted to money, she'd tried to win me over.

I gazed into her violet eyes, considered her clothes, her car, her villa, her long *farniente* beneath the Italian sun, smiled and told her, in that case, we'd both been deceived. She grabbed me by my rich man's thumb and squeezed it tight. "No, no," she said, her laughter spilling around us like smoky red wine. "It wasn't for me. It was for my project. How does Jean-Pierre put it? *Mon péché mignon....*" Two weeks ago—on the evening of the day we'd met—she'd hoped I'd come to the fundraiser she was throwing in the ballroom of the Grand Hotel.

"Come on," she said, pushing away from the restaurant table. "I'll explain."

We walked all afternoon beneath the hazy circle of the sun. The waters of the Ligurian flicked at my feet and at the hem of Sandy's dress, tossed up flecks of yellow foam, garlands of seaweed, the broken glass and shattered wood of countless human dreams. The gusts of wind caught in the lido chairs and fanned them out like sails, the rigging sang on the swaying masts and the birds flew out to sea. A child with dark curls and shiny brown skin chased the waves and screamed.

"My faith," Sandy said, "is in people."

"Your gods, then, are neither immortal nor infallible."

"Why waste my worship on perfect gods?"

"Why worship an undeserving god?"

"It's by my worship he is made deserving. By my sacrifice he is made whole."

"Your god is a very lucky man."

"Child, you mean. Woman. And man."

And this is how, on a windswept stretch of Italian beach, in the early days of the post-Renaissance, post-Christian, post-humanistic twenty-first century, I stumbled upon philanthropy in the guise of a small, tough, worldly-wise blonde. And blushed to think of my useless words, my childish loves, my crass and bare-faced selfishness.

~

Her guests are all gone. Only Kenneth is left, and he flies to Nairobi tomorrow. Last night, Sandy threw a farewell party for him and, as I moved among her friends, listening, smiling and drinking too much, I learned a number of fascinating things. Sandy's project, first of all, is Kenneth. He's a virologist working in an AIDS clinic in Nairobi. While he bends over a microscope in the African heat, his sister raises money among her well-connected friends to underwrite his research, to fly him home between six-month stints, to give hope to a dying world. I also learned most of the money she bankrolls comes from her ex-lovers and husbands—four of whom happened to be in the room last night. I met these handsome gentlemen, some young, some not so young, all of them urbane and well-heeled, all of them clearly in love, who kept talking in glowing terms about the very same woman. It took me only a minute to figure out who she was.

Kenneth tells me that it's the quality of her attention. She listens, he says, with a very attentive heart, she listens and remembers. When she moves on, the men she loved feel lost at sea, calling and calling and no one there to answer.

Kenneth and I stayed up late, talking about Nairobi. And I'm not sure, this morning, what, in the effulgence and largesse of liquor, I may have promised him—what amount of money, how much time committed, what peace of mind forever sacrificed. He told me about the African dawn, and the earth so dry it crackles with the sound of fire, the skies so loud they thrum with animal voice. And he set up a longing in me for the thin sleek cats and their jungle spots, for the tribal manes and the beads and the drums, for the zeal that burns on the edge of night, pushing with linked arms and hands against the onslaught of the dark.

This afternoon, later, now, I will ask him what I offered to give and be amazed, or ashamed, at the dimensions of my unthinking heart.

Villa Saena Julia
Sunday 26 May

I am sitting here, in my room, with ice packs pressed to my lip and my groin, listening carefully through the walls for angry voices or slamming doors. The boys who gave me a lift home were a tad rowdy after the game. Their blaring car horn and cheers and laughter most certainly broke through the professors' snores. I'm sure I'll hear about it tomorrow.

Though my head is still full of the smell of the sea, and my blood still rocks with its dip and swell, I find myself once again in the fold of the Tuscan hills. I have brought with me a thousand images of the ocean and the strand, of the fishing boats and the nets, of the olive-limbed children who rise out of the surf and lift their hands to the sun. We sailed till nightfall yesterday, watched the birds cut across the deepening sky, spreading darkness beneath their wings, watched one star bleed and another star glow. We didn't speak, our hands busy with the sheets and the halyards, our lips burning with the sting of salt, our eyes full of indigo heaven. It's only when we slipped into shore, releasing the lines and the stays and gathering the sails in our arms that I remembered to ask.

"What," I said, "did I promise you, Kenneth, when that bourbon ran like water in my veins?"

He looked at me in surprise, checked a smile and said, "Your life, man, nothing less than your life."

I thought a moment, then replied, "So how soon can I begin?"

But Sandy heard me. She dropped the rope she was coiling, stepped into the fringe of wave at the shore and came to stand beside her brother. She peered at me through the darkness, her mouth set, her eyes severe, and said, "So what are you running away from this time, Clevenger?"

And I knew the game was up.

~

Kenneth went to bed early. The wind, he said, had played him out and tomorrow was a travelling day. We had a last drink together, exchanged addresses and said goodbye. In the morning, I would be gone before he woke.

Sandy and I were left alone. We broke out the Marsala, settled into loveseats and faced each other across a wide divide.

"So," she said. "It appears I was wrong about you. You are not as rich as your thumb seems to claim, you believe in God and mistrust man, you are not only not unattached, but deeply and completely in love with two women at the same time."

I closed my eyes and nodded.

"So what's the problem?" she asked. "Just choose one."

I placed my elbows on my knees, folded my hands beneath my chin and looked her in the eye. "Oh, but I have, Sandy," I said. "I already have."

"So what are you waiting for?"

"The homecoming."

"And in the meantime?"

"Precisely."

That's when she stood up, wrapped her pashmina more tightly around her shoulders and nudged me over with her hip. She sat down beside me, leaned with all her weight against my heart and said, "Let me tell you a story."

It went something like this. When she was twelve years old, she died. A routine appendectomy, but someone made a mistake with the anaesthesia and, for a few minutes, she was gone. She experienced it all, she said: the tunnel, the white light, the sense of peace, the inexpressible love. And then, she saw her grandmother's hands. She recognized them right away, their gnarled joints, their parchment skin, the soft pink curve of their palms. They were open, but not to receive. They reached out, but not to take hold. Gently, the way one releases a bird, they pushed her back into the world. The next thing she knew, she was staring up into her mother's anxious face.

"An ordinary story," Sandy said. "A common occurrence."

"But it marked you for life."

"Why?"

"Because it's comfort for the heart."

"How?"

"It proves that we're not alone. That death is life on another plane. That our deceased loved ones hover nearby, watching over us. That they are not indifferent to our struggle. That there is only a thin veil between this world and the other."

"A membrane," Sandy said. "A dark glass."

"A fold in the fabric of time."

"And so, I learned, at twelve years of age, this adventure we call life is exactly that. A side trip, a day excursion, a quick plunge into the physical world. Our real purpose—our real life—lies elsewhere."

"And what is the nature of that place, do you think?"

"I don't think," Sandy said. "I know. Because I felt it. I was filled, I was suffused with it."

"With light?" I asked.

"No," she said. "With love. A love so great, so pervasive, everything on this earthly plane pales into insignificance."

I took a minute to consider this. And then I said, "Our sorrow?"

"A passing cloud on the face of the sun."

"Our pain?"

"A tiny sliver beneath the skin."

"Our love?"

"A blind fumble in the dark."

By this time, she was curled up against me, her head tucked into my shoulder. She folded her legs beneath a length of her shawl, moved in a bit closer, and soon was drowsy with the warmth. Before drifting off completely, she reached one hand to my face, stroked my cheek with her fingertips and said, "Let her go, Dan. You're keeping her here against her will."

And then she slept, while I sat still beside her and opened wide eyes on the night.

~

When I woke up, the sun was coming through the French doors with a tentative May morning kind of light, and the air was filled with the cries of hungry gulls. At some point during the night,

Sandy had placed a cushion behind my head and covered me up with a blanket. My back was sore, my neck was stiff, I needed a shower and a shave, but the sea was there, just beyond the window, and the smell of coffee was everywhere.

Sandy and I sat in the sunshine, drinking latte, eating *sticciata* and licking the taste of orange blossoms from our fingers. She was wrapped in a white terry-towel robe and her hair was a dark, sleek cap worn tight against her skull. She asked me if I'd dreamt. I told her, No. She asked where I was going. I told her, Home. Good, she said. And she looked at me with those *pervenche* eyes, one eyebrow cocked in query. I told her No, again, and promised, I'm not going to run anymore.

By the time I stood on the highway, my deceitful thumb up in the air, the sun had heaved itself up over the tops of the trees and sat there throbbing, a yellow, pulsing star. At my insistence—it was her last day with Kenneth; the next time they'd see each other again, it would be Christmas in Manhattan—Sandy dropped me off on the S68. The first car to pick me up—an older man in a vintage Spider—took me all the way to Volterra. But from there, I had to walk. It was Sunday, the tourists were crowding into the cathedrals and the village churches to hear Mass, the families were lingering around the breakfast table, making the morning last with laughter and desultory talk. I could hear the soft voices through the open shutters of the houses I passed, hear the clatter of cutlery and the thud of plates on tabletops and I felt it, the sudden stab of nostalgia, the reeling homesickness that always tastes of tears. I was the outsider, a passing figure on a morning road, looking in with envy on a happiness I, too, had known, but somehow misplaced.

About mid-afternoon, a car full of young men in soccer jerseys slowed to pick me up. They were good-looking kids with the healthy glow of athletes and the easy camaraderie of teammates. They piled up on the backseat to give me room, and smiled and nodded, their gleaming dark eyes full of friendly curiosity. Each of them tried out their English on me, singing lines from American pop songs, or reciting slogans from advertising jingles, and I attempted a few phrases in very bad Italian. One of them asked me a question, probably in dialect. I thought, for some obscure reason, he wanted to know my age. I told him, and the whole bunch of them laughed uproariously. As it turned out, he was asking my name. So for the rest of the day, they called me Fifty-two.

We stopped at a field on the outskirts of Siena. I tried to explain that it was time for me to head home, but they pretended not to understand, insisted the game would be a short one and promised to drive me to the villa after it was over. Before I knew it, I was outfitted in shorts, shin guards and somebody's ragged old cleats. They barely had enough players to field a team and needed another body on defence—so there I was, with my greying hair and my stiff joints, creaking through the stretches of a warm-up while, all around me, the boys ran and jumped and moved with the suppleness of panthers.

I touched the ball twice during the game, both times in weak passes to the mid-fielder. The rest of the time, I watched with amazement as the boys moved the ball around with an easy, consummate skill, using their feet better than most of us can use our hands. I cheered the good plays of both teams, which earned me a few glowering glances from our side, and clapped and whistled whenever the ball was kicked home. More of a delighted spectator, really, than a player, I stumbled into the thick of things a number of times and took a couple of hits for my trouble. A forward and I collided as he leapt in the air to head a ball and my bottom lip split on contact with his chin. Later, I foolishly lunged for the ball with my right leg, did a modified splits and pulled a groin muscle. That one sidelined me at last, and I was able to watch the rest of the game from the safety of the bleachers, feeling oddly redeemed, somehow, the throbbing pain from my wounds filling me with grim satisfaction.

"Bravo, *Signore*," the boys kept saying as I hobbled to the car. "Good game, Fifty-two." And with the back of their hands, they kept trying to wipe away the blood splattered on my jersey.

We ended up at a sports bar in Siena, where fiery-eyed *signorinas* made much of my swollen lip. They gave me ice for my injuries and wine for my soul and, while the young men flirted with the girls and the old men shouted and raised their fists at the TV screens, I was treated to plate after plate of piping hot pastas and sauces, of mushrooms and salamis, of breads fragrant with garlic and butter. As I ate, I listened to the Italian surging around me in waves of rich, unctuous sound, I watched the expressions—the pouting lips, the histrionic shrugs, the eloquent hands—I watched the boys move in on their women, the sultry slash of their mouths, their hungry lips, their beseeching eyes. And at that moment, I wanted more than anything to be twenty-two again, to be the local soccer star, to be Italian and to be in love.

It was quite late when they finally agreed to take me home. The driver had had his share to drink, and his girl sat close beside him, her soft muzzle pressed into his sweat-streaked neck. More than once, I thought my final hour had come, I thought I would breathe my last in a spectacular wreck on an Italian highway in the heavy nighttime musk of wild Tuscan lilies. And how surprised everyone would be, I thought, to discover amongst the long, light bones of the young my old flesh, my hollow grey fossils, the sunken pools of my eyes.

We raced up the villa's drive and stopped in the screaming scrunch of gravel. The lads leaned on the car horn, sang loud snatches of "Fratelli d'Italia," while the girls touched their pulpy mouths to my broken lip. I clambered out of the car, shook hands through the windows, then limped off to the side of the road. The car wheeled around in a wide circle, all four tires screeching against stone and sending up spinning wreaths of dust. I stood and watched them from the top of the drive, a stupid smile on my face, my bloodied jersey in my hands.

And now I am too full of adrenaline and grappa to sleep. My groin hurts like a bitch and my lip bleeds every time I grimace with the pain. So while I sit here, slowly numbing with the ice, I will try to catch the images that rise up in me unbidden and flash before my eyes like sunlight glancing off seaglass. And instead of dreaming, I will spin a tale made of seashore and sea wind, of simmering desire and slow surrendering, of hard lust and harder hate.

SAN SALVI

XV

DURING THE SUPPER AT THE INN, SAN SALVI HAD BEEN TREATED with the derision masters usually reserved for their ignorant *garzoni*. Since he had not served an apprenticeship as a young boy, he had never been on the receiving end of that special brand of humiliation before. The experience had been decidedly unpleasant. While the other painters had contributed comments and questions to the masters' discussions, San Salvi, for his part, had not been able to place a word. Masolino had continually interrupted him, or glared him down, and, with a sickening, fawning look upon his face, had turned again and again towards Masaccio to ask his opinion or simply to smile on him, an infuriating, avuncular smile. San Salvi had wanted to smash him in the mouth. By the time the serving girl had brought around the bread and honey, he had had enough. Without saying a word to anyone, he'd left the inn and made his way back to the cathedral.

A few assistants would still be at work. While they prepared the wall and moved the scaffolding in place for the next *giornate*, he would concentrate on drawing sketches of the Annunciation, the very scene Masaccio had stuttered and stumbled over earlier that day. In the morning, when the masters arrived at the church, he would show them the work he had tossed off during the night and, like the Pope before Giotto's "o," they would be forced to recognize its superiority. He would be given the commission and Masaccio, the rough painter from the hills, would be sent back to his wilderness.

San Salvi's talent was, like everything else about him, a lying, cheating thing. His vocation as a painter had not been the result of some deep, undeniable necessity, but had simply been the means by which he'd hoped to keep his life safe. Born in Santa Marinella, a fishing village outside of Civitavecchia, he had spent his life as a child and a young man casting nets into the Tyrrhenian sea. He'd been a beautiful boy, strikingly different from the scrawny children who fought the gulls for fish scraps down on the water front, their spindly arms and legs flailing like sticks among the bird wings, their misshapen heads bobbing on the shore like wooden floats out on the sea. His body was solid and square and his limbs gleamed like polished oak. In his olive complexion, the even row of his little white teeth made a startling smile that won mothers over, that made them think of milk and of small, sweet mouths tugging at their nipples. The village women loved to run their fingers through the heavy curls on his brow. They would push away their own children to take him in their arms and press his dark head to their breast.

San Salvi was very young when he discovered the power of his black eyes. They were smouldering, sullen stars that gazed out on the world in mild reproof. Those he looked upon with his dark, reproachful eyes invariably felt stricken with some vague remorse and quickly took the blame. San Salvi was never punished, or found fault with, he was never lonely, or afraid, was denied nothing and forgiven everything. Sometimes, when it was time for his brothers and sisters to spread the great fish nets on the strand and wear the skin off their fingers weaving and knotting the coarse fibres of the mesh, or when, hour after hour, they lifted their young arms to hang small fishes in the sun to dry, sometimes, on those days, San Salvi would slip away unseen. He would run down to the northern cove where the clampickers' children lived, throw off his tunic and fling himself into the surf that came crashing there on a small heel of beach. Playing among the waves, as free as a young seal, he'd spend the day diving beneath the surface to search out with wide, salt-stung eyes the seashells and starfish that clung to the tide-swept sand. And as the sea receded, he would linger in the pools warmed by the sun and pluck with small fingers at the scuttling fish the ocean had left behind. All the day, while his brothers' arms streamed with sweat and his sisters' palms grew raw with weaving, he would let the sun burnish his young body and the ocean dance him upon its back. When he'd return at dusk, the shine of his black curls dulled with sea salt and every fold in his skin rimed with white, his father would look at him with thunder in his brow but never say a word. Young San Salvi would gaze up into his father's lined face, his dark eyes gleaming their silent reproach and, before long, he would feel the old man's rough fingers in his hair. And when at the evening meal, in the very face of his brothers' hunger, he looked with longing eyes at the last piece of bread or the largest slice of golden squash, his mother would slap away the weary hands that reached for it and give it instead to her black-eyed son.

It was because of his beautiful eyes that laziness was never beaten out of him. Though he loved the fisherman's life—the rocking of the sea beneath his feet, the spill of early-morning sunlight on the dark face of the water, the wind and the sun and the salt upon his lips—he loved drinking and carousing and making love to other men's wives even more. At the hour when the village men were setting out for a night's fishing, San Salvi was still in his house, oiling his hair and his skin and polishing his teeth, preparing for a night's revelry. And while he drank red wine and bedded young girls, night turned into day, summer into fall, and his boats and nets rotted on the shore. When hunger forced him at last to take to the sea again, he preferred to risk death by borrowing other people's boats and stealing from other people's nets than to put in an honest day's work. The women who lay with him behind their husband's back did so because they found him irresistible, of course, but also because they knew—as San Salvi knew perfectly well himself—his cheating days were numbered. If the plague had not swept out of the east to save him, he would have been found dead among the seaweed, a stiletto slipped between his ribs.

It was a rat that jumped ship somewhere up the Ligurian coast that carried the flea of death to Civitavecchia. When the fevers and the chills first declared themselves in the winter of 1400, the villagers believed they had fallen under the influence of an unusual conjunction of planets. But what they took to be the innocuous, if uncomfortable, symptoms of influenza soon metamorphosed into the nastier characteristics of plague. At midday, old men came staggering out of their houses, blind with pain, their armpits and groin thick with throbbing ganglions, the skin of their face a mass of congested pustules. And as they writhed in the dust of the roadway, convulsing like poisoned dogs, women gathered their children about them and ran into the woods to hide. San Salvi, more afraid of disfigurement than he was of death, abandoned his mother and sisters to their fate and took to the sea in a borrowed fishing boat. He planned to wait out the slaughter at a safe distance, cured and pickled in ocean brine.

He barely survived the fever when it finally fell upon him. Dehydrated and delirious, with fresh water in short supply, with no one to hold his head to help him drink, he nearly succumbed to its ravages. Lying in the bottom of the boat, its hard ribs digging into his back, he had spent many days and nights floating in and out of consciousness while the fishing skiff was pulled this way and that by the currents and the tides. When he'd swum up out of the darkness, like some monstrous deep-water fish rising to the surface of the sea, he had stared out at the blank blue canvas of the sky or the star-encrusted night and felt death gaining on him. Burning with fever, he'd cried out in horror as he'd felt its icy grip around his ankles, its slithering chill coil around the long bones of his legs. That's when he'd begun to pray. His dry lips cracking as he murmured his *aves* and *paternosters*, his mouth full of the metallic taste of blood, he had invoked Mary and all the saints, he had begged Christ himself to save him from disfigurement and death. In return, San Salvi promised, his head pulsing with fever and his skin roiling with blisters, he would be a good son and brother, he would be an honest fisherman, he would stop fornicating and carousing, he would say his morning prayers and kneel by his bed at night, he would attend Mass, would receive communion, would ask forgiveness of all those against whom he had sinned. In spite of these solemn vows, the cold had kept rising through his flesh, flicking at his heart and squeezing at his throat, while some wicked, fallen sun filled his skull with blazing fire. And so he'd promised more. If God rescued him, he vowed to spend the rest of his life bearing witness to His greatness. He would become a painter committed to depicting the marvels of God's love on all the walls of Christendom. His hands and his heart, he promised, would become God's instruments, to do with as He pleased.

On the morning of the seventh day of the fever, San Salvi opened his eyes on the pitiless gaze of the sun and knew he would live. He ate and he drank, and he watched as the pustules on his body broke, bled water and dried. Then, with trembling arms, he rowed to land.

He was met by offshore winds that carried to his nostrils the smell of putrefaction and the stench of burning flesh. The villages north and south of Santa Marinella had been devastated by the plague and nothing moved there among the houses but fire, the only living thing to cast a shadow beneath the sun. As San Salvi ran from the line of pyres burning along the coast, he saw the black smoke curling at his back and imagined it was the dark arms of all the women he had lain with reaching out to hold him. In those wreathing fumes, all the laughing girls he'd kissed, their high, sweet voices dead in their throats. What a waste, he'd thought. That beautiful, yielding, hungry flesh. Gone to rot and ashes. Then he'd imagined the throngs of young women, untouched by disease or death, who awaited him in Rome and, turning his back on the fouled sea, made inland for God and all His earthly pleasures.

✣

It was easy to locate the painters in the workshops and the inns of Rome, easier still to win their trust. They were a faceless lot, underfed and underpaid, but guileless and quick to warm to praise. San Salvi would seek them out in the dim halls of hostelries where they sat in a lump with the carters and the grooms and, sharing in their cheese soups and their cheese pies, would draw them into conversation. In a very short time, he had picked up their jargon and understood a thing or two about technique. He had also commmitted to memory the names of the most illustrious painters of the day, and the locations of the most notable Roman frescoes. Above all, he had acquired from his association with these rough and tumble artisans a respect for work well done. He spent hours in the churches of Rome, copying and recopying details of the great mediaeval frescoes on pieces of parchment purloined from nearby workshops. He hung about work sites, eavesdropping on patrons' recommendations and masters' instructions, watching carefully as tradesmen prepared plaster and assistants ground pigment. He haunted the ateliers of the city, identified the young lions—the brightest stars, the most promising talents—and devoted himself to picking their brains and stealing their drawings.

He'd had doubts, at first, about the necessity of all this. About the binding nature of his promise to the Lord. But as he'd learned more about the trade, had come to appreciate the articulateness of a simple line of charcoal, he'd found pleasure, despite his resolutely carnal tastes, in pursuing the shadowy images of his mind. It was exacting work, requiring a discipline that was totally foreign to his temperament. It was also physically demanding, drawing relentlessly on the diminished strength his disease had left as legacy. But whenever he threw up his hands in frustration, or grew impatient with the painstaking nature of the work, he would recall the scantily clad young nymphs he'd glimpsed through the arched windows of the city's workshops—the round young women who sat as models for the apprentices' lessons—and he would feel his resolve harden. He was determined, then, to be counted among the painters of the city, and, through stealth and deceit and a smattering of talent, even hoped one day to figure prominently among them.

While his arrogance and his large portfolio of (mostly) stolen drawings allowed him, in time, to pass himself off as an eminent painter from the north, he found, to his surprise, that a reputation as a great lover was rather more difficult to establish. Putting it down to his newness to Rome and to the worldly wariness of big-city women, he did not at first consider that their aloofness might have anything to do with him. It was only after he'd been repeatedly cold-shouldered and turned away from with distaste that it had occurred to him to have a look in the mirror. He knew the fever had eroded the flesh off him like the ocean eats the shore, and he remembered, too, that after his illness, hanks of his hair had fallen out in handfuls. But it was only the day he'd studied his reflection in a sheet of polished metal in a goldsmith's shop that he'd been able to measure the full extent of the damage.

At first glance, he had not recognized his face. His eyes, most of all, had undergone the most profound alteration: the shining black stars that had lit up his figure with a dark lustrous gleam were now two dull pewter disks. They were large and lifeless, two cold stones set deeply in the bony pockets of his face. His thin hair hung around his scrawny forehead and cheeks, lanky lengths devoid of curl or shine or sway. The skin on his jaw lay slack, small sagging pouches marring the fine, hard line of his chin. And he was of an ashen colour, his golden body turned grey like the burned bodies of his young seashore lovers, and his white teeth had gone black. As he held the plate of metal between his shaking hands, tilting it to catch the sun, he saw with a gasp of horror that the skin of his face was no longer smooth and clean as an apple peel, but was as pitted and pockmarked as an ocean sponge.

His heart broke as he took in the depth and breadth of the ravages. Turning away from the shop in the marketplace, he let his empty grey gaze fall to the ground and wished himself dead. Wished Brigitta's husband had caught them the last time, had gone into a frenzied rage and stabbed him between the shoulders even as he lay upon her. He wished a fishbone had stuck in his gullet as the cooking fire had burned low on the beach and the sun had sunk into the sea, and the taste of bread and olives from Simonetta's lips still lingered in his mouth. He wished the current had grabbed him as he swam too far from shore, had pulled him down and held him there, turning his big black eyes to jelly. He wished the fever had nailed him to the bottom of the boat and left his bones to bleach beneath the burning midday sun. And he wished now that the earth beneath his feet would open wide its yawning gullet and swallow him up in darkness.

He found his way home and threw himself down upon his bed. Taking neither food nor drink, he lay there for three days and three nights, rigid upon his bed of husks, one arm thrown across his ugly face. Despite his best efforts to will himself dead, he discovered instead that there lay within him a frighteningly stubborn desire to live. To possess, to command and to conquer. When he rose on the evening of the third day, leaned upon the windowsill of his room and turned his face to the wind and the first stars, his mind was made up. Though men would look upon him and cringe and women flee from his touch, there was no power beneath the sun that would keep him from obtaining what he wanted. Men's respect and women's favours, fame and glory and praise, he would wrest it all, even from the most unwilling hands.

XVI

POOR SLUT, HE THOUGHT. BAREFOOT AND ALONE IN A STRANGE city. Oh well. It would teach her to go lusting after fame like a bitch in heat. San Salvi gathered up the shreds of his drawing, picked up the piece of charcoal and stood there, weighing it in the palm of his hand. He thought of the sketch of the Annunciation he had gone to the chapel to work on earlier in the evening. He had had the time to draw only a few lines before Cecilia had walked in and turned his thoughts to revenge. He did not feel like drawing now, but curiously enough, felt more vindictive than ever. His fingers closed upon the vial of poison he had taken from the girl. He doubted very much it could kill a man, but perhaps it contained enough venom to seriously sicken. Young Masaccio sidelined by a prodigious case of indigestion would throw Masolino into a panic. The cold season was nearly upon them, the Cardinal was growing impatient, the master would not have time to send to Siena or Pisa or Florence for some other famous painter. He would have to rely on the talent he'd had here in Rome, before Masaccio's arrival.

Namely, San Salvi, who waited, poised like a cat in the shadows, waiting for a chance to prove his worth.

San Salvi knew Masaccio would still be at the inn. When he'd left earlier in the evening, wine was being poured liberally, talk was running high, he was sure the two old friends would drink to themselves till early dawn. While they clinked cups and plotted their immortality, San Salvi would make a visit to their rooms. He would leave a small token of friendship by Masaccio's bed. A few fruits, a skin of wine. That handsome girl, that Miuccia, would be there to let him in. If she was alone, San Salvi thought, and if she was halfway willing, he'd take her fast, up against the wall, her skirts bunched above her belly like the petals of a rose.

On the way to the Cardinal's palace, San Salvi entertained himself by imagining a grovelling Masolino, begging him to undertake the work a terribly ill Masaccio would be forced to give up. He quickened his pleasure by recalling, word by vitriolic word, the barbs and criticisms Masolino had cast his way in the space of one short day. The old man's patience had been cruelly tried by San Salvi's arrogant ways but until Masaccio had appeared on the scene, Masolino had suffered them in silence. The presence of his young friend had suddenly given him the confidence to speak his mind freely and he had not waited long to avail himself of the privilege. San Salvi could only imagine what it would be like in the days to come. The two of them, thick as thieves, praising and congratulating one another, laughing in private at their corny, bumpkin jokes, dismissing everyone's work but their own with an amused look and a wave of the hand.

San Salvi knew, as well, it would be impossible for him to conceal his meagre talents from Masaccio. He had a sharp eye, San Salvi gave him that much, and it would not take long for him to discover the truth about the tiresome assistant Masolino had been forced to take on.

✢

Miuccia appeared in the doorway as soon as he called out a greeting. San Salvi noticed she'd changed her gown. Instead of the blue one she'd worn at noon, snug at the waist and cut low on her breasts, she was dressed now in a kind of sack. A white muslin affair, tied with a drawstring at the throat and at the wrists, something prudish, something a nun might wear to bed. San Salvi suppressed a sigh of displeasure. When he lifted his eyes from Miuccia's bosom to her face, he saw that, unlike himself, she was suppressing nothing. Her whole expression was a study in mingled disappointment and disgust. He understood at once she'd been expecting someone else, and his appearance at her door, with his ugly face and his cutting tongue, filled her with a kind of despair.

Over time, he had become accustomed to that kind of reception on the part of women, had even learned to wait for it with a kind of perverse joy, but even he could not have guessed the depth of the revulsion he inspired in Miuccia. When he'd called to her from the doorway, she'd been lying in quiet wait, nursing a bruised and brimming heart. In the hours since she'd learned of Masaccio's betrayal, Miuccia had been feeding on very bitter fruit. Anger, rejection and the salty pulp of grief, they'd filled her mouth with their ashy taste and brought burning tears to her eyes. She had wept and sobbed and thrown herself about the place, she had beaten her breast and covered her face with her hair, she had hated, detested, loathed and despised and, in the end, she had come again to love. Oh, how she had loved. And so, hearing a man's voice at the door, she had run to greet Masaccio with forgiveness in her heart and love on her lips and had discovered in his place an ugly, vile rat of a man.

Everything about San Salvi made her shudder. But on this evening, when her emotions lay raw as freshly flayed skin, the very sight of him brought her heart to the edge of her lips. Her head began to spin. A sudden warmth filled her mouth and set her stomach churning. But when she saw one of San Salvi's small, vulgar hands spring out of its sleeve to steady her, she backed quickly out of its reach and willed away her queasiness. Raising the candle level with his face, and looking him directly in the eye, she forced herself to speak. "San Salvi. What do want from this house at such an hour of the night?"

"Forgive me for disturbing you, Miuccia. Even a blind man could see you are not well." He let his glance wander the length of her body, then raised one hand to show her what it held. "Look, Miuccia: Trebbiano, from Florentine vines. It is a gift of welcome for Masaccio—with humble love, from me to him.... But seeing you standing there, so shaky and pale, has given me a better idea." He held up the goatskin and waggled it obscenely in her face. "Why don't we drink it, you and I, and to hell with Masaccio?"

Miuccia made a tight knot of her arms and laid them hard against her chest. "Be gone with you, San Salvi. Masaccio wants none of your gifts, and nor do I."

"Now, now, Miuccia. I only want to make you smile.... Here. Take this for your old friend, and let it wait upon his return. He will be back at dawn—or sooner—if he tries the innkeeper's patience."

Miuccia's eyes grew wide with surprise. "Masaccio is still at the inn? And his wife? Does he keep her by his side while he drinks and talks the whole night through?"

"Wife? What wife?"

"I met a woman at the church. She told me she was Masaccio's wife."

San Salvi laughed darkly. "I also met a woman at the church. And I swear to you, she is nobody's wife—at least, not Masaccio's. Just some little tramp panting after fame. But I sent her on her way. She will not be bothering us again."

Miuccia grew thoughtful. That small, elegant lady a liar and a tramp? It seemed hardly possible. Having lived among artificers all of her life, masterful creators of illusion, she of all people should have known how deceiving appearances could be. She felt shame, now, at the thought that she had let herself be taken in by nothing more than a fine face. One elegantly turned phrase dropped from the lips of a "lady" and she had believed the worst of her own, dear Masaccio.

All at once, as the significance of San Salvi's words sunk in, she felt her heart swell with sweet relief. Masaccio was not married, Masaccio would still be hers to love. A changed woman, she now smiled upon San Salvi, pressed his arm with a warm hand. "Be assured I will give Masaccio your gift, San Salvi. Go now, and take with you his heartfelt thanks. And mine, San Salvi. And mine."

San Salvi looked at her and cocked an eyebrow. Some transformation had come over Miuccia and he wondered if it was too late to take advantage of this sudden softer mood. He stepped towards her, touched a thin finger to her cheek. She turned towards him with shining eyes, smiled kindly and caught the candle's flame between her fingers. When San Salvi raised a blind hand to touch her again, Miuccia had disappeared.

He stood a moment on the threshold, raised his eyes to the bloated moon and wished Masaccio's soul good passage. The man was as good as dead, he decided, and it would be up to him, San Salvi, to make sure Rome didn't mourn him long. Sniffing contentedly, he went on his way, immensely pleased at the thought that it sometimes sufficed, in this world where all is passing, to linger a little longer than the rest.

✣

Too excited to sleep, Miuccia lay in her bed and prayed. She prayed to Masaccio as though he were a god, entreating pardon and vowing to make amends. Today, when she first saw him, her first impulse had been to throw herself in his arms and to hold him close. Instead, she had let foolish pride rein in her heart and leave unspoken the words of love that had risen like a blessing to her lips. She had wanted to punish her sweet, absent-minded Masaccio for one night's forgetfulness, as though he were a stranger, as though she did not know he was the most easily distracted of men. And today, when a Jezebel had made her believe he had betrayed her by marrying another, she had gone so far as to entertain thoughts of murder. She kill Masaccio! She might as well turn the knife against herself. For Miuccia's life was all bound up with her love for the dear, bewildered man. Nothing else mattered. The seas could rear up and the skies rain down fire, the earth could split and the rivers dry up, she could go hungry and thirsty and be naked in the cold, as long as Masaccio's lean, lumbering shadow touched the edges of her life, she knew she would be whole. In his befuddled, endearing way, he'd stumbled into her very heart. And she held him there, like a chalice holds wine, and she was the altar and he, her perfect sacrament.

When she awoke at first light, the men had not returned. She guessed they had gone directly from the inn to the chapel in San Clemente without taking the time to wash or to eat. It was typical of them to round off a night of drinking and discussion with impassioned work at dawn. By mid-morning, the inspiration of the midnight hours would have worn off, they would be feeling the effects of wine and sleeplessness, and they would crumple into mindless heaps on the chapel floor. Miuccia had often seen them in that condition. She had been the one to slip a folded sack beneath their heads and lay a cloak across their shoulders and wait among the scaffolds and the bags of plaster for them to wake and eat the food she'd brought them. While she watched over them, she would gaze up at the work they'd executed in their exalted, overwrought state and every time, she would be stricken to her very soul by the wonder of their art. That is how she had come to know the gods that lived within them, and how she had come to understand that, for the gift of such grace, much could be forgiven.

She would go to the chapel this very morning and watch Masaccio work. He would not see her, he would have eyes only for the images inside his head, but when at last he'd break and fall to pieces, she would be there to gather him up in her arms. She would cradle his weary head, cover up his aching limbs, and wait upon his waking to feed him bread and wine. And today, it would not be the fruit of dusty Roman vines he'd drink, but Trebbiano, wine pressed from Tuscan grapes. Thanks to San Salvi, Miuccia would be able to give her bone-tired, yearning Masaccio the soft, sweet taste of home. His eyes widening with delight, he would smile at her, thank her for the gift and settle in her arms to sleep.

Wednesday 29 May
My lip is almost healed, my leg is feeling a little stronger. This morning, I bummed a ride to Montevarchi with the cook, parted company with her at the wine merchants and made my way to the marketplace. I found my bicycle exactly where I'd left it and pushed it through the streets and piazzas to the edge of town. Then, pedalling slowly, and keeping the s69 always in sight, I followed a secondary road through fields and vineyards till I came upon the cobblestoned streets of San Giovanni Valdarno. The door of No. 83 Corso Italia stood open, and I could hear voices echoing in the empty chambers of the house.

Masaccio's boyhood home has been converted into an art gallery that showcases local talent. Today, there were paintings in tempera and dry brush by a Luccan artist named Matteo Scaletta hanging on the walls of the three storeys of the house. I spent some time admiring them—amazingly detailed works of garden vegetation—while waiting for the other tourists to move on. I'd gone there with the intention of spending a few minutes in quiet communion with the spirit of the place.

The visitors were in no rush to leave. So I placed a wooden kitchen chair in the middle of the largest exhibition room, settled myself on it as comfortably as I could and let my eyes fill with the images around me. The artist had focused his attention on the subtleties of composition in an apparently random growth of plants. He had captured the symmetry and dissonance in the thick veins of the cabbage leaves, in the sweat on the tomato skins, in the purple velvet of the aubergines. He had studied the underlying abstraction in the tangle of stem and leaf, had studied, and understood, the physics of vegetable skin. And I marvelled, once again, at the artist's ability to see beyond the ordinary and into the very newness of things. He reveals for us—the blind, the insensitive, the unloving—the dynamics of forms, the negative spaces, the modulation of light, the texture of darkness, the breathtaking beauty of the commonplace. And it occurred to me, as I sat on that hard wooden chair in the stark emptiness of an old, old house, that the art of living consists of nothing more, and nothing less, than the art of seeing. Our life is richer, our love deeper if, like the artist who sees the bone structure in the landscape, we learn to see what lies beneath. With those sharper eyes, that keener sense, we can see the light emanating from blue snow, the lay and the angle of the blades of grass, the wind, the rain and all the sea in the lustre of a mussel shell. We can see the god in man, the spirit in flesh, the life pulsing on the other side of death. And with kinder eyes, more loving sense, we can see into the labyrinth of the human heart.

When I woke from my meditation, the house was silent, the tourists were gone.

I set the kitchen chair against the wall and climbed the stairs to the third floor.

For some reason, I felt the room up there, under the roof, would have been his. I paced across the floor, ran my fingers along the walls, breathed in the smell of dust and terra cotta. Then I chose the gloomiest corner, the one where shadows gathered and painted the walls with a patina of age, and sat with my back tucked into its angle. I closed my eyes and let the silence build around me. Sounds from the street wafted up to me, and odd smells besieged my nose, a telephone jangled somewhere in the distance and a cock crowed from a nearby rooftop. I waited and listened, willed the space around me to widen, I wanted to feel it hollow out and swell and be filled, suddenly, with another presence. Though I sat there a long time, my mind empty, my blood slowed, my nerves loose, no spirit came to visit me, no phantom, no angel, no ghost. Only time—immortal time that looks upon the finite with a vast and benevolent patience. I could feel it breathing in the room where I sat, like the ocean breathes, or the forest, with the perfect serenity of a god.

~

On the slow ride back to the villa, I felt it grow with each kilometre I covered—the certainty that I would finish Masaccio's story. The afternoon I'd spent in his house confirmed my suspicions. My lies, my distortions, my weak and puny words can't touch him where he lives. He has moved far beyond the place where human voice can reach him. And besides, I reflected as my bad leg pumped up and down on the bicycle pedal, it wasn't his story I had written, it was ours, Christie's and mine. (In the telling of the final three days of Masaccio's life, I tried to write everything you taught me about love, Christie, and, therefore, about immortality. As he journeyed to Rome, as he travelled toward death, Masaccio moved ever closer to the knowledge I found in your arms.) I made him leave all that was familiar and comfortable in his life—the sweet habits of existence—and brought him into an alien land of dust and stone. I gave him false love and illusory kinship, I took from him the instruments of his science and his art, I stripped him of his glory, his identity, his life. I forced him to detach himself from all that is of this world, so that he would turn, and turn again, towards the light. The one he'd received as gift, the one I embodied in Francesca, the one that burns forever in the deepest reaches of my heart.

Like me, Masaccio will die with a sigh on his lips. Like me, he will dwell where he loved best. And his story, like mine, will end as it began. With love.

PART THREE

XVII

THE ANGEL WOULD COME TO MARY IN THE FIELDS. SHE WOULD BE holding the corners of her apron tightly in her hands and it would be bulging with the fruit she had just gathered. Her head would not be bowed, but lifted towards the angel, and she would look upon his face, her eyes unblinded by his radiance. And he, he would be a fall of golden water, his wings wet with light, his white feathers sprinkled with bright drops that each contained a world. The sun would play in the fields around Mary, and the wind would move among the vine leaves, and "the landscape, Maso, even the landscape. You will be able to hear it breathe." Masaccio had spoken these words as he and Masolino pushed through the chapel doors, passionate men, their eyes full of passionate fire.

But San Salvi had been waiting for them there. He'd started in on them as soon as they'd appeared, dispelling at once the fervent mood the night had inspired. Masaccio had immediately gone weak, his energy seeping out of him, softening his bones. Unable even to speak, weary beyond reckoning, he had simply left the room.

At the church door, a great, dark beast of a man hesitated. Masaccio would have walked right by him, but the stranger unaccountably began to tug at his sleeve. Annoyed, Masaccio turned to scowl at him, a sharp word springing to his lips, and came face to face with Eloisa's brother. He felt his blood run hot with guilt, felt his mouth go dry with fear. Raising his hands in the air, waving them in front of his face, he began to stammer excuses. But all of a sudden, he let out a cry. A body come hurtling out of the street had rushed into his arms and thrown him off balance. Catching himself before he stumbled, he took a step back and looked down into a woman's face. It was Miuccia, smiling and laughing, adjusting her body to his, wrapping her long, fine arms around his neck. He couldn't help but smile, too. Disregarding the stranger, she pulled Masaccio's head to hers and kissed him on the mouth. Then, tucking a wineskin into a fold of his robe, she buried her face in his long untidy locks, and spoke some simmering words into his ear. Masaccio felt his skin tingling with her heat. He caught her small head in his hands, closed his eyes and bent his face to her lips. But she slipped away from him, laughing as she ran and, as he watched her disappear without a backward glance, he felt a tightening at the heart. The one familiar thing in this foreign street, gone without a trace.

"It's about your horse, *Signor*. Whenever you should need her again, she will be waiting for you."

Eloisa's brother still stood there, a humble look smudging up his dark face. Masaccio shook his head to clear his mind. It was a strange wine he had drunk, to leave him with such muddled thoughts. He tried to focus on Vittorio's face, saw only the ingrown hairs of his beard and the large pores on his Roman nose, then found himself thinking about the mare. He had better take her home in one piece or Giovanni would have his hide. With his thoughts on his brother and on Florence, he did not hear the speech Vittorio had come to make. He heard only goodbye before finally noticing his hands were piled high with gifts. A couple of curious-looking packages and a second goatskin of wine. He watched Vittorio walk away and thanked the Lord he had not come in anger. There goes a man, Masaccio thought, who would not shrink from murder.

His first impulse was to take the gifts into the chapel to share them with the others. But before he had crossed the threshold, the image of San Salvi's unappetizing face reared up before him and chased him from the door. Taking a turn in the fresh morning air would do him good, he decided. He would walk to the inn and sit down to breakfast, put something solid in the slopping wash of his guts.

Vittorio's wineskin slipped in beside Miuccia's, Masaccio turned his attention to the packages that fit so neatly in the palm of his hand. With a jerk of his thumb, he unwrapped the heavier one, hoping to find among its greasy folds a piece of sausage or good, hard cheese. The paper flipped up to reveal small golden morsels of what appeared to be meat. He sniffed at them and flicked his tongue at them, and knew at once that Vittorio, bless his generous heart, had given him a gift of sweetbreads. Massacio had only tasted them once before, at a patron's house in Florence, and had been amazed offal could melt so sweetly upon the tongue. He tried one piece, wondered while he chewed whether it was calf, lamb or kid that had been sacrificed for his pleasure. Took another, marvelled at its fullness in the mouth, at its richness against the palate, like freshly pressed oil, then, nuzzling into the greasy paper, proceeded to finish off the four remaining pieces. With the last swallow, he found himself wishing ardently for a piece of bread. Something, anything, to peel away the thick coating lining his mouth. He unwrapped the second package, found a handful of chocolates, felt his heart rise up warm in his throat. Folding them up again, he tucked them in beside the wine, and headed for the marketplace to buy a few citrons or some sour green grapes. A clean astringency to cut through the cloying taste of deep-fried animal glands.

In the market street, he very nearly gave up his breakfast. A young man pushing a barrow laden with clothing was weaving his way among the crowds converging on the merchants' stalls. When Masaccio stepped aside to let him pass, he saw that the bottom half of the boy's face was missing. His stomach heaved at the sight, he felt the sweetbreads climbing up his throat, spreading a nauseous warmth behind his teeth. Turning quickly away, his eyes fell upon the figure of the small woman trotting along at the boy's side. She was at once familiar and strange. It was Eloisa—he did not doubt it for a moment—but somehow transformed. As she passed before him, her face bent to the grimy urchins clinging to her white hands, he realized she'd exchanged her fine clothing for rags. She walked barefoot, too, and the hem of her gown dragged in the dirt. Impelled by some mysterious urge, Masaccio lifted a hand to touch her. To stop her a moment, to speak to her. To say exactly what, he wondered. I am sorry? Adieu? *Grazie*? His fingers brushed against her sleeve, but she did not see him there. She walked on, smiling into the upturned faces of the beggar children. Masaccio gathered his fingers to his face and breathed deeply. A scent of violets, rising strong above the smell of grease, lifted off his flesh like incense. Pressing his hand to his heart, he watched her go, leading her orphans home.

Noon-tide found him leaning on the parapet of the Sant'Angelo bridge, looking down into the dancing current of the Tevere. It was a warm fall day, the sun lay bright upon the surface of the water, anyone could have been fooled into thinking it was still summer. Perfect weather for fresco, thought Masaccio for the hundredth time that morning. In a few moments, I will leave this bridge, turn my back on this castel, this fortress, this tomb, and retrace my steps to San Clemente. By evening, I will have completed the sketch of the Annunciation and by this time tomorrow morning, I will have begun to paint.

But something held him there. Was it the water, he wondered, its slow eddies lulling him into a trance, or was it Vittorio's decidedly wicked chocolates? He had eaten them all, one after the other, as he'd wandered through the streets of Rome. He felt a little wobbly in the legs now, as though his blood ran thicker and slower, sludged up as it was with deep, dark fat. He decided he would linger awhile, let the feeling pass.

The sun was warm on his face, and it was pleasant here on the bridge, with the farmers and the pilgrims and the priests going to and fro behind him. He closed his eyes. He could smell the smoke of the peasants' fires lift off their clothing as they went by. He could hear the whistle of the goatherds' willow switches as they moved them through the air. He could hear the high, swirling stridency of the young girls' voices and the trembling rumble of the old women's talk. Those smells, he thought, those sounds. I can see them, I can see their colours so clearly that I could paint them. The old familiar ache awoke in his hands, he opened his eyes and watched the dark water flow beneath the bridge.

And how would you capture that in paint, Masaccio, that shimmering sunlit river and, in the shadows, the looming darkness of its depths? How, with pigment and brush, would you capture what lies beneath?

He wondered now, had he ever been able to catch the spirit that hovered beneath the skin of things? Or paint a face illuminated by the life within? What did a dab of carmine upon *verdaccio* flesh reveal? Or a stroke of light upon a darkened face?

These poor, mortal eyes, thought Masaccio. Failing ever and always to see what lies just inside the light.

The night's drinking had left his mouth as dried and puckered as a she-goat's teat. Reaching for a wineskin, he thought of Miuccia, felt again the heat of her embrace. She had poured words sweet as honey into his ear, had promised him more Trebbiano when he would come to her that night. More wine, more love, more life. Such a clever girl, to get her hands on sunny Florentine wine in the stark, cold ruin of Rome. He really should marry her, he thought, settle into his own home and bring daughters into the world, laughing girls gifted with their mother's dark eyes.

His face turned to the sun, his eyes closed against the light, he smiled up at the sky. He wasn't fooling anyone. He knew, God knew, the whole world knew, he would die an unmarried man. Devoted, as always, to only one thing. Possessed, inspired, overruled, by one single undying passion.

The wine he'd tipped to his lips had been Vittorio's, he decided. Not Miuccia's. A good wine, too, very full and fruity, but with an acidic bite that lingered in the throat. Certainly not Trebbiano. He reached for the second skin, helped himself to a quenching draught. Knew at once this wine, like the other, had not been pressed from Tuscan grapes. It was a powerful drink, though. It went searing through his blood and exploded in his brain. He caught the bridge wall in his hands, he fought to catch his breath. A sudden collusion of the light and the mist off the dancing water dropped a veil before his eyes. His elbows digging hard into the brickwork of the wall, he leaned out over the water, went searching for air like a newborn routs for milk. Breathing deeply, blinking like Lazarus pulled from the grave, he looked out over the river, willing his eyes to see. Everything was shrouded in shadow, lines blurred, darkened, then vanished. His heart burned, his heart caught on fire, he knew he was going to die.

He fell in a heavy heap upon the ground, felt his flesh turn to stone, felt his cheek break against the stony earth. And still he stared, his eyes open in wide amazement at the strange familiarity of death. He watched it move towards him, saw it hover, saw it take a woman's shape. Raising white arms against the darkness, she took the veil in her hands and tore it from top to bottom.

Poor mortal eyes, no more, he thought, as Francesca bent towards him, took him by the hand and drew him into the light.

Saturday 1 June
I suggested she not wait up for me. It would probably be very late by the time I wrote the last lines of the final chapter. But she told me to come to her at any hour of the day or night. The champagne would be on ice, she said, and we would toast the conclusion of another book.

The conclusion of one story, and the shy and halting beginning of another. We had our heart-to-heart, Magda and I, in long walks through the countryside, talking about everything from Swedish colleagues and children and age, to God and Sandy (and you, my forever love). We let our glances linger, we exchanged gentle kisses, we held on to each other as the earth rolled away from the sun. She was glad, she said, I'd made my peace with my beloved dead.

So on the last day of May, in a beautiful Tuscan spring, I finished Masaccio's story. It was dark when I looked up from my desk, the sky outside my window already pierced with the first stars. Those suns, I thought, those burning worlds, that fill the daytime heavens with invisible fire. They go on glowing, beyond the light, and it is only by night that we see what is always there.

The halls of the villa were empty. I could hear voices and the sound of laughter, could feel the day's heat seeping out of the stone. Outside Magda's door, I paused a moment and listened. Nothing breathed but the night. I knocked, once, softly. The door opened on an unlit room, Magda's silhouette deep against the deepness of the shadows. And I hovered there, on the threshold, waiting for her to reach for me and draw me into the dark.

GLOSSARY OF FOREIGN TERMS

ITALIAN

arricio—in fresco, the first coat of coarse plaster that must be rough (have "tooth") in order for the *intonaco* to adhere

arti—guilds

a secco—in fresco, method that uses a binder and paint on dry plaster; some pigments such as blue could only be applied *a secco*; often used for fine details of costume and anatomy

astratissima—distracted, absent-minded

bottega—workshop

belleza—beauty

biscotti / cantucci alla mandorla—dry biscuits flavoured with almonds

cantambanco—minstrel or public storyteller

cantarella—subtle, fast-acting poison

capella—chapel

cartone—cartoon, or parchment for drawing

caccuicco—fish soup

prosciutto di cinghiale—ham made from wild boar

crostini—day-old salted Tuscan bread grilled and drizzled with olive oil

chiaroscuro—light and shade effects

cassone—wooden wedding chests

cucina—kitchen; cuisine

Dio mio—my God

dipintore (pittore)—painter

discepolo—apprentice in a guild

enoteci—wine shops

finocchione—dry sausage flavoured with anise

farniente—sweet idleness

fama—fame

garzoni—boys or companions to the maestro in a guild

gesso—plaster mould

giornate—different patches of a fresco; the size of each giornate depended on the time it would take to paint it before the plaster dried. For example, heads, which required more work and time, tended to be painted on smaller giornate than less detailed features such as background.

gloria—glory, fame

grido—a cry; fame

in nome di Dio—in God's name

intaglio—carving, incision, engraving

intonaco—final thin, smooth layer of plaster; the actual painting surface

mezzogiorno—midday

nominanza—repute

nostalgia del cupolone—nostalgia for the dome; homesickness

onore—honour

pecorino—Italian cheese made from sheep's milk

ponentino—light westerly sea breeze

pulchritudine—beauty

puta—prostitute

rumore—noise, talk

sampietrini—cobblestones

sinopie—brush drawing done with charcoal and then with red ochre dissolved in water used to lay out the plan of a fresco; never meant to be seen by anyone other than the artists

sfumato—shaded, soft

spolveri—dusted pounce marks

sticciata—brioche flavoured with marsala and orange flower

verdaccio—greenish tone recommended by Cennino for the underpainting of flesh

vermiglio—wine from the town of Vermiglio

vicolo—alleyway; back lane

vignarola—spring vegetable casserole

zucotto—sponge pastry filled with cream, chocolate and candied fruit

FRENCH

à rebours—backwards

au courant—aware of

avant-goût—foretaste

bises—kisses

coup de hasard—stroke of luck

dépaysement—removal from the natural sphere, country, home, etc.

distrait—distracted, absent-minded

effeuilleuse—stripteaser

engouement—infatuation

fille de joie—prostitute

frisson—shudder

fugue—flight, escapade

malentendu—misunderstanding

marcheurs de Dieu—pilgrims

mégot—cigarette-end

moue—pout

naïf—naïve, artless, ingenuous

par hasard—by chance

péché mignon—a harmless, pleasant fault

pêle-mêle—disordered, jumbled

quiproquo—mistake, blunder, taking a thing for something else

le regretté—the recently deceased

sans crier gare—without giving warning

ACKNOWLEDGEMENTS

I would like to thank Wayne Tefs for his expert editorial advice, and David Welham for reading the manuscript in its early stages. And my warmest thanks to Craig, as always, for his constant love and support.

The following resources were very helpful in providing background information on Tuscany and the fresco painters of the quattrocento: *Léonard de Vinci* by Serge Bramly (J.C. Lattes, 1988); *The Civilization of the Renaissance in Italy* by Jacob Burckhardt (Harper, 1958); *The Italian Renaissance. Culture and Society in Italy* by Peter Burke (Princeton University Press, 1987); *The Florentine Renaissance* by Vincent Cronin (E. P. Dutton & Co. Inc., 1967); *Biblical Holy Places* by Rivka Gonen (Collier Books, 1987); *The Light of Early Italian Painting* by Paul Hills (Yale University Press, 1987); *Medieval Pilgrims* by Alan Kendall (Putnam, 1970); *The Brancacci Chapel, Florence* by Andrew Ladis (George Braziller, 1993); "The Madonna Puzzle" by Douglas Preston (*The New Yorker*, December 18, 2000); *All the Paintings of Masaccio* by Ugo Procacci, trans. Paul Colacicchi (*The Complete Library of World Art*, v. 6, Hawthorn Books, 1962); *Selections from The Notebooks of Leonardo da Vinci*, edited by Irma A. Richter (Oxford University Press, 1977).

Excerpt from the poem "The Man Who Married Magdalene" by Louis Simpson appears on page 3. From *Modern Poems,* Richard Ellman, Robert O'Clair eds., W.W. Norton & Company Inc., 1973, page 381.

Excerpt from the poem "To His Coy Mistress" by Andrew Marvell appears on page 7. From *Seventeenth Century Poetry*, Hugh Kenner, ed., Holt, Rinehart and Winston, Inc., 1964, page 457.

On page 12, the quotation is taken from John Keats's epitaph.

Excerpt from the poem "Sailing to Byzantium" by W.B. Yeats appears on page 16. From *The Collected Poems of W.B. Yeats*, Macmillan London Ltd., 1977, page 218.

Excerpt from the poem "The Tower" by W. B. Yeats appears on page 37. From *The Collected Poems of W.B. Yeats,* Macmillan London Ltd., 1977, page 218.

Excerpt from the poem "In Memory of W.B. Yeats" by W.H. Auden appears on page 42. From *Selected Poetry of W.H. Auden,* Vintage Books, 1970, page 53.

Excerpt from the poem "Booz Endormi" by Victor Hugo appears

on page 45. From *La légende des siècles*. Tome I. J. Hetzel, 1880, page 51.

Excerpt from "A New Refutation of Time" by Jorge Louis Borges appears on page 47. From *Labyrinths: Selected Stories & Other Writings*, Donald A. Yates and James E. Irby, eds., New Directions Publishing, 1964.

Excerpts from the novel *More Die of Heartbreak* by Saul Bellow appear on pages 48, 66, 92, and 118. Morrow, 1987.

Excerpt from "La forma de la espada" by Jorge Luis Borges appears on page 76. From *Cuentos Espanoles, Angel Flores*, ed., Dover Publications, Inc., 1987, page 233.

Excerpt from "Adonais" by Percy Bysshe Shelley appears on page 90. From *English Romantic Writers*, David Perkins, ed., Harcourt, Brace & World, Inc., 1967, pages 1051-1052.

Excerpt from the poem "The Letter" by W. H. Auden appears on page 95. From *Selected Poetry of W.H. Auden,* Vintage Books, 1970, page 3.

Excerpt from the poem "L'invitation au voyage" by Charles Baudelaire appears on page 98. From *Les Fleurs du mal,* Editions Gallimard et Librairie Générale Française, 1964, page 66.

Excerpt from "Ode: Intimations of Immortality" by William Wordsworth appears on page 117. From *English Romantic Writers*, David Perkins, ed., Harcourt, Brace & World, Inc., 1967, page 281.

Excerpt from the unpublished poem "To Chi: on passing through" by Paul Savoie appears on page 123.

Excerpt from the poem "The Relique" by John Donne appears on page 126. From *Seventeenth Century Poetry,* Hugh Kenner, ed., Holt, Rinehart and Winston, Inc., 1964, page 28.

Excerpt from the novel *Le premier homme* by Albert Camus appears on page 145. Gallimard, 1994.

An excerpt from "Doomsday Song" by W.H. Auden appears on page 147. From *Selected Poetry of W. H. Auden,* Vintage Books, 1970, page 74.

An excerpt from *Henderson the Rain King* by Saul Bellow appears on page 150. Penguin Books, 1978.

George's comments on Botticelli's Venus on page 154 are taken from *The Story of Art* by E.H. Gombrich, Phaidon Press Limited, 1995, page 264.

Excerpt from the poem "Ribblesdale" by Gerard Manley Hopkins appears on page 180. From *Poems and Prose of Gerard Manley Hopkins*, Penguin Books, 1963, page 52.

Excerpt from *The English Patient* by Michael Ondaatje appears on page 187. McClelland & Stewart Inc., 1992, page 190.

Excerpt from poem #44 by Gerard Manley Hopkins appears on page 188. From *Poems and Prose of Gerard Manley Hopkins*, Penguin Books, 1963, page 62.